HIS
MASTER'S
VOICE

Stanislaw LEM

HIS MASTER'S VOICE

**Translated from the Polish by
MICHAEL KANDEL**

*Northwestern University Press
Evanston, Illinois*

Northwestern University Press
Evanston, Illinois 60208-4170

Printed in the United States of America
10 9 8 7 6 5
ISBN 0-8101-1731-2

Library of Congress Cataloging-in-Publication Data

Lem, Stanisław.
　　[Głos pana. English]
　　His master's voice / Stanisław Lem ; translated from the Polish by
Michael Kandel.
　　　　p. cm.
　　ISBN 0-8101-1731-2 (pbk. : alk. paper)
　　I. Kandel, Michael. II. Title.
PG7158.L39G613 1999
891.8'5373—dc21　　　　　　　　　　　　　　　　99-41917
　　　　　　　　　　　　　　　　　　　　　　　　　　CIP

The paper used in this publication meets the minimum requirements of the
American National Standard for Information Sciences—Permanence of
Paper for Printed Library Materials, ANSI Z39.48-1992.

HIS
MASTER'S
VOICE

Editor's Note

THE MANUSCRIPT WAS found among the papers of the late Professor Peter E. Hogarth. That great mind, alas, was unable to put it into final form, though he had labored long over it. The illness that claimed him made the book's completion impossible. Because the deceased was reluctant to speak of the work—a work unusual for him, and undertaken more out of a sense of duty than by choice—and reluctant, even, to speak of it to those near him, in whose number I am honored to have been included—certain obscurities and points of contention arose during the preliminary efforts to prepare the manuscript for publication. I must state, to be truthful, that in the circle of those who were made acquainted with the text there were voices raised in opposition to its publication: they claimed that such was not the intention of the deceased. There is to be found, however, no written testimony of his to this effect; one can only conclude that such opinions are without foundation. It was obvious, on the other hand, that the thing was unfinished, for it had no title, and one particular fragment existed only in a rough draft, which fragment was to have served—and here lies one of the principal doubts—as either a preface or an afterword to the book.

As friend and colleague of the deceased, and mentioned by him in his will, I have decided, finally, to make of this fragment, necessary for an understanding of the whole, the preface. The title, *His*

1

Master's Voice, was suggested to me by the publisher, John Keller, whom I wish to take this opportunity to thank for the great care he has given to the publication of this last work of Professor Hogarth. I should also like to express here my gratitude to Mrs. Rosamond Schelling, who so painstakingly assisted in the initial editing and in the final proofreading.

Professor Thomas V. Warren
Mathematics Department
Washington University, D.C.
June 1966

Preface

THOUGH I MAY shock many readers with the words that follow, it is my duty, I am convinced, to speak them. I never before wrote a book like this; and, since it is not the custom for mathematicians to introduce their works with statements of a personal nature, I could have spared myself the trouble.

It was as a result of circumstances beyond my control that I became involved in the events that I wish to relate here. The reasons I preface the account with a kind of confession should become evident later on. In speaking of myself, I must choose some frame of reference; let this be the recent biography of me penned by Professor Harold Yowitt. Yowitt calls me a mind of the highest caliber, in that the problems that I attacked were always, among those currently available, the most difficult. He shows that my name was to be found wherever the heritage of science was in the process of being torn down and the edifice of new concepts raised—for example, in the mathematical revolution, in the field of physico-ethics, or in the Master's Voice Project.

When I came, in my reading, to the place where the subject was destruction, I expected, after the mention of my iconoclastic inclinations, further, bolder inferences, and thought that at last I had found a biographer—which did not overjoy me, because it is one thing to strip oneself, and another, entirely, to be stripped. But Yowitt, as if frightened by his own acumen, then returned—

inconsequently—to the accepted version of me as the persistent, modest genius, and even trotted out a few of the old-standby anecdotes about me.

So I could set this book on the shelf with my other biographies, calmly, little dreaming, at the time, that I would soon be entering the lists with my flattering portraitist. I noted, also, that not much space remained on the shelf, and recalled what I had once said to Yvor Baloyne, that I would die when the shelf was filled. He took it as a joke, and I did not insist, though I had expressed a genuine conviction, no less genuine for being absurd. And therefore—to return to Yowitt—once again I had succeeded, or, if you like, failed, in that at the age of sixty-two I had twenty-eight volumes devoted to my person and yet remained completely unknown. But am I being fair?

Professor Yowitt wrote about me in accordance with rules not of his making. Not all public figures may be treated the same. Great artists, yes, may be drawn in their pettiness, and some biographers even seem to think that the soul of the artist is perforce a scurvy thing. For the great scientists, however, the old stereotype is still mandatory. Artists we view as spirits chained to the flesh; literary critics are free to discuss the homosexuality of an Oscar Wilde, but it is hard to imagine any historian of science dealing analogously with the creators of physics. We must have them incorruptible, ideal, and the events of history are no more than local changes in the circumstances of their lives. A politician may be a villain without ceasing to be a great politician, whereas a villainous genius—that is a contradiction in terms. Villainy cancels genius. So demand the rules of today.

True, a group of psychoanalysts from Michigan did attempt to challenge this state of affairs, but they fell into the sin of oversimplification. The physicist's evident propensity to theorize, these scholars derived from sexual repression. Psychoanalytic doctrine reveals the pig in man, a pig saddled with a conscience; the disastrous result is that the pig is uncomfortable beneath that pious rider, and the rider fares no better in the situation, since his endeavor is not only to tame the pig but also to render it invisible. The notion that we have within us an ancient Beast that carries upon its back a modern Reason—is a pastiche of primitive mythologies.

Psychoanalysis provides truth in an infantile, that is, a school-boy fashion: we learn from it, roughly and hurriedly, things that scandalize us and thereby command our attention. It sometimes happens, and such is the case here, that a simplification touching upon the truth, but cheaply, is of no more value than a lie. Once again we are shown the demon and the angel, the beast and the god locked in Manichean embrace, and once again man has been pronounced, by himself, not culpable, as he is but the field of combat for forces that have entered him, distended him, and hold sway inside his skin. Thus psychoanalysis is, primarily, sophomoric. Shockers are to explain man to us, and the whole drama of existence is played out between piggishness and the sublimation into which civilized effort can transform it.

So I really ought to be thankful to Professor Yowitt, for maintaining my likeness in the classical style and not borrowing the methods of the Michigan psychologists. Not that I intend to speak better of myself than they would speak; but there is, surely, a difference between a caricature and a portrait.

Which is not to say that I believe a man who is the subject of biographies possesses any greater knowledge of himself than his biographers do. Their position is more convenient, for uncertainties may be attributed to a lack of data, which allows the supposition that the one described, were he but alive and willing, could supply the needed information. The one described, however, possesses nothing more than hypotheses on the subject of himself, hypotheses that may be of interest as the products of his mind but that do not necessarily serve as those missing pieces.

With sufficient imagination a man could write a whole series of versions of his life; it would form a union of sets in which the facts would be the only elements in common. People, even intelligent people, who are young, and therefore inexperienced and naïve, see only cynicism in such a possibility. They are mistaken, because the problem is not moral but cognitive. The number of metaphysical beliefs is no greater or less than the number of different beliefs a man may entertain on the subject of himself—sequentially, at various periods of his life, and occasionally even at the same time.

Therefore, I cannot claim to offer anything other than the notions of myself that I have formed over the space of roughly forty years, and their only singularity, it seems to me, is that they are not flattering. Nor is this uncomplimentariness limited to "the pulling off of the mask," which is the only trick available to the psychoanalyst. To say, for example, of a genius that morally he was a bastard may not necessarily hit him in the place of his private shame. A mind that "reached the ceiling of the age," as Yowitt puts it, will not be bothered by that type of diagnosis. The shame of a genius may be his intellectual futility, the knowledge of how uncertain is all that he has accomplished. And genius is, above all, constant doubting. Not one of the greats, however, bent beneath the pressure of society, has pulled down the monuments raised to him in his life, calling himself thereby into question.

As one whose genius has been duly certified by several dozen learned biographers, I think I may say a word or two on the topic of intellectual summits; which is simply that clarity of thought is a shining point in a vast expanse of unrelieved darkness. Genius is not so much a light as it is a constant awareness of the surrounding gloom, and its typical cowardice is to bathe in its own glow and avoid, as much as possible, looking out beyond its boundary. No matter how much genuine strength it may contain, there is also, inevitably, a considerable part that is only the pretense of that strength.

The fundamental traits of my character I consider to be cowardice, malice, and pride. As it turned out, this triumvirate had at its disposal a certain talent, which concealed it and ostensibly transformed it, and intelligence assisted in this—intelligence is one of life's most effective instruments for masking inborn traits, once it decides that such a course is desirable. For forty-odd years I have been an obliging, modest individual, devoid of any sign of professional arrogance, because for a very long time and most persistently I schooled myself in precisely this behavior. But as far back into childhood as I can recall, I sought out evil, though of course I was unaware of it.

My evil was isotropic, unbiased, and totally disinterested. In places of veneration, such as churches, or in the company of particularly worthy persons, I liked to think forbidden thoughts. That the content of these thoughts was ludicrously puerile does not matter in the least. I was simply conducting experiments on a scale practically accessible to me. I do not remember when I began these experiments. I remember only the deep sense of injury, the anger, and the disappointment that came upon me some years later, when it turned out that a head filled with wickedness would never, not in any place nor in any company, be struck by lightning; that breaking free of and not participating in the Proper brought with it no—absolutely no—punishment.

If it is at all possible to speak thus of a child of less than ten, I wanted that lightning or some other form of dire retribution; I summoned it, challenged it, and grew to despise the world, the place of my existence, because it had demonstrated the futility of all action and thought, evil included. Thus I never tormented animals, or hurt even the grass underfoot; on the other hand, I lashed out at stones, the sand, I abused furniture, subjected water to torture, and mentally smashed the stars to pieces, to punish them for their indifference to me, and as I did so my fury became more and more helpless, for my understanding increased, of how ridiculous were the things I did.

Somewhat later on, with self-knowledge, I came to the realization that my condition was a kind of keen unhappiness that was utterly useless to me, because it could serve no purpose. I said before that my rancor was unbiased: I bestowed it first upon myself. The shape of my arms, of my legs, the features of my face, seen in the mirror, galled me in a way in which usually only the features of others cause us anger or impatience. When I grew a bit older, I saw that it was impossible to live like this; I determined, through a progression of decisions, exactly what I ought to be, and from then on strove—true, with variable results—to adhere to that established plan.

An autobiography that begins by listing cowardice, malice, and pride as the foundations of one's psyche entails, from the deterministic point of view, a logical error. If one says that everything in us is predetermined, then predetermined also must have been my resistance to my inner meanness, and the difference between me and other, better people is then reduced to nothing but a variation in the localized source of the behavior. What those better people did voluntarily, at little cost, for they but followed their own natural inclination, I practiced in opposition to mine—hence, as it were, artificially. Yet since it was I who dictated conduct to myself, I was, in the overall balance—in this formulation—nevertheless predestined to be as good as gold. Like Demosthenes with the pebbles in his stammering mouth, I put iron deep in my soul, to straighten it.

But it is precisely in this equalizing that determinism reveals its absurdity. A phonograph record of angelic singing is not an iota better morally than one that reproduces, when played, a scream of murder. According to determinism, he who desired and was able to be better was no more or less fated beforehand than he who desired but was unable, or than he who did not even attempt to desire. This is a false image, for the sound of battle played on a record is not an actual battle. Knowing what it cost me, I can say that my struggle to be good was no semblance. Determinism simply deals with something altogether different; the forces that operate according to the calculus of physics have nothing whatever to do with the matter—just as a crime is not made innocent by its translation into the language of amplitudes of atomic probabilities.

About one thing Yowitt is definitely right: I always sought difficulty. Opportunities for me to give free rein to my natural malice I usually forwent, as too easy. It may sound strange, or even nonsensical, but I did not suppress my inclination to evil with my eyes fixed on the Good as a higher value; rather, I suppressed it for the precise reason that I felt so powerfully its presence in me. What counted for me was the calculus of resistance, which had nothing in common with the arithmetic of morality. Therefore I really cannot say what would have become of me had the principal trait of my nature been the inclination to do only good. As usual, reasoning that attempts to picture ourselves in a form other than what is given breaks the rules of logic and must quickly founder.

Once only did I not eschew evil; that memory is connected with the protracted and horrible death of my mother. I loved her, yet at the same time I followed with an unusually keen and avid attention the process of her destruction in the illness. I was nine then. She, the personification of tranquillity, of strength, of a composure almost sovereign, lay in a lingering agony, an agony prolonged by the doctors. I, at her side in the darkened bedroom filled with the stink of medicine, still kept a grip on myself; but when I left her, as soon as I had shut the door behind me and found myself alone, I stuck out my tongue joyfully in the direction of her bed, and, that being insufficient, ran to my room and breathlessly jumped up and down in front of the mirror, fists clenched, making faces and giggling with delight. With delight? I understood perfectly that my mother was dying; since that morning I had fallen into despair, and the despair was as real as my stifled giggling. I remember how the giggling frightened me, yet at the same time it took me beyond everything I had known, and in that transgression there was a dazzling revelation.

That night, lying alone, I tried to comprehend what had taken place; unable to do this, I worked up a befitting pity for myself and my mother, and tears flowed until I fell asleep. I considered these tears to be an expiation; but then, later, the whole thing repeated itself, when I overheard the doctors conveying worse and worse news to my father. I dared not go up to my room; deliberately I sought the company of others. Thus the first person I ever shrank from was myself.

After my mother's death I gave myself up to a child's despair that was untroubled by any qualms. The fascination ended with her last breath. With her died my anxiety. This incident is so confusing that I can only offer a hypothesis. I had witnessed the fall of the Absolute—it had been shown to be an illusion—and witnessed a shameful, obscene struggle, because in it Perfection had come apart like the most miserable rag. This was the trampling of life's Order, and although people above me supplied the repertoire of that Order with special evasions even for so dismal an occasion, these additions failed to fit what had happened. One cannot, with dignity, with grace, howl in pain—any more than one can in ecstasy. In the messiness of loss I sensed a truth. Perhaps I saw, in that which disrupted, the stronger side, and so sided with that side, because it had the upper hand.

My hidden laughter had no connection with the actual suffering of my mother. I only feared that suffering; it was the unavoidable concomitant of the expiring—that I could understand, and I would have delivered her from the pain had I been able. I desired neither her suffering nor her death. At a real murderer I would have thrown myself with tears and pleas, like any child, but since there was none, I could only absorb the cruel treachery of the blow. Her body, bloated, turned into a monstrous, mocking caricature of itself, and it writhed in that mockery. I had only one choice: either to be destroyed with her or to jeer at her. As a coward, then, I chose the laughter of betrayal.

I cannot say whether it really was this way. The first paroxysm of giggling seized me at the sight of the destruction; perhaps the experience would have skipped me had my mother met her end in a fashion more aesthetic, like quietly falling asleep, a form that is much favored by people. It was not like that, however, and, forced to believe my own eyes, I proved defenseless. In earlier times a chorus of hired mourners, brought in quickly, would have drowned out the groans of my mother. But the decline of tradition has reduced magical measures to the level of hairdressing, because the undertaker—and I overheard this—suggested to my father the various facial expressions into which her frozen grimace could be reworked. My father left the room then, and for a brief moment I felt a tremor of solidarity, because I understood him. Later I thought of that mortal agony many times.

The idea of my laughter as a betrayal seems incomplete. Betrayal is the result of conscious decision, but what causes us to be drawn to destruction? What black hope, in destruction, beckons man? Its utter inutility rules out any rational explanation. This hunger has been suppressed in vain by numerous civilizations. It is as irrevocably a part of us as two-leggedness. To him who seeks a reason but cannot abide any hypothesis of a design, whether in the form of Providence or of the Diabolical, there remains only the rationalist's substitute for demonology—statistics. Thus it is from a darkened room filled with the smell of corruption that the trail leads to my mathematical anthropogenesis. With the formulae of stochastics I strove to undo the evil spell. But this, too, is only conjecture, therefore a self-defensive reflex of the mind.

I know that what I am writing here could be, with slight shifts in emphasis, turned to my favor—and that some future biographer will try to do this. He will show that with intellect I conquered my character, achieved a great victory, but defamed myself out of a desire to do penance. Such labor follows in the steps of Freud, who has become the Ptolemy of psychology, for now, with him, anyone can explain human phenomena, raising epicycles upon epicycles: that construction speaks to us, because it is aesthetic. He converted the pastoral model into one that was grotesque, unaware that he remained a prisoner of aesthetics. It was as if the purpose had been to replace the opera, in anthropology, with tragicomedy.

Let my posthumous biographer not trouble himself. I require no apologia; all my effort was born of curiosity, untouched by any feeling of guilt. I wanted to understand—only to understand, nothing more. For the disinterestedness of evil is the only support, in man, for the theological argument; theology answers the question where does a quality come from that has its origin neither in nature nor in culture. A mind immersed totally in the human experience, and therefore anthropocentric, might finally agree with the image of Creation as a somewhat sick joke.

It is an attractive idea, that of a Creator who merely amused Himself, but here we enter into a vicious circle: we imagine Him sadistic not because He made us that way, but because we are ourselves that way. Meanwhile the utter insignificance and smallness of man vis-à-vis the Universe, of which science informs us, makes the Manichean myth a concept so primitive as to be trivial. I will put it in another way: if a creation were to take place—which personally I cannot conceive—then the level of knowledge that it would require would be of such an order that there would be no place in it for silly jokes. Because—and this really is the whole credo of my faith—nothing like the wisdom of *evil* is possible. My reason tells me that a creator cannot be a petty scoundrel, a conjurer who toys ironically with what he has brought into being. What we hold to be the result of a malign intervention could only make sense as an ordinary miscalculation, as an error, but now we find ourselves in the realm of nonexistent theologies—that is, theologies of fallible gods. But the domain of their constructional practices is nothing other than the field of my lifework, i.e, statistics.

Every child unwittingly makes the discoveries from which have sprung the worlds of Gibbs and Boltzmann, because to a child reality appears as a multitude of possibilities, where each can be taken separately and developed so easily that it seems almost spontaneous. A child is surrounded by a great many virtual worlds; completely alien to him is the cosmos of Pascal, a rigid corpse with even, clocklike movements. The ossified order of maturity later destroys that primal richness. If this picture of childhood seems onesided, for example, in that the child owes his inner freedom to ignorance and not choice—well, but every picture is one-sided. With the demise of imagination I inherited its residue, a kind of permanent disagreement with reality, more like an anger, though, than a rejection. My laughter had already been a denial, and a more effective kind, perhaps, than suicide. I acknowledge it, at the age of sixty-two; and the mathematics was only a later consequence of this attitude. Mathematics was my second desertion.

I speak metaphorically—but hear me out. I had betrayed my dying mother, betrayed all people, opting, with the laughter, for a thing of power greater than theirs, however hideous it was, because I saw no other way out. Later I would learn that this enemy of ours—which was everything, which had built its nest in us as well—I could also betray, at least to a certain extent, because mathematics is independent of the world.

Time showed me that I had been doubly mistaken. Genuinely to opt for death, against life, and for mathematics, against the world, is not possible. The only true option is one's own annihilation. Whatever we do, we do in life; and, as experience has demonstrated, neither is mathematics the perfect retreat, because its habitation is language. That informational plant has its roots in the world and in us. This comparison has always been with me, even before I was able to put it into the language of a proof.

In mathematics I searched for what I had valued in childhood, the multiplicity of worlds, which broke contact with the imposed world, but so gently that it was as if the latter had been stripped of its force—a force that lay within us as well, yet was hidden enough for us to forget its presence. Later, like every mathematician, I learned to my surprise how unpredictable and incredibly adaptable is that activity, which at first resembles a game. One enters into it proudly; without apologies and unequivocally one shuts out the world; with arbitrary propositions that rival, in their uncontestableness, Creation, one performs a definitive closure; this is to separate us from the vortex in which we are forced to live.

And lo, that denial, that most radical break, leads us precisely to the heart of things, and the flight turns out to have been an attainment, the desertion—an appreciation, and the break—a reconciliation. We make the discovery, then, that our escape was apparent only, since we have returned to the very thing we sought to flee. The enemy metamorphoses into an ally; we are purified; the world gives us to understand, silently, that only by means of it may we conquer it. Thus our fear is tamed and turns to joy, in that special refuge whose deepest interiors intersect the surface of the only world.

Mathematics never reveals man to the degree, never expresses him in the way, that any other field of human endeavor does: the extent of the negation of man's corporeal self that mathematics achieves cannot be compared with anything. Whoever is interested in this subject I refer to my articles. Here I will say only that the world injected its patterns into human language at the very inception of that language; mathematics sleeps in every utterance, and can only be discovered, never invented.

What constitutes its crown may not be cut free from its roots, because it arose not in the course of the three hundred or eight hundred years of civilized history, but through the millennia of linguistic evolution: at the loci of man's encounter with his environment, from the time of tribes and rivers. Language is wiser than the mind of any one of us, just as the body is wiser than the discernment of any of its units as it moves, self-aware and many-faceted, through the current of the life process. The inheritance of both evolutions, of living matter and of the matter of informational speech, has not yet been exhausted, but already we dream of stepping beyond the boundaries of both. These words of mine may make poor philosophizing, but that cannot be said of my proofs of the linguistic genesis of mathematical concepts, of the fact, in other words, that those concepts arose neither from the enumerability of things nor from the cleverness of reason.

The factors that contributed to my becoming a mathematician are complex, no doubt, but one major factor was talent, without which I could have accomplished in my profession no more than could a hunchback in a championship track-and-field competition. I do not know whether the factors that had to do with my character, rather than with my talent, played a role in the account I intend to give—but I should not rule out the possibility, for the importance of the affair itself is such that neither natural modesty nor pride ought to be considered.

As a rule, chroniclers become extremely honest when they feel that what they have to say about themselves is of monumental importance. I, on the contrary, with the premise of honesty arrive at the complete immaterialness of my person; that is, I am forced into an insufferable garrulity simply because I lack the ability to tell where the statistical caprice of personality composition leaves off and the rule of the behavior of the species begins.

In various fields one can acquire knowledge that is real, or the kind only that provides spiritual comfort, and the two need not agree. The differentiation of these two types of knowledge in anthropology borders on the impossible. If we know nothing so well as ourselves, it is surely for this reason: that we constantly renew our demand for nonexistent knowledge, i.e., information as to what created man, while ruling out in advance, without realizing it, the possibility of the union of pure accident with the most profound necessity.

I once wrote a program for an experiment of one of my friends. The idea was to simulate, in a computer, families of neutral beings; they would be homeostats, cognizant of their "environment" but possessing, initially, no "emotional" or "ethical" qualities. These beings multiplied—only in the machine, of course, therefore in a way that a layman would call "arithmetically"—and after a few dozen "generations" there continually appeared, over and over again, in each of the "specimens," a characteristic that made no sense at all to us, a sort of equivalent of "aggression." After many painstaking but fruitless checking calculations, my friend, at his wit's end—really grasping at straws—began examining the most trivial circumstances of the experiment; and then it turned out that a certain relay had reacted to the changes of humidity in the air, and thus those changes had become the hidden producer of the deviation.

I cannot help thinking of that experiment as I write, for is it not possible that social evolution lifted us from the Animal Kingdom in an exponential curve—when we were fundamentally unprepared for the ascent? The socialization reaction began when the human atoms had barely given evidence of their first cohesiveness. Those atoms were a material strictly biological, a material made and prepared to satisfy typically biological criteria, but that sudden movement, that upward shove, seized us and carried us off into the space of civilization. How could such a start not have bound onto that biological material accidental convergences, much as a probe that, lowered to the ocean floor, scoops up from it, along with the desired object, debris and chance pieces of junk? I recall the damp relay in the sophisticated computer. And the process that engendered us—why, pray, must it have been in every respect perfect? Yet neither we nor our philosophers dare consider the idea that the finality and singularity of the existence of our species do not at all imply a perfection under whose aegis the species originated—just as such perfection is not present at the cradle of any individual.

It is a curious thing that the marks of our imperfection, which identify the species, have never been, not by any faith, recognized for what they simply are, that is, the results of uncertain processes; on the contrary, practically all religions agree in the conviction that man's imperfection is the result of a demiurgic clash between two antagonistic perfections, each of which has damaged the other. The Light collided with the Dark, and man arose: thus runs their formula. My conception sounds ill-natured only if it is wrong—but we do not know that it is wrong. The friend whom I mentioned caricatured it; he said that according to Hogarth humanity is a hunchback who, in ignorance of the fact that it is possible not to be hunchbacked, for thousands of years has sought an indication of a Higher Necessity in his hump, because he will accept any theory but the one that says that his deformity is purely accidental, that no one bestowed it upon him as part of a master plan, that it serves absolutely no purpose, for the thing was determined by the twists and turns of anthropogenesis.

But I intended to speak about myself, not about the species. I do not know where it came from or what caused it, but even now, after all these years, I find within myself that malice, as vigorous as ever, because the energies of our most primitive impulses never age. Do I shock? Over many decades now, I have acted like a rectification column, producing a distillate composed of the pile of my articles as well as of the articles occasioned by them—hagiography. If you say that you are not interested in the inner workings of the apparatus which I unnecessarily bring out into the light, note that I, in the purity of the nourishment I have vouchsafed you, see the indelible signs of all my secrets.

Mathematics for me was no Arcadia; it was, rather, a court of last resort, a church that I entered, unbelieving, because it offered sanctuary. My principal metamathematical work has been called destructive, and not without reason. It was no accident that I called into question, irreversibly, the foundations of mathematical deduction and the concept of the analytic in logic. I turned the tools of statistics against these basic notions—until at last they crumbled. I could not be a devil underground and an angel in the light of day. I created, yes, but on ruins, and Yowitt is right: I took away more truths than I ever gave.

For this negative balance the epoch was held to account, not I; because I had followed in the steps of Russell and Gödel—after the former had discovered the cracks in the foundation of the Crystal Palace, and after the latter had shaken it. It was said that I had acted in the spirit of the time. Well, of course. But an emerald triangle does not cease to be an emerald triangle when it becomes a human eye—in an arranged mosaic.

More than once I have wondered what would have become of me had I been born within any one of the four thousand cultures we call primitive, which preceded ours in that gulf of eighty thousand years that our lack of imagination contracts to the foreground, the foyer, of history proper. In some of them I would no doubt have languished; but in others, who knows, I might have found greater personal fulfillment, as one visited, as one creating new rites, new magic, thanks to the talent I brought into the world, that of combining elements. Perhaps, in the absence of a restraining curb, which in our culture is the relativism of every conceptual entity, I could have consecrated, with no trouble, orgies of havoc and debauchery; because in those ancient societies they practiced the custom of a temporary, periodic suspension of daily law, by dissolving their culture (it was the bedrock, the Constant, the Absolute of their lives, and yet, remarkably, they knew that even the Absolute required holes!) in order to give vent to the festering mass of excesses that could not be fitted into any codified system, and of which only a portion found expression in war masks and family masquerades, under the bit and bridle of morality.

They were sensible, rational, those severings of societal bonds and rules, the group madness, the pandemonium liberated, heightened by the narcotics of rhythm and poison. It was the opening of a safety valve, out of which poured the factor of destruction; through this particular invention barbarity was adapted to man. But the principle of a crime from which one could retire, of a reversible madness, of gaps rhythmically repeated in the social fabric, has been done away with, and now all those forces must go in harness, work treadmills, play roles that are too tight for them and always ill-suited. So they corrode everything quotidian; they hide in every place; for nowhere is it permitted them to emerge from anonymity. Each of us is, from childhood, fastened to some publicly allowed piece of himself, the part that was selected and schooled, and that has gained the *consensus omnium*; and now he cultivates that fragment, polishes it, perfects it, breathes on it alone, that it may develop as well as possible; and each of us, being a part, pretends to be a whole—like a stump that claims it is a limb.

As far back as I can remember, no ethics ever took root in my sensitivity. Cold-bloodedly I built myself an artificial ethics. But I needed to find a reason to do this, because setting up rules in a desert is like taking Communion without faith. I am not saying that I planned out my life in as theoretical a manner as I present it here. Nor did I attach axioms to my behavior—retroactively. I proceeded always in the same way, at first unawares; the motivations I later guessed.

Had I considered myself a person who was basically good, I would have been quite unable to understand evil. I would have believed that people perpetrated it always with premeditation— that is, that they did what they had resolved to do—because I would have found no other source of vileness within my personal experience. But I had better knowledge; I was aware of my own inclinations, as well as of my blamelessness for them—blamelessness because I was, after all, the way I was to begin with, and no one had ever consulted me in the matter.

Now, for one slave to strangle another slave to satisfy the forces implanted in both; for one blamelessness to torture another if there existed any chance whatever to resist such a compulsion—to me this was an offense against reason. We are given to ourselves and it is fruitless for us to question what is given, but if there should open up the minutest chance to oppose the Way Things Are—how can one not seize it? Only such decisions and such actions are our exclusive human property, as is the possibility, also, of suicide. This is the sector of freedom where our unasked-for inheritance meets with contempt.

Please do not tell me I contradict myself—the self who saw in the Stone Age a time of dreams come true. Knowledge is irreversible; one cannot go back into the darkness of sweet ignorance. In that time I would have had no knowledge and would have been unable to obtain it. One must make use of the knowledge one possesses. I know that Chance fashioned us, put us together as we are—and what, am I to follow submissively all the directives drawn blindly in that endless lottery?

My *principium humanitatis* is curious in that if someone basically good wished to apply it to himself, he would be obliged—in keeping with the policy of "conquering one's own nature"—to do evil in order to affirm his human freedom. My doctrine therefore is not suited for general application; but I do not see why I have to provide humanity with an ethical panacea. Diversity, heterogeneity, is a given in mankind; thus Kant's declaration that the basis of individual actions could be made a general law means a varying violence done to people; in sacrificing the individual for a superior value—the culture—Kant dispenses injustice. But I am not saying that one is a man only to the extent that he is a self-chained monster. I have presented a purely private argument, my own strategy, which, however, has changed nothing in me. To this day my first reaction, upon hearing of someone's misfortune, is a spark of pleasure, and I no longer even attempt to stifle such twitches, because I know that I cannot reach the place where that mindless chuckle lives. But I respond with resistance and act contrary to myself, for the reason that I am able to do so.

Had I truly intended to write my own biography—which would have turned out to be, in comparison with the volumes on my shelf, an *anti*biography—there would have been no need for me to justify these confessions. But my object is different. The adventure I am to relate boils down to this: humanity came upon a thing that beings belonging to another race had sent out into the darkness of the stars. A situation, the first of its kind in history, important enough, one would think, to merit the divulging, in greater detail than convention allows, of who it was, exactly, who represented *our* side in that encounter. All the more since neither my genius nor my mathematics alone sufficed to prevent it from bearing poison fruit.

1

THE MASTER'S VOICE Project has an enormous literature, more extensive and diverse than ever had the Manhattan Project. Upon its public disclosure, America and the world were inundated with articles, treatises, and essays, so numerous that the bibliography alone is a tremendous tome, as thick as an encyclopedia. The official version is the *Baloyne Report*, which the American Library later published in ten million copies; but the essence of it appears in the eighth volume of the *Encyclopedia Americana*. And there have been books about the Project by others who held high positions in it, such as Rappaport's *The First Interstellar Communication*, Dill's *Inside His Master's Voice*, or Prothero's *HMV: The Implications for Physics*. This last work, authored by my late friend, is among the most accurate, though it really belongs more to the professional literature—professional meaning that the thing studied is clearly separated from the one who studies it.

There are too many historical treatises even to mention. The four-volume work of the historian of science William Angers, *749 Days: A Chronicle*, is monumental. It amazed me with its meticulousness; Angers had got hold of all the former workers of the Project and done a compilation of their views. But I did not read his opus to the end—that seemed to me as impossible as reading a telephone book.

In a separate category are books not factual but interpretive, ranging from the philosophical and theological even to the psychiatric. The reading of such publications never fails to weary and annoy me. It is no coincidence, I am sure, that those who have the most to say about the Project are the ones who have had no direct contact with it.

Which is similar to the attitude physicists have regarding gravitation or electrons—as opposed to that of the "well-informed" who read popular science. The "well-informed" think they know something about matters that the experts are reluctant even to speak of. Information at second hand always gives an impression of tidiness, in contrast with the data at the scientist's disposal, full of gaps and uncertainties. The writers on HMV who come under the interpretive heading as a rule crammed the information they acquired into the corsets of their convictions; what did not fit they lopped off without ceremony or hesitation. A few such books one can at least admire for the authors' inventiveness. But this type imperceptibly turns into a characteristic form that one might term the graphomania of the Project. Science, from its very beginning, has been surrounded by a halo of pseudo science, which rises like steam from various half-educated heads; it is not surprising, then, that HMV, as a phenomenon completely unprecedented, evoked so violent a ferment among addled minds, a ferment crowned by the appearance of a series of religious sects.

The amount of information that is necessary for even a general grasp of the questions dealt with in the Project exceeds, to tell the truth, the brain capacity of a single individual. But ignorance, while it checks the enthusiasm of the sensible, in no way restrains the fools; thus in the ocean of published papers that His Master's Voice has called into existence, a man can find whatever suits him, as long as he is not overly concerned about the truth. And even the most venerable personages have tried their hand at literature devoted to the Project. *The New Revelation*, by the respected Patrick Gordiner, is at least logical and lucid, which I *cannot* say of *The Epistle of the Antichrist* by Father Bernard Pignani. The pious priest reduces HMV to demonology (using for the purpose the *nihil obstat* of his church superiors), and its concluding failure he attributes to Divine Intervention. This resulted, I guess, from Lord of the Flies, that name jokingly made up at the Project, which Father Pignani took seriously, acting like a child who thinks the names of the stars and planets are written on them, and that the astronomers read these off through their telescopes.

To say nothing of the swarm of sensational versions—which are like those frozen meals one heats and serves, practically pre-chewed, which look a great deal better under the cellophane than they taste. The ingredients are seasoned with an ever-novel but always fabulously colored sauce. *Look* used the spy-political to season its series of articles (putting into my mouth words I never said); *The New Yorker* served up a dish more refined, adding certain essences of philosophy; and, again, in *HMV: Between the Lines*, Dr. Shapiro provided a psychoanalytic interpretation, from which I learned that the people of the Project were driven by a libido made unnatural by the projections of the newest—cosmic—mythology of sex. Dr. Shapiro is also in possession of precise information concerning the sex life of cosmic civilizations.

I cannot for the life of me understand why, while people without driver's licenses are not allowed on public roads, in bookstores one can find any number of books by persons without decency—let alone knowledge. The inflation of the printed word has been caused, no doubt, by the exponential increase in the number of those writing, but in equal degree by editorial policies. In the childhood of our civilization only select, well-educated individuals were able to read and write, and much the same criterion held after the invention of printing; and even if the works of imbeciles were published (which, I suppose, is impossible to avoid completely), their total number was not astronomical, as it is today. Today, in the flood of garbage, valuable publications must go under, because it is easier to find one worthwhile book among ten worthless than a thousand among a million. Moreover, the phenomenon of pseudo plagiarism becomes inevitable—the unintentional repetition of the ideas of others who are unknown.

I can have no certainty that what I write is not similar to what already has been written. This is one hazard of an age of population explosion. If I have decided to present my reminiscences in connection with the work of the Project, it is because nothing I have read on the subject so far has satisfied me. I do not promise to "tell the truth and nothing but the truth." Had our labor been crowned with success, that might have been possible, but success at the same time would have made such an undertaking unnecessary, for then the concluding truth would have eclipsed the circumstances of its attainment; it would have become a material fact nailed in the center of our civilization. But the failure somehow has cast all our efforts back to their sources. Since we do not understand the mystery, nothing really remains to us but those circumstances that were to have been the scaffolding—and not the edifice itself—or the process of translating—and not the content of the work. And yet the former turned out to be all that we returned with from our quest for the Golden Fleece of the Stars. It is here that I part company as well with the versions that I called objective, beginning with the *Baloyne Report*, because the word "failure" does not appear in them. Did we not leave the Project incomparably richer than when we entered it? New chapters opened up in the physics of colloids, in the physics of strong interactions, in neutrino astronomy, in nucleonics, biology, and, above all, the new knowledge of the Universe—this represents but the first interest that has accrued to us from the informational principal, which, according to the experts, promises huge profits to come.

No doubt. But there are benefits and there are benefits. Ants that encounter in their path a dead philosopher may make good use of him. If the example is shocking, I intend it to be. Literature, from the very beginning, has had a single enemy, and that is the restriction of the expressed idea. It turns out, however, that freedom of expression sometimes presents a greater threat to an idea, because forbidden thoughts may circulate in secret, but what can be done when an important fact is lost in a flood of impostors, and the voice of truth becomes drowned out in an ungodly din? When that voice, though freely resounding, cannot be heard, because the technologies of information have led to a situation in which one can receive best the message of him who shouts the loudest, even when the most falsely?

I had not a little to say about the Project, but hesitated a long time before sitting down at my desk, aware that I would be adding to what already was a swollen sea of paper. I had assumed that someone more adept with words would perform the task for me; but after years passed I realized that I could not remain silent. The most important works dealing with His Master's Voice, the objective versions, with the Congressional at the head, admit that we did not learn everything; but the amount of space devoted to the achievements, with occasional footnote mentions of what remained unknown—those very proportions suggested that we had mastered the Labyrinth, with the exception of a few corridors—dead ends, no doubt, probably buried in rubble—whereas in fact we did not get as far as the entrance. Doomed forever to conjecture, having chipped a few flecks from the lock that sealed the gate, we delighted in the glitter that gilded our fingertips. But of what was locked we know nothing. And yet, surely, one of the first duties of a scientist is to determine the extent not of the acquired knowledge, for that knowledge will explain itself, but, rather, of the ignorance, which is the invisible Atlas beneath that knowledge.

I have no illusions. I fear that I will not be listened to, because no longer are there universal authorities. The distribution—or disintegration—of specialization has advanced so far that the experts declare me unqualified whenever I encroach upon their particular territory. It has been said that a specialist is a barbarian whose ignorance is not well-rounded. My pessimism is based on personal experience.

Nineteen years ago I published, with a young anthropologist named Maxwell Thorpe, who later died tragically in an automobile accident, a paper in which I proved the existence of a complexity threshold for finite automata with algedonic control, to which class belong all the animals as well as man. Algedonic control means an oscillation between punishment and reward, as between pain and pleasure.

My proof showed that if the number of elements of a regulatory center (a brain) exceeds the maximum of four billion, the set of such automata displays a distribution between the opposing parameters of control. In each such automaton one of the poles of control can become dominant; or—to put it in more popular language—sadism and masochism cannot be avoided, and their appearance in the anthropogenetic process was inevitable. Evolution "chose" such a solution because it operates statistically: what matters to it is the survival of the species, and not the defective states, the ills, the sufferings of separate individuals. Evolution is, as an engineer, an opportunist, not a perfectionist.

I was able to show that in any human population, assuming panmixia (random interbreeding), at most 10 percent will manifest a good equilibrium of algedonic control, while the rest must deviate from the norm. Inasmuch as I belonged, even at that time, in the forefront of the mathematical world, the impact of this proof on the communities of anthropologists, ethnologists, biologists, and philosophers was equal to zero. For a long time I could not understand it. My work was no hypothesis but a formal—therefore irrefutable—proof demonstrating that certain human characteristics, over which a legion of thinkers through the centuries had racked their brains, were accounted for entirely by a process of statistical fluctuation, a process—whether in the construction of automata or of organisms—impossible to circumvent.

Later I expanded the proof to include, as well, the phenomenon of the appearance of ethics in social groups, and there I was able to rely on the excellent material that had been prepared by Thorpe. But this paper, too, was ignored. After a number of years, having had a great many discussions with the specialists who dealt with man, I came to the conclusion that my discovery had failed to gain their recognition for the reason that none of them wanted *that kind* of discovery. The style of thinking that I represented was in those circles a repugnant thing, because it provided no scope for rhetorical counterargument.

It had been tactless of me to prove something on the topic of man—mathematically! At the very best my work was called "interesting." Not one of those specialists was willing to accept that the venerable Mystery of Man, the unexplainable aspects of his nature, is a consequence of the General Theory of Regulation. Of course, this opposition was not expressed outright, but the proof was held against me. I had behaved like a bull in a china shop, because that which could not be figured out by anthropology and ethnography, with their field research, or by the profoundest philosophical reflection-meditation on "human nature," and which defied propositional formulation in both neurophysiology and ethology, and which provided fertile ground for ever-proliferating metaphysics, for psychological abstrusity, and for psychoanalysis classical and linguistic, and God knows what other esoteric study —I had attempted to cut through, like the Gordian knot, with my proof contained in nine printed pages.

They had grown accustomed to their high office of Keepers of the Mystery, whether the Mystery was called the Transmission of

Archetypes, Instinct, the Life Force, or the Death Wish; and I, crossing out these holy words with some sort of transformational groups and ergodic theorems, claimed to possess the solution to the problem! Therefore they took a decided dislike to me (though scrupulously concealed)—an indignation toward that crude heathen who lifted his hand against the Enigma, who sought to stop up its perennially vital wellspring, and silence lips that with such satisfaction posed unending questions. Since the proof allowed no refutation, it became necessary to ignore it.

These remarks are not occasioned by a wounded vanity. The works for which I was hoisted up on a pedestal belong in another field—that of pure mathematics. But the experience was most enlightening. We tend to underestimate the inertia of the style of thought in different branches of science. Psychologically, of course, it is to be expected. The resistance we offer to the statistical model is much more easily overcome in atomic physics than in anthropology. We gladly accept a lucid, well-constructed statistical theory of the atomic nucleus, if experimentation supports it. Becoming acquainted with such a theory, we do not ask, "Fine, but how are the atoms *actually* behaving?"—because we know the foolishness of such a question. But similar revelations in the realm of anthropology we will fight with our last breath.

It has been known, for forty years now, that the difference between a noble, upright man and a maniacal degenerate can be pinpointed at the site of a few clumps of white matter in the brain, and that the movement of a lancet in the supraorbital area of the brain, if it damages those clumps, can transform a splendid soul into a loathsome creature. Yet what an enormous portion of anthropology—not to mention the philosophy of man—refuses to take cognizance of this circumstance! But I am no exception here; whether scientists or laymen, we agree finally that our bodies deteriorate with age—but the mind?! We would like to see it different from any earthly mechanism subject to defect. We crave an ideal —even one carrying a minus sign, even one shameful, sinful, so long as it delivers us from an explanation worse than the Satanic: that what is taking place is a certain play of forces perfectly indifferent to man. And because our thinking moves in circles from which it is impossible to leap free, I admit that there is some truth in the words of one of our foremost anthropologists. He said to me once—I remember it well—"The satisfaction with which you parade your proof of the lottery origin of human nature is not pure. It is, besides the joy of knowledge, a pleasure in befouling that which others consider lovely and hold dear."

Whenever that unrecognized work of mine comes to mind, I cannot help thinking, sadly, that there must be many other such works in the world. Rich lodes of potential discoveries no doubt lie in various libraries, but have gone unnoticed, untapped, by competent people.

We are at home with this simple image: what is dark and unknown stretches out before the monolithic front line of science, while what has been acquired and understood constitutes its rear. But it really makes no difference whether the unknown lies in the lap of Nature or, instead, is buried among the pages of worthless manuscripts read by no one; because an idea that has not entered the bloodstream of science, and does not circulate seminally in it, in practice does not exist for us. The receptivity of science, at any time in history, to a radically different interpretation of phenomena has in fact not been great. The madness and suicide of one of the creators of thermodynamics is an example of this.

Our civilization, in its "advanced" scientific part, is a narrow construct, a vision repeatedly constricted by a historically stiffening conglomeration of multiple factors, among which sheer coincidence, though considered to be in strict accordance with inflexible methodologies, may play a major role. All that I write here is to the point.

Given that our civilization is unable to assimilate well even those concepts that originate in human heads when they appear outside its main current, although the creators of those concepts are, after all, children of the same age—how could we have assumed that we would be capable of understanding a civilization totally unlike ours, if it addressed us across the cosmic gulf? The metaphor of an army of tiny creatures that put to good use their encounter with the corpse of a philosopher—still seems to me very fitting. Until such an encounter took place, my view might have been judged extreme, the attitude of a crackpot. But the meeting did come to pass, and the defeat we suffered in it represented a true *experimentum crucis*, a proof of our resourcelessness, and *still* the result of that proof was ignored! The myth of our cognitive universality, of our readiness to receive and comprehend information absolutely new—absolutely, since extraterrestrial—continues unimpaired, even though, receiving the message from the stars, we did with it no more than a savage who, warming himself by a fire of burning books, the writings of the wisest men, believes that he has drawn tremendous benefit from his find!

And so the recording of the history of our *vain* efforts may prove useful—if only to some later, future student of the First Contact—because the published accounts, those official reports, concentrate on the so-called successes, that is, on the pleasant warmth that emanates from the burning pages. Of the hypotheses we tried, one after another, practically nothing is said there. Such a course of action would have been permissible—I alluded to this already—had the thing investigated been kept separate, in the end, from its investigators. Those who study physics are not burdened with information about what incorrect, imprecise hypotheses, what false notions, were advanced by its creators; for how long Pauli groped about before he formulated, in the right way, his Principle; or the number of abortive conceptions Dirac tried before the fortunate guess of his electron "holes." But the history of His Master's Voice is the tale of a defeat: of wrong turns that were not followed by a straightened path. Thus one should not wipe away the zigzags of our journey, because those zigzags are all that is left us.

A considerable amount of time has passed since these events. I have waited patiently for a book like this one. But I cannot wait—for reasons purely biological—any longer. I availed myself of certain notes taken immediately after the closing of the Project. As for why I did not include them in one of my papers, that will become evident. There is one thing I would like to make clear. It is not my intention to raise myself above my colleagues. We stood at the feet of a gigantic find, as unprepared, but also as sure of ourselves, as we could possibly be. We clambered up on it from every side, quickly, hungrily, and cleverly, with our time-honored skill, like ants. I was one of them. This is the story of an ant.

2

A **PROFESSIONAL COLLEAGUE** to whom I showed my preface remarked that I had painted myself black in order to be able afterward to give free rein to my outspokenness, on the principle that those whom I took to task could not easily hold it against me if first I did such honors for myself. Though said half in jest, the observation struck me. So devious a design had not entered my head, and yet we are familiar enough with the mechanics of the mind to know that such protestations are worthless. It is possible that the remark was true, that an unconscious cunning had been in operation. The ugliness of my malice I made public; I localized it, in order to divorce myself from it—but I did this only in words.

Meanwhile, by stealth, it penetrated, permeated my "good intentions," and all the time guided my pen, so that I proceeded like a preacher who, calling fire and brimstone down upon the foulness of man, finds a secret pleasure in at least describing what he dares not participate in actively himself. In this diametrically opposed view of the matter, what I held to be an unpleasant necessity dictated by the gravity of the subject becomes the primary motive, while the subject itself—His Master's Voice—is a pretext that came conveniently to hand. But the framework of this reasoning, which one could call carrousellike—in that it goes in circles, the premises and conclusions changing places—can in turn be attributed to the very substance of the Project. Our thinking must come up against some hard focal point of facts that sobers it and corrects it; in the absence of such a corrective, it easily turns into a projection of private flaws (or virtues, it doesn't matter)—onto the plane of the thing studied. The reduction of a philosophical system to the biographical vicissitudes of its creator is considered (I know something of this) an occupation as petty as it is unsporting. But at the core of philosophy—which always wants to say more than is possible at a given time, because it represents an effort to "capture the world" in a closed conceptual net—even in the works of the most illustrious thinkers, there lies hidden an acute vulnerability.

Man's quest for knowledge is an expanding series whose limit is infinity, but philosophy seeks to attain that limit at one blow, by a short circuit providing the certainty of complete and inalterable truth. Science meanwhile advances at its gradual pace, often slowing to a crawl, and for periods it even walks in place, but eventually it reaches the various ultimate trenches dug by philosophical thought, and, quite heedless of the fact that it is not supposed to be able to cross those final barriers to the intellect, goes right on.

How could this not drive the philosophers to despair? One form of that despair was Positivism, remarkable in its hostility, because it played the loyal ally of science but in fact sought to abolish it. The thing that had undermined and destroyed philosophy, annulling its great discoveries, now was to be severely punished, and Positivism, the false friend, passed that sentence—demonstrating that science could not truly discover anything, inasmuch as it constituted no more than a shorthand record of experience. Positivism desired to muzzle science, to compel it somehow to declare itself helpless in all transcendental matters (which, however, as we know, Positivism failed to do).

The history of philosophy is the history of successive and nonidentical retreats. Philosophy first tried to discover the ultimate categories of the world; then the absolute categories of reason; while we, as knowledge accumulates, see more and more clearly philosophy's vulnerability: because every philosopher must regard himself as a model for the entire species, and even for all possible sentient beings. But it is science that is the transcendence of experience, demolishing yesterday's categories of thought. Yesterday, absolute space-time was overthrown; today, the eternal alternative between the analytic and the synthetic in propositions, or between determinism and randomness, is crumbling. But somehow it has not occurred to any of our philosophers that to deduce, from the pattern of one's own thoughts, laws that hold for the full set of people, from the eolithic until the day the suns burn out, might be, to put it mildly, imprudent.

This initial equating of oneself with the norm of the species—an unknown—was, to be plain, irresponsible. One justification for it became the incessant desire to understand "everything"—a desire having only psychological value. Thus philosophy speaks of human hopes, fears, and longings at much greater length than it does of the essence of the completely indifferent world, a world that is an eternal constant of laws only for the news media.

And even were we to find such laws, laws that future advances would not supplant, we would not be able to distinguish them from those that eventually will be discarded. For this reason I could respect philosophers only as people driven by curiosity, never as propounders of truth. When, in formulating their theses of categorical imperatives, of the relationship of thought to perception— when did they conscientiously undertake to question, first, a large number of human subjects? No—they consulted always and only themselves. It is this repeated self-enthronement of theirs, this tacit setting up of themselves as models of *Homo sapiens*, that has always aggravated me and made it hard for me to read "profound" works—because in them I quickly reach the place where the author's *obvious* is no longer mine, and thereafter he speaks only to himself, tells only of himself, appeals only to himself, and loses the right to deliver pronouncements that are valid for me, not to mention the rest of the bipeds that populate the planet.

I had to laugh, for instance, at the assurance of those who determined that all thought was linguistic. Those philosophers did not know that they were creating a subset of the species, i.e., the group of those not gifted mathematically. How many times in my life, after the revelation of a new discovery, having formulated it so solidly that it was quite indelible, unforgettable, was I obliged to wrestle for hours to find for it some verbal suit of clothes, because the thing had been born, in me, beyond the pale of all language, natural or formal?

I call this phenomenon "surfacing." It defies description, because what emerges from the unconscious with difficulty, slowly, finds nests of words for itself; it exists as an entity before it settles inside those nests; yet I can give no indication, no hint, to explain in precisely what form that non- and preverbalness appears; it is heralded only by a keen presentiment that the expectation of it will not be in vain. The philosopher who does not know such states from introspection is, with respect to the quality of certain mechanisms in the brain, a man unlike me; we may belong to the same species, but we differ far more than such thinkers could wish.

It was precisely with regard to the vulnerability and the huge risk that the philosopher takes upon himself that the situation of the people of the Project was similar, in the face of its central problem. What did we have to work with? A mystery and a jungle of guesses. From the mystery we chipped off a few slivers of fact, but when they did not increase, or amount to any solid edifice that could correct our hypotheses, the hypotheses began gradually to assume the upper hand, and in the end we wandered lost in a wilderness of conjectures, of conjectures based upon conjectures. Our constructs became more and more inspired and bold, more and more removed from the store of accumulated knowledge—we were prepared to raze that store, to lay in ruins the most sacred principles of physics or astronomy, if only we could possess the mystery. So it seemed to us.

The reader who has plowed his way to this point and is waiting, with growing impatience, to be led into the inner sanctum of the famous enigma, in the hope that I will regale him with thrills and chills every bit as delightful as those he experiences viewing horror movies, I advise to set my book down now, because he will be disappointed. I am writing no sensational story, but telling how our civilization was subjected to a test of cosmic—or at least of more-than-terrestrial—universality, and what came of this. From the beginning of my work in the Project, I believed that the Project was just such a test, quite apart from the question of what benefits were anticipated from my activity and that of my friends.

He who has been following me closely may have noticed that in shifting the problem of "carrousellike reasoning" from the relationship between myself and my theme, to the theme itself (i.e., to the relationship between the scientists and His Master's Voice), I extricated myself from an embarrassing position, widening the accusation of "undisclosed sources of inspiration" until it covered the entire Project. But that had been my intention even before I heard such criticism. With an exaggeration that is necessary for the clarification of my meaning, I will say that in the course of my work (it is difficult to say exactly when this occurred) I began to suspect that the "letter from the stars" was, for us who attempted to decipher it, a kind of psychological association test, a particularly complex Rorschach test. For as a subject, believing he sees in the colored blotches angels or birds of ill omen, in reality fills in the vagueness of the thing shown with what is "on his mind," so did we attempt, behind the veil of incomprehensible signs, to discern the presence of what lay, first and foremost, within ourselves.

This suspicion hampered my work, and now has compelled me to make confessions I would have much preferred not to make; I realize, however, that a scientist baffled to that degree can no longer regard his professional ability as a kind of isolated gland or molar; he may not, therefore, conceal even the most embarrassing of his personal problems. A botanist who classifies flowers has not much of a field on which to project schemata of his fantasies, illusions, and perhaps even dishonorable passions. The researcher of ancient myths runs a greater risk, because—given their abundance—the very choice he makes may testify more to what pervades his dreams and unscientific thoughts than to what constitutes the structural invariables of the myths themselves.

The people of the Project were forced to take the next, reckless step—accepting a risk of the nature mentioned above but on a scale hitherto unknown. None of us knows, therefore, to what extent we were the instruments of an objective analysis, to what extent the delegates of humanity (in that we have been shaped by and are typical of our society), and to what extent, finally, each of us represented only himself, with the inspiration for his hypotheses about the contents of the "letter" being supplied by his own—possibly raving, possibly wounded—psyche in its uncontrolled regions.

Misgivings of this kind, when I voiced them, were treated by many of my colleagues as pure drivel. They may have used other words, but that was what they meant.

I understood them perfectly. The Project constituted a precedent in which, like those Russian wooden dolls-within-dolls, sat other precedents, and primarily this: that never before had physicists, engineers, chemists, nucleonicists, biologists, or information theorists held in their hands an object of research that represented not only a certain material—hence natural—puzzle, but which had been intentionally made by Someone and transmitted, and where the intent must have taken into account the potential addressee. Because scientists learn to conduct so-called games with nature, with a nature that is not—from any permissible point of view—a personal antagonist, they are unable to countenance the possibility that behind the object of investigation there indeed stands a Someone, and that to become familiar with that object will be possible only insofar as one draws near, through reasoning, to its completely anonymous creator. Therefore, though they supposedly knew and freely admitted that the Sender was a reality, their whole life's training, the whole acquired expertise of their respective fields, worked against that knowledge.

A physicist never thinks that Someone has set the electrons in their orbits for the express purpose of making him, the physicist, rack his brains over orbital configurations. He knows that the hypothesis of a Setter of Orbits is, in physics, completely unnecessary—more, altogether inadmissible. But in the Project such an impossibility turned out to be an actuality; physics stood by useless in its prior posture; genuine agonies were suffered because of this. What I have said should, I think, make it clear that inside the Project I occupied a rather isolated position (in the theoretical, general sense, of course, not administratively).

I have been accused of being "counterproductive" because I constantly had my two cents' worth to stick in, and did so in the course of other people's reasonings, causing those to grind to a halt; whereas I introduced little of my own of any use, few ideas that "someone could do something with." Baloyne, though, speaks highly of me in the Congressional Report (not only out of the friendship that unites us, I hope), which may in part have stemmed from his position (administrative as well as scientific). In each particular research group different views, after a period of oscillation, converged to some collectively held opinion, but any-one who sat (as Baloyne did) on the Science Council saw clearly that the opinions of the various groups were often diametrically opposed. The organizational structure of the Project, with its mu-tual isolation of the different groups, I considered wise, because it prevented any kind of "epidemic of error." This informational quarantine, however, did have its negative aspects. But here I am entering into details—prematurely. It is time we went on to an account of the events.

3

WHEN BLADERGROEN, NORRIS, and Shigubov's team discovered the inversion of the neutrino, a new chapter in astronomy was opened up, in the form of neutrino astrophysics. Overnight it became extremely fashionable; throughout the world people began to study the cosmic emission of these particles. The observatory on Mount Palomar installed one of the first apparatuses, a thing highly automated and with a resolution, for those days, of exceptional power. At this apparatus—more precisely, at the so-called neutrino inverter—there formed a line of eager scientists, and the director of the Observatory, who at that time was Professor Ryan, had his hands full with astrophysicists, young ones in particular, each of whom felt that *his* research project should be given priority.

Among the fortunate few was a duo of such youngsters, Halsey and Mahoun, both ambitious and quite capable (I knew them, though only briefly); they recorded the maxima of the neutrino emission from certain selected patches of the sky, looking for traces of the so-called Stöglitz Effect (Stöglitz was a German astronomer of the previous generation).

This effect, supposed to be the neutrino equivalent of the "red shift" in photons, somehow never was found; and indeed, it turned out several years later that Stöglitz's theory was wrong. But the young men had no way of knowing this, so they fought like lions to

35

hold on to the apparatus; thanks to their initiative, they had the use of it for almost two years—only to leave, in the end, empty-handed. Miles of their recording tape went into the Observatory archives at that time. Several months later a considerable portion of those tapes found their way into the hands of a shrewd but not particularly talented physicist—actually, the man had been dismissed from a little-known institution in the South, in connection with the commission of certain immoral acts; the matter was not taken to court, because it involved several highly respected persons. This physicist *manqué*, by the name of Swanson, obtained the tapes in circumstances that remain unclear. He was questioned afterward, but nothing was ever learned, since he kept changing his testimony.

An interesting individual, nevertheless. He made his living as a supplier, and banker, and even spiritual comforter for the kind of maniacs who in earlier times confined themselves to building perpetual-motion machines and squaring the circle, but who nowadays discover various forms of health-giving energy, think up theories of cosmogenesis, and devise ways of commercially utilizing telepathic phenomena. Such people need more than pencil and paper; to construct "orgonotrons," detectors of "supersensitive" fluids, or electronic dowsing rods that locate water, petroleum, and buried treasure (dowsing rods of ordinary willow are an anachronism now, worthless antiques), one needs numerous raw materials, which are often expensive and difficult to obtain. Swanson was able, for an appropriate amount of cash, to move heaven and earth to get them. His bureau was frequented by paraphysicists and ectoplasmologists, builders of teleportation stations and of pneumatographs that made possible the opening of communications with the spirit world. Circulating in this way in the lower regions of the kingdom of science, where it merges imperceptibly with the realm of psychiatry, he acquired an amount of quite useful information; he knew, with surprising accuracy, where lay the greatest demand among his crippled titans of intellect.

Not that he turned up his nose at more mundane sources of revenue; for example, he supplied small chemistry laboratories with reagents of unknown origin. There was no period in his life in which he was not involved in legal difficulties, although he was never jailed, managing to balance at the very brink of criminality.

The psychology of people like Swanson has always fascinated me. As far as I can tell, he was neither a "simple crook" nor a cynic who preyed on the aberrations of others, though he must have had intelligence enough to know that the great majority of his clients would never carry out their ideas. Some he took under his wing and gave equipment on credit, even when that credit was worn awfully thin. Apparently, he had a weakness for his protégés, just as I have for individuals of his type. His aim was to serve his client well, so if someone absolutely had to have horn of rhinoceros, because the instrument assembled with any other horn would remain deaf to the voice of the departed, Swanson did not deliver bull or ram—or so, at least, I have been told.

Receiving—perhaps purchasing—the tapes from an unknown person, Swanson showed good business sense. He had enough of an acquaintance with physics to know that what had been recorded on them represented what is called "pure noise," and he hit upon the idea of producing—with the aid of the tapes—tables of random numbers. Such tables, also known as random series, are used in many areas of research; they are produced either by specially programmed digital computers or with the help of rotating disks marked with numbers on the rims and illuminated by an irregularly flashing beam of light. And there are other ways to produce them, but anyone who undertakes this frequently runs into problems, because the series obtained rarely are "sufficiently" random. Upon closer examination they display, more or less plainly, regularities in the appearance of particular numbers, because—in long series, especially—certain numbers "somehow" tend to show up more often than others, which is enough to disqualify such a table. No, deliberately creating "complete chaos," and in a "pure state" at that, is not easy. At the same time, the demand for random tables is constant. Therefore Swanson counted on turning a nice profit, all the more so since his brother-in-law was a linotype operator in a university print shop. The tables were printed up there, and Swanson sold them by mail, avoiding the middleman of a bookseller.

One of the copies of this publication ended up in the hands of Dr. Sam Laserowitz, another very dubious individual. Like Swanson, he was a man of uncommon enterprise, possessing also, in his own way, a touch of idealism; not everything that he did was for money. He belonged to—and occasionally had also founded—numerous organizations, on the order of the Flying Saucer Society, and was in and out of financial hot water, since the budgets of those associations often showed unaccountable losses; embezzlement, however, was never proved. It is possible that the man was simply careless.

Despite the "Dr." before his name, he had completed no course of study and received no degree. When people tried to pin him down about this, he would say that the letters were merely an abbreviation of his first name—Drummond—which he did not use. But it was as "Dr." Sam Laserowitz that he appeared in a number of science-fiction magazines; he was also known, in the circles of the fans of that genre, as a lecturer, and spoke on "cosmic" themes at their many conferences and conventions. Laserowitz's specialty was earthshaking discoveries, which he happened upon two or three times a year. Among other things, he established a museum in which the exhibits were items allegedly left by passengers of flying saucers at various locations in the United States. One of these was a shaved, dyed-green monkey fetus floating in alcohol—I saw a photograph of it. We really have no idea what a multitude of con men and crackpots inhabit the domain that lies halfway between contemporary science and the insane asylum.

Laserowitz was, in addition, the coauthor of a book about the "conspiracy" of the governments of the Great Powers to suppress all information on saucer landings, not to mention contacts between our high-placed political figures and emissaries from other planets. Collecting all possible (more or less ridiculous) "evidence" of the activity of "Others in the Universe," he finally hit on the trail of the recordings from Mount Palomar and sought out their present possessor, who was Swanson. Swanson did not wish to lend them to him at first, but Laserowitz presented him with a powerful argument in the form of six hundred dollars—one of Laserowitz's "cosmic foundations" was backed by a generous eccentric.

Before long, Laserowitz was publishing a series of articles with screaming headlines, declaring that on the Mount Palomar tapes certain areas of noise were interspersed with sections of silence, so that together they formed the dots and dashes of Morse code. Then, in increasingly sensational pronouncements, he cited Halsey and Mahoun, authorities in astrophysics, as proof of the authenticity of his revelation. When this news was reprinted in a few local papers, an angered Dr. Halsey sent them a correction. He advised them, with an economy of words, that Laserowitz was a complete ignoramus (how would the "Others" know Morse code?), that his society for communicating with the Universe was imbecilic, and that the "sections of silence" on the tapes were blanks that occurred because from time to time the recording machine would shut off. Laserowitz would not have been himself had he borne meekly such a dressing-down; unfazed, he added Halsey to his blacklist of the foes of "cosmic contact," which already contained quite a number of enlightened people who had unwisely stood in opposition to Laserowitz's past triumphs.

Meanwhile, independently of this business, which in the press had acquired a circulation of sorts, a truly curious incident came about. It began when Dr. Ralph Loomis, a statistician by education, who had his own agency, doing, mainly, market research for smaller companies, wrote to Swanson with a complaint. It seemed that nearly a third of volume two of Swanson's random tables was a perfect duplication of a previous series found in volume one. Loomis suggested that perhaps Swanson, not wanting to labor over the systematic transcription of "noise" into columns of figures, had done it only once, and then, instead of providing further random sequences, mechanically copied the first series, bothering only to shuffle a couple of pages. Swanson, at least in this particular case, had a clear conscience; he rejected Loomis's demand for reimbursement and in indignation wrote him a few choice words. Loomis, in turn indignant, and considering himself swindled, took the matter to court. Swanson was fined for personal abuse; moreover, the court agreed with the plaintiff that the second installment of the series tables was a fraudulent repetition of the first. Swanson appealed, but five weeks later withdrew his appeal and, paying the fine, disappeared without a trace.

The Topeka *Morning Star* several times gave coverage of the litigation of Loomis versus Swanson, because it was the silly season then and there were no better stories. One of these articles was read by Dr. Saul Rappaport of the Institute for Advanced Study on his way to work (as he told me, he found the paper on a seat in the train—he never would have purchased it).

It was Saturday, and the *Morning Star*, having additional column space to fill that day, included, besides the court proceedings, Laserowitz's "Brothers in Reason" declaration, along with an irate rebuttal from Dr. Halsey. Rappaport therefore was able to see the whole of this strange if insignificant affair. As he put down the paper, a thought came to him, a thought so queer that it was comical: Laserowitz, taking the "sections of silence" on the tapes for signals, was without question raving. And yet it was conceivable that at the same time the man could be right, seeing in the tapes a "communication"—if that communication was the very noise!

An insane idea, but Rappaport could not rid himself of it. A stream of information—human speech, for example—does not always tell us that it is information and not a chaos of sounds. Often we receive a foreign language as complete babble. Individual words can be distinguished only by someone who understands the language. For someone who does not, there exists but one way to make possible that all-important recognition. In the case where we receive true noise, individual signals never repeat themselves in the same order. In this sense a "noise series" would be, say, a thousand numbers that show on a roulette wheel. It would be quite impossible for the next thousand turns of the wheel to repeat, in the same sequence, the results of the preceding series. This is precisely the essence of "noise," that the order of appearance of its elements—be they sounds or other signals—is unforeseeable. If, however, the series repeats itself, it proves that the "noise" quality of the phenomenon is superficial, that in fact we have before us a transmitter acting as a channel of information.

Dr. Rappaport thought to himself that, just possibly, Swanson had not lied to the judge and had not copied, in a circle, one single tape, but had used sequentially the tapes that resulted from those many months of recording cosmic radiation. If the radiation was an intentional signaling, and if, in that period of time, one series of emissions of the "communication" concluded and then the transmission of the communication was resumed from the beginning, the result would be what Swanson swore to. The subsequent tapes would record the exact same series of impulses, which by their *repetition* would reveal that their noise aspect was only an illusion!

It was in the highest degree unlikely, but nevertheless possible. Whenever he experienced brainstorms like this, Rappaport, usually an easygoing sort of person, showed unusual initiative and energy. The paper gave the address of Dr. Halsey, so it was simple to get in touch with him. The main thing Rappaport needed was to get his hands on one of the tapes. He wrote to Halsey, but without revealing his idea—it would have sounded too fantastic—and asked only whether Halsey would mind lending him the tapes that remained in the archives of Mount Palomar. Halsey, put out by having got involved in the Laserowitz business, refused. It was then that Rappaport took up the matter in earnest; he wrote directly to the Observatory. His name was well enough known in scientific circles, and in no time he acquired a good kilometer of tape, which he handed over to his friend Dr. Hense, so that he could run a computer analysis of the frequency distribution of its elements.

But the problem, even in this phase, was much more complex than I have presented it here. Information resembles pure noise to a greater degree the more thoroughly (economically) the transmitter makes use of the channel of the transmission. If the channel is made use of totally—if, in other words, there is no redundancy—the signal, for one uninformed, in no respect differs from utter chaos. As I have said, it is only possible to reveal such noise as information if the emissions of the message repeat themselves in a circle and one can set them side by side for comparison. That was exactly Rappaport's intention. He was to be assisted in this by equipment at the computer center where Hense worked. Rappaport did not tell Hense at first what he was about, preferring to keep it quiet; this way, if his idea fizzled, no one would ever know. This amusing beginning of what later became a most unamusing affair was related by Rappaport many times; he even kept, like a sacred relic, a copy of the newspaper that had led him to his famous revelation.

Hense, burdened with work, was not particularly eager to take on an arduous analysis without even knowing the purpose; so Rappaport finally decided to let him in on the secret. Hense's first reaction was to laugh at Rappaport; but, impressed by the latter's arguments, he at length agreed to the request.

When Rappaport returned, several days later, to Massachusetts,

Hense greeted him with news of negative results, which, in Hense's opinion, refuted the fantastic hypothesis. Rappaport—I know this from him—was ready to abandon the whole thing, but, nettled by the gibes of his friend, began to argue with him. After all, he told him, the entire neutrino emission of one quadrant of the firmament is a veritable ocean covering an enormous spectrum of frequencies, and even if Halsey and Mahoun, combing that spectrum once, had by sheer luck pulled out from it a "piece" of emission that was artificial, coming from an intelligent sender, it would be a miracle indeed for them to accomplish the same thing—again by luck—a second time.

Therefore they should try to get the tapes that were in Swanson's possession. Hense went along with this reasoning, but observed (he, too, wanted to be right) that, given the alternative of "message from the stars" versus "Swanson's fraud," the second proposition had a probability a few billion times greater than the first. He added that obtaining the tapes would do Rappaport little good: Swanson, when he received the court summons, and no doubt wanting to build himself a good defense, could simply have copied the tape he had and then presented that copy as another original neutrino recording.

Rappaport had no answer to that, but he knew someone in the field of long-sequence semiautomatic recording devices. He telephoned the man and asked if it was in any way possible to distinguish a tape on which certain natural processes were registered from tapes onto which similar impressions had been transferred secondhand. (In other words, what was the difference—if any existed—between an original recording and a copy of it?) It turned out that such a distinction could sometimes be made. Rappaport then went to Swanson's lawyer and in a week had the full set of tapes at his disposal. As it turned out, all were pronounced original by the expert; thus Swanson had committed no fraud, and thus the emission had in fact repeated itself periodically.

Rappaport informed neither Hense nor Swanson's lawyer of this finding, but that very same day—or, rather, that very night—he flew to Washington. Well aware of the hopelessness of trying to force his way through the bureaucracy's obstacle course, he went straight to Mortimer Rush, the President's science adviser and the former director of NASA, whom he knew personally. Rush, a physicist by education, a man with a first-rate head on his shoulders, received Rappaport despite the lateness of the hour. For three weeks Rappaport waited in Washington while the tapes were examined by specialists of increasing importance.

Finally, Rush requested his presence at a conference in which a total of nine people participated, among whom were the shining lights of American science—Donald Prothero the physicist, Yvor Baloyne the linguist and philologist, Tihamer Dill the astrophysicist, and John Baer the mathematician and information theorist. At that conference it was decided, informally, to set up a special commission to study the "neutrino letter from the stars," which was given then the code name—Baloyne's half-joking suggestion —His Master's Voice. Rush urged discretion on the participants of the conference, for the time being, because he feared that the media's giving the matter a sensational cast could only harm its chances of gaining the necessary funding; the thing would immediately become a political football in Congress, where Rush's position, as he represented a much-criticized administration, was shaky.

It appeared that the matter had been put on as sensible a course as possible, when, without warning, who should become mixed up in it but Dr. Sam Laserowitz. From the whole account of Swanson's trial, the one thing Laserowitz noted was that the court expert had said nothing in his testimony to the effect that the "sections of silence" on the tapes were "blanks" brought about by the periodic shutting-off of the apparatus. He drove, then, to Melville, where the trial was in process, and sat in the hotel lobby laying siege to Swanson's lawyer; Laserowitz wanted the tapes, feeling that they should be placed in his museum of "cosmic curiosities." The lawyer, however, refused to give them to Laserowitz, a person of no importance. Laserowitz, who smelled "anticosmic conspiracy" everywhere, hired a private detective to tail the lawyer; he thereby learned that some man from out of town, who had arrived on the morning train, was closeted with the lawyer at the hotel, received the tapes from the lawyer, and subsequently took them away with him, to Massachusetts.

The man was Dr. Rappaport. Laserowitz dispatched his detective on the trail of the unsuspecting Rappaport, and when the latter turned up in Washington and paid several visits to Rush, Laserowitz decided it was time to act. And a most unpleasant surprise it was, too, for Rush and the HMV candidates, that article from the *Morning Star* reprinted by one of the Washington tabloids, in which, under a suitably shrill headline, Laserowitz revealed how the administration was using every dirty trick at its disposal to hush up a tremendous discovery—exactly as, more than ten years earlier, it had buried beneath the official statements of the Department of Aviation the so-called unidentified flying objects, the famous saucers.

Only now did Rush realize that the matter could take on an ugly aspect in the international arena if the thought occurred to anyone that the United States was attempting to conceal from the world the fact that it had established contact with a cosmic civilization. He was not greatly concerned about the article itself, since its ludicrous tone discredited not only the author but the information as well; he calculated, therefore, relying on his considerable experience in the field of publicity, that if silence was maintained, the commotion would soon die down of itself.

But Baloyne decided to go see Laserowitz, in a purely personal capacity, because—he told me this himself—he felt sorry for the cosmic-contact maniac. He thought that if he offered him, in private, some minor position in the Project, everything would be set to rights. A foolish step, as it turned out, though dictated by the best intentions. Baloyne, who did not know Laserowitz, was taken in by the "Dr.," and believed that, though the man he had to deal with might be somewhat touched in the head, publicity-hungry, and not overly fastidious about how he made a buck, he was nevertheless a colleague, a scientist, a physicist. Instead he found himself face to face with a feverish little man who, upon hearing that the "letter from the stars" was genuine, informed him with a kind of hysterical nonchalance that the tapes, and consequently the "letter," too, were his property, of which he had been robbed. As the conversation progressed, he drove Baloyne into a rage. Laserowitz, seeing that he would gain nothing from Baloyne by words, ran out into the hall shouting that he would turn the matter over to the United Nations, to the Tribunal of Human Rights, then got into an elevator and left Baloyne to his unpleasant reflections.

Baloyne, seeing the mischief he had done, went immediately to Rush and told him everything. Rush feared for the future of the Project. However unlikely it was that someone somewhere would listen seriously to Laserowitz, the possibility could not be ruled out, and if the affair ever made its way into a major metropolitan newspaper, it would for certain assume a political character. The initiates could well imagine the hue and cry that would be raised: that the United States was seeking to appropriate for itself what by rights belonged to all humanity. Baloyne suggested that this might be forestalled by a brief, at least semiofficial press release; but Rush did not have the authorization to issue one, nor did he intend to request it, because—he explained—the thing still was not absolutely certain. Even if the government wished to back the undertaking with the full weight of its influence before the forum of nations, it could not do so until preliminary work had proved the truth of what so far were assumptions. However, since the matter was of a highly sensitive nature, Rush *nolens volens* had to turn to his friend Barnett, the Democratic minority leader in the Senate, who, in turn, after consulting with his people, turned to the FBI; who, however, referred him to the CIA. A top FBI legal adviser told him that the Universe, lying mainly outside the nation's borders, did not fall under the jurisdiction of the Bureau; it was the CIA that concerned itself with foreign problems.

The unfortunate consequences of this step did not show themselves at once, but the process, once begun, was irreversible. Rush, as an individual at the interface of science and politics, well knew the undesirable ramifications of placing the Project under such protection; therefore, asking the Senator to wait twenty-four hours, he sent two trusted men to Laserowitz in an effort to talk some sense into the man. Laserowitz not only refused to listen, he caused such a scene with his visitors that fisticuffs ensued and the hotel manager had to call the police.

The following days saw a flood of articles that were altogether fantastic—ridiculous accounts of various "dyads" and "triads" of silence sent to Earth by the Universe, of lights in the sky, of the landing of little green men wearing "neutrino clothes," and similar nonsense, in which reference was made, over and over, to Laserowitz, now promoted to Professor. But shortly thereafter, in less than a month, the "renowned scientist" turned out to be a paranoiac and was placed in a psychiatric hospital. Nor was this, unfortunately, the conclusion to his story. The syndicated press and the national magazines carried echoes of Laserowitz's phantasmagorical struggle (twice he escaped from the hospital, the second time in a radical manner, leaving via a window eight floors up) to defend his discovery, a discovery so insane—according to the versions published later—and yet so near the truth. I confess I get the shivers when I recall that fragment of the prehistory of our Project.

It is not hard to guess that filling the newspaper columns with items one more nonsensical than the next was nothing more or less than a diversionary tactic engineered by the skilled professionals of the CIA. Because to deny the business, and in the pages of the major publications at that, would have meant focusing attention on it in absolutely the most undesirable way. But to show that the thing was all delirium, to bury the grain of truth under an avalanche of imbecilic fictions—all attributed to "Professor" Laserowitz—was a clever move, particularly when the operation could be crowned with the insertion of a brief paragraph about the suicide of the madman, which, with its simple eloquence, completely laid to rest all rumors.

The fate of that fanatic was truly horrible. I did not at first believe that either his insanity or his last step from the window into an emptiness of eight stories was genuine, but people whom I have to trust convinced me of that version of events. Yet the sign of the times had been stamped at the head of our great undertaking —times that mix, perhaps as no other, the seamy and the sublime. The zigzag of coincidences, before it threw into our hands that colossal opportunity, crushed like a flea a man who, albeit in blindness, was still the first to approach the threshold of the discovery.

If I am not mistaken, Rush's emissaries had thought Laserowitz crazy at the point when he refused to accept a considerable sum of money in exchange for giving up his claims. But in that case he and I were of the same faith, with this one difference, that we practiced it in different monasteries. Had it not been for that great wave in which he became caught, Laserowitz would undoubtedly have prospered, a low-grade maniac devoting himself, undisturbed, to his flying saucers and all the rest of it, for there is surely no shortage of such people. But the knowledge that he was being relieved of his most sacred possession, a discovery that divided the history of mankind into two parts, tore his hardiness like an explosion and drove him to his death. In my opinion we owe more than a sneer to the man's memory. Every great matter has, among its circumstances, some that are ludicrous or pitifully banal, which does not mean that they do not play an integral role. Ludicrousness, anyway, is a relative thing. I, too, cut a ludicrous figure every time I spoke of Laserowitz in this vein.

Of all the dramatis personae of this prologue, Swanson probably came out the best, because he was satisfied with money. His fine was paid (whether by the CIA or the Project administration, I do not know), and, with a generous sum as compensation for the mental anguish he had suffered in being falsely accused of fraud, he was dissuaded from filing an appeal. All this so that the Project could begin its work in peace and quiet, in the complete isolation finally allotted it.

4

NOT ONLY THESE events, whose description here in general
—though not in every respect—agrees with the official version, but
the whole first year of the Project as well, passed without my
participation. As to why I was approached only after the Science
Council had become convinced of the necessity of acquiring academic reinforcements, I was told so many different things so often,
and given such weighty reasons, that probably none of it was the
truth. My exclusion, however, I did not hold against my colleagues, particularly not against Yvor Baloyne. Though they were
for quite some time unaware of it, their organizational activity was
not entirely free. Not that there was any open interference then,
any obvious pressure. But the whole thing was of course managed
by specialists in stagecraft. In my exclusion, I believe, High Places
had a hand. The Project, practically from the beginning, was
classified—an operation, that is, whose secrecy was a *sine qua non*
of government policy, vital to the national security. The scientific
directors of the Project, it should be emphasized, learned of this
gradually, and as a rule separately, one by one, at special meetings
during which discreet appeal was made to their political wisdom
and patriotic feelings.

How it was exactly, what means of persuasion, what compli-
ments, promises, and arguments were enlisted, I do not know,
because that side of things the official record passes over with

absolute silence; nor were the people of the Science Council quick to come forward later on, now as my fellow workers, with admissions touching that preliminary phase of research in His Master's Voice. If one or another turned out to be a bit uncooperative, if appeals to patriotism and the national interest were insufficient, resort was made to conversations "at the highest level." At the same time—and this perhaps was the most important factor contributing to the psychological accommodation—the hermetic nature of the Project, its severance from the world, was seen purely as a stopgap, a temporary, transitional arrangement that would be changed. Psychologically effective: for despite the misgivings felt by this or that scientist about the administration's representatives, the attention given the Project now by the Secretary of State and now by the President himself, the warm words of encouragement, expressive of the hope placed in "such minds"—all this created an atmosphere in which the posing of a plain question as to the time limit, the deadline for lifting the secrecy on the work, would have sounded discordant, impolite, positively boorish.

I can also imagine, though in my presence no one ever breathed a word on that delicate subject, how the noble Baloyne gave instruction in the principles of diplomacy (coexistence, that is, with politicians) to his less worldly colleagues, and how with his characteristic tact he kept putting off inviting and qualifying me to join the Council. He must have explained to the more impatient that first the Project had to win the trust of powerful patrons; only then would it be possible to follow what in all conscience the scientific helmsmen of HMV considered the most appropriate course. And I do not say this with irony, for I can put myself in Baloyne's shoes: he wished to avoid friction on both sides, and was well aware that in those high circles I had the reputation of being unreliable. So I did not take part in the launching of the enterprise; this, however— as I was told a hundred times—was all to my advantage, because the living conditions in that ghost town situated a hundred miles east of the Monte Rosa mountains were at first quite primitive.

I think it best to present what happened in chronological order, and therefore will begin with what I was doing just before the arrival at New Hampshire, where I was teaching, of the emissary from the Project. Best, because I entered its course when many of the general concepts had already been formed; as a "greenhorn" I needed to be introduced to—to acquaint myself with—everything, before I could be harnessed, like a new draft horse, to that huge machine (numbering twenty-five hundred people).

I had only recently come to New Hampshire, invited there by the chairman of the Mathematics Department, my old classmate Stewart Compton, to conduct a summer seminar for doctoral candidates. I accepted the offer; with a load of only three hours a week, I could spend whole days roaming the woods and fields in the area. Even though I had a full vacation coming to me, having completed, that June, a year-and-a-half collaboration with Professor Hayakawa, I knew—knowing myself—that I would not be able to relax unless I had at least some intermittent contact with mathematics. Rest gives me, immediately, the guilty feeling that I am wasting valuable time. Besides, I have always enjoyed meeting new practitioners of my esoteric discipline, about which prevail more false notions than about any other field.

I cannot call myself a "pure" mathematician; too often have I been tempted by outside problems. Such temptation led to my work with young Thorpe (his contribution to anthropology remains unappreciated, because he died young: in science, too, one's biological presence is required, because, despite appearances, a discovery needs credentials louder than its own merit)—and, later on, with Donald Prothero (whom I found at the Project, to my great surprise), and with James Fenniman (who subsequently received the Nobel Prize), and, finally, with Hayakawa. Hayakawa and I had built a mathematical backbone for his cosmic-origin theory, which was, unexpectedly, to make its way—thanks to one of his rebellious students—into the very center of the Project.

Some of my colleagues looked down their noses at these guerrilla raids of mine into the preserves of the natural sciences. But the benefit usually was reciprocal: the empiricists not only received my aid, but I, too, in learning their problems, began to see which directions of our Platonic Kingdom's development lay along the lines of the main strategic assault on the future.

One frequently encounters the sentiment that in mathematics all that is needed is "naked ability," because the lack of it there cannot be hidden; while in other disciplines connections, favoritism, fashion, and—most of all—the absence of that indisputability of proof which is supposed to characterize mathematics, cause a career to be the resultant vector of talents and conditions that are nonscientific. In vain have I tried to explain to such enviers that, alas, in our mathematical paradise things are not ideal. Cantor's beautifully classical theory of plurality was for many years ignored, and for quite unmathematical reasons.

But every man, it seems, must envy another. I regretted that I was weak in information theory, because in that sphere, and especially in the realm of algorithms governed by recursive functions, phenomenal discoveries were in the air. Classical logic, along with Boole's algebra, the midwives of information theory, were from the beginning burdened with a combinatorial inflexibility. Thus the mathematical tools borrowed from those domains never worked well. They are, to my taste, unwieldy, ugly, awkward; though they yield results, they do it in a graceless way. I thought that I would be better able to study the subject by accepting Compton's offer. Because it was precisely about this region of the mathematical front line that I would be speaking at New Hampshire. It sounds odd, perhaps, that I intended to learn through lecturing, but this had happened to me more than once before. My thinking always goes best when a link forms between me and an active and critical audience. Also, one can sit and read esoteric works, but for lectures it is imperative to prepare oneself, and this I did, so I cannot say who profited more from them, I or my students.

The weather that summer was good, but too hot, even out in the fields, which became dreadfully parched. I am particularly fond of grass. It is thanks to grass that we exist; only after that vegetation revolution that covered the continents with green could life establish itself on them in its zoological varieties. But I do not claim that this fondness of mine derives only from evolutionary considerations.

August was at its height when one day there appeared a herald of change—in the person of Dr. Michael Grotius, who brought me a letter from Yvor Baloyne as well us a secret communication delivered orally.

It was on the second floor of an old, pseudo-Gothic building of dark brick, with a pointed roof half-concealed by reddening vines, in my rather poorly ventilated room (the old walls contained no ducts for air conditioning), that I received the news—from a small, quiet young man as delicate as Chinese porcelain and wearing a little black crescent beard—that an announcement had reached Earth, but whether good or not, no one yet knew, for despite more than twelve months of effort, they had not succeeded in deciphering it.

Though Grotius did not say so, and though in the letter of my friend I found no mention of it, I understood that here was research under very high protection—or, if you prefer, supervision. How else could a thing of such importance not have been leaked to the press or other media channels? It was obvious that experts of the first order were engaged in keeping the lid on tight.

Grotius, his youth notwithstanding, showed himself to be an accomplished fox. Since it was not certain that I would agree to participate in the Project, he could tell me nothing concrete. He had to appeal to my vanity, to emphasize that twenty-five hundred people had chosen—out of all the remaining four billion—me as their potential savior; but even here Grotius knew moderation and did not lay it on too thick.

Most believe that there is no flattery that the object of the flattery will not swallow. If that is a rule, I am an exception to it, because I have never valued praise. One can praise—to put it this way—only from the top down, not from the bottom up. And I know well my own worth. Grotius either had been warned by Baloyne or simply possessed a good nose. He spoke at length, seemed to answer my questions fully, but at the end of the conversation all that I had got out of him could be written on two index cards.

The main scruple was the secrecy of the work. Baloyne realized that that would be the sore point, so in his letter he wrote of his personal meeting with the President, who had assured him that all the research of the Project would be published, except information that might be detrimental to the national interest of the United States. It appeared that in the opinion of the Pentagon, or at least of that section of the Pentagon which had taken the Project under its wing, the message from the stars was a kind of blueprint for a superbomb or some other ultimate weapon—a peculiar idea, at first glance, and saying more about the general political atmosphere than about galactic civilizations.

I sent Grotius away for three hours and went, without hurrying, to my fields. There, in the strong sun, I lay on the grass and deliberated. Neither Grotius nor Baloyne in his letter had said a word about the necessity of binding myself by oath to preserve the secret, but that there was some such "initiation" into the Project was self-evident.

It was one of those typical situations of the scientist of our time—zeroed in on and magnified, a prime specimen. The easiest way to keep one's hands clean is the ostrich-Pilate method of not involving oneself with anything that—even remotely—could contribute to increasing the means of annihilation. But what we do not wish to do, there will always be others to do in our place. Yet this, as they say, is no moral argument, and I agree. One might reply, then, with the premise that he who consents to participate in such work, being full of scruples, will be able to bring them to bear at the critical moment, but even should he be unable, no such possibility would exist if in his place stood a man who was devoid of scruples.

But I have no intention of defending myself in that way. Other reasons prompted me. If I know that something is happening that is extremely important but at the same time a potential menace, I will always prefer to be at that spot than to await the outcome with a clear conscience and folded hands. In addition, I could not believe that a civilization incommensurably above us would send out into the Cosmos information convertible to weaponry. If the people of the Project thought otherwise, that did not matter. And, finally, this chance that had suddenly opened up before me was totally beyond anything I could still expect from life.

The next day Grotius and I flew to Nevada, where a military helicopter stood waiting. I had got myself into the gears of an efficient and unerring machine. This second flight lasted about two hours, practically all of it over desert. Grotius, to keep me from feeling like a man roped into joining a criminal gang, was deliberately low-key; he refrained from giving me any feverish briefing on the dark secrets that waited at our destination.

From the sky, the compound presented itself as an irregular star half sunken in sand. Yellow bulldozers crept about the dunes like beetles. We landed on the flat roof of the highest building there, whose architecture made no pleasant impression. It was a cluster of massive concrete blocks, erected back in the fifties as the operation center and living quarters for a new atomic testing ground, the old testing grounds having become obsolete with the increase in explosive charge. Even as far as Las Vegas, windows would be knocked out after every major detonation. The new testing ground was to be situated in the heart of the desert, about thirty miles from the compound, which was fortified against possible shock waves and fallout.

The entire complex of buildings was surrounded by a system of slanted shields that faced the desert; their function was to break up the shock waves. All the structures were windowless and double-walled, the space between filled, probably, with water. Communications were put below the ground. As for staff housing and the buildings designated for operations, they were oval and placed so that no dangerous resonance would result in the event of repeated reflections and deflections of a wave front.

But that was the prehistory of the site, because before construction was completed a nuclear moratorium was signed. The steel doors of the buildings were then bolted shut, the air shafts capped, and the machines and shop equipment packed carefully in lubricant-filled containers and taken below ground (beneath the streets was a level of storage areas and magazines, and beneath that, another level, for a high-speed subway). The place guaranteed complete isolation for research, and therefore someone in the Pentagon assigned it to the Project—perhaps also because, in this way, some use could be made of the many hundreds of millions of dollars that had gone into all that concrete and steel.

The desert had not gained access to the compound, but had buried it in sand, so at the beginning there was a great deal of sweeping and cleaning to do. It also turned out that the plumbing did not work, because the water table had changed, and it was necessary to drill new artesian wells. Meanwhile, water was carried in by helicopter. All this was told me in great detail, so that I should appreciate my good fortune in having been invited late.

Baloyne was waiting for me on the roof of the building that housed the Project administration. This was the main heliport. The last time we had seen each other was two years before, in Washington. He is a person that physically you could make two of, and intellectually—four, at least. Baloyne is and, I think, will always remain greater than his achievements, because it very rarely happens that in so gifted a man all the psychical horses pull in the same direction. A little like Saint Thomas, who, as we know, did not fit through every door, and a little like young Ashurbanipal (but without the beard), he constantly wanted to do more than he was able. This is pure supposition, but I suspect that he—albeit on a different principle and possibly a larger scale—performed upon himself, over the course of the years, the kind of psychocosmetic operations that I spoke of, in reference to my own person, in the Preface. Secretly grieved (but this, I repeat, is my hypothesis) at his physical appearance as well as personality—he was a butterball and painfully timid—he assumed a manner that could be called circular irony. Everything he said, he said in quotes, with an artificial, exaggerated emphasis, and with the elocution of someone playing a succession of improvised, ad hoc roles. Therefore, whoever did not know him long and well was confounded, for it seemed impossible ever to tell what the man thought true and what false, and when he was speaking seriously and when he was merely amusing himself with words.

This ironic quote-unquote became at last a part of him, and enabled him to utter things that no one else would have been forgiven. He could even ridicule himself at any length, since this trick, in principle very simple, through consistent application rendered him quite impossible to pin down or catch.

With humor, with self-irony, he built up around his person such a system of invisible fortifications that even those—like me—who had known him for years could not predict how he would react. I think that he strove particularly for this, and that the things he did, which sometimes indeed bordered on the clownish, he did with secret design, though they seemed perfectly spontaneous.

Our friendship resulted from the fact that Baloyne first looked down on me and later envied me. Both the one and the other I found amusing. At the beginning he believed that as a philologist and humanist he would never in his life need mathematics; concerned with things of the spirit, he placed knowledge of man over knowledge of nature. But then he became involved in linguistics as in an illicit love affair; he began to wrestle with the currently reigning fashions of structuralism and developed a taste, however reluctantly, for mathematics. And thus arrived, unwillingly, on my territory. Realizing that there he was weaker than I, he was able to admit this in such a way that it was I, with my mathematics, that was the butt of the joke. Did I say that Baloyne was a Renaissance figure? I loved his exasperating home, where there were always so many people that you could not talk to the host in private earlier than midnight.

What I have so far said touches the fortifications Baloyne raised about his personality but not the personality itself. A special hypothesis is needed to divine what lives *intra muros*. It was, I think, fear. I do not know what he feared. Himself, perhaps. He must have had a great deal to hide, surrounding himself as he did with such a labored din; he always had so many ideas, plans, projects, and got himself into so many unnecessary things, was a member of all sorts of societies, conservatories, a professional respondent to academic questionnaires and polls of scientists; he overburdened himself intentionally, because in that way he would not have to be alone with himself—there would never be time. He dealt with the problems of others, and understood people so well, one naturally assumed he understood himself well, too. A mistaken assumption, I believe.

Over the years he imposed upon himself various constraints, until they hardened into his external, publicly visible nature—that of the universal activist of reason. He was, then, a Sisyphus by choice; the magnitude of his efforts disguised any failure, because if he himself established the rules and laws of his activity, no one could know with any certainty whether he was accomplishing all that he set out to do, or sometimes stumbled, particularly since he boasted of his defeats and made much of the littleness of his intellect, but in quotes of ostentation. He had the special penetration of the richly endowed, who are able to take hold of any problem, even one foreign to them, immediately from the proper angle, as if instinctively. He was so haughty that he was forever bending himself—as in a game—to humility, and so anxious that over and over again he had to prove himself, to assert his merit— while at the same time denying it.

His study was like a projection of his soul. Everything in it was gargantuan: the chest of drawers, the desk; you could have drowned a calf in his cocktail pitcher. From the huge window to the opposite wall was one battlefield of books. Apparently he required this chaos pressing from all sides—and in his correspondence, too.

I speak this way of my friend and risk his displeasure, though before I spoke no differently of myself. I do not know what it was among the people of the Project that determined finally the Project's fate. Therefore, just in case, thinking of the future, I am also presenting here those bits and pieces that I have not been able to put into any coherent whole. Perhaps someone else, someday, will manage that.

In love with history, rapt in history, Baloyne drove backward, as it were, into the time coming. For him modernity was a destroyer of values, and technology an instrument of the Devil. If I exaggerate, it is not by much. He was convinced that the culmination of humanity had already taken place, long ago, possibly in the Renaissance, and that a long, accelerating downhill career had begun. Although he was a Renaissance *homo animatus* and *homo sciens*, he took pleasure in contacts with people whom I would rank among the least interesting, though they present the greatest threat to our species; I mean politicians. He had no political ambitions himself; or, if he did, he kept them even from me. But various and sundry gubernatorial candidates, their spouses, Congressional hopefuls or "in" Congressmen, and gray-haired, doddering Senators, as well as those hybrid types only half politico, or a quarter, who occupy positions veiled in mist (but mist of the best quality), were all to be found, all the time, at his house.

My attempts to keep up a conversation with such people (like holding up the head of a corpse, but I did it for Baloyne) collapsed after five minutes, whereas he was able to jabber with them for hours on end—God only knows for what reason! Somehow I never asked him point-blank about this, but now it turned out that those contacts bore fruit, because during the screening of candidates for the post of science director of the Project it came to light that they all—all the advisers, experts, board members, committee chairmen, and five-star generals—wanted only Baloyne, trusted only Baloyne. He, however, and I know this, was not at all eager to assume the post, smart enough to realize that sooner or later there would be conflict, and ugly conflict, between the two groups that it would be his job to keep united.

One had only to remember the Manhattan Project and the fate of people among those who directed it but were scientists, not generals. While the latter were all promoted and could tranquilly set about writing their memoirs, the former, with surprising regularity, met with "ostracism from both worlds," i.e., the worlds of politics and science. Baloyne changed his mind only after a meeting with the President. I do not believe that he allowed himself to be taken in by any kind of argument. It was simply that the situation in which the President made the request—a request Baloyne was able to fulfill—possessed for him sufficient justification to risk the most he had to risk: his whole future.

But here I am falling into journalese, because, besides everything else, he must have been driven by a genuine curiosity. A part of it, too, was that a refusal would have seemed like cowardice, and only a man to whom fear, day by day, is a stranger can be cowardly with the full knowledge that he is being cowardly. One who is timorous and unsure will lack the courage to expose himself so horribly, confirming, as it were—to himself as well—the ruling feature of his character. But even if this sort of desperation played a role in Baloyne's decision, he undoubtedly proved to be the right man to occupy what was the most uncomfortable office in the entire Project.

I have been told that General Oster, the chief administrator of HMV, was so unable to deal with Baloyne that he voluntarily stepped down from his post; Baloyne meanwhile fostered the image of a man desiring above all else to quit the Project, and made so much noise lamenting the fact that Washington would not accept his resignation that Oster's successors, anxious to avoid unpleasant exchanges at the top, deferred to him as much as possible. When he felt himself more secure in the saddle, he proposed that I be included in the Science Council; the threat of resignation was no longer needed.

Our meeting took place without reporters and flash bulbs; but, of course, any sort of publicity was quite out of the question. As I stepped from the helicopter onto the roof, I saw that he was truly moved. He even attempted to embrace me (which I cannot stand). His retinue stood at a respectful distance; I was being received like a sovereign lord, but had the feeling that we were both aware of the ineradicable ridiculousness of the situation. On the roof there was not a single man in uniform; the thought occurred to me that Baloyne had carefully kept them out of sight so that I would not be antagonized. But I was mistaken—mistaken, however, only regarding the extent of his influence, because, as I discovered later, he had removed uniforms from the entire area under his jurisdiction.

On the door of his office someone had written in lipstick, in giant letters, COELUM. Baloyne spoke to me, of course, nonstop, but lit up expectantly when the retinue, as if cut off with a knife, remained outside the door and we could look each other in the eye—alone.

As long as we regarded each other with what I might call a purely animal sympathy, nothing marred the harmony of our reunion. But, though curious about the secret, I first questioned him on the Project's position with respect to the Pentagon and the Administration, and, specifically, about the extent of freedom allowed in using the possible results of the research. He tried, though halfheartedly, to avail himself of that ponderous dialect employed by the State Department; I became, therefore, more acerbic with him than I intended, as a result of which a tension arose between us, and it was washed away only by the red wine (Baloyne must have wine) at dinner. I learned later that he had not at all contracted the infection of officialdom, but had spoken so as to invest the maximum amount of sound with the minimum of meaning—because his office was riddled with bugging devices. Practically all the buildings, and the labs, too, were packed with that electronic upholstery.

It was only after several days that I learned this, from the physicists, who were not in the least perturbed by the fact; they considered it a natural phenomenon, much like the sand in the desert. But none of them went anywhere without a little scrambling apparatus; they took a childish delight in foiling the ubiquitous protection placed over them. Out of humanitarian considerations, so that those occult minions (I never saw one in the flesh) who had to sit and listen through all that was recorded would not be too bored, the antibugging units were turned off—such was the custom—during the telling of jokes, particularly those off-color. But the telephones, I was advised, were not to be used for matters other than making dates with the girls that worked in administration. There were no people in uniform, as I said, not even the type who brought uniforms to mind, in the entire community.

The only nonscientist who took part in the sessions of the Science Council was Dr. (but of Law) Eugene Albert Nye, the best-dressed man in the Project. He represented Dr. Marsland (who, by strange coincidence, also was a four-star general). Nye was well aware that the younger scientists in particular liked to play jokes on him, passing index cards with cryptic diagrams and numbers, or secretly confiding to one another—ostensibly failing to notice him —outlandishly radical views.

The jokes he bore with saintly composure, and was able to conduct himself admirably when someone at the hotel canteen showed him a tiny transmitter with a microphone, not bigger than a safety match, which had been dug out from behind an outlet in one of the rooms. All this did not amuse me in the least, though I have a fairly active sense of humor.

Nye represented a very real power, and neither his manners nor his love of Husserl made him likable. He knew, of course, that the jokes, digs, and little incivilities shown him by his associates were compensatory, because in fact it was he who was the quietly smiling *spiritus movens* of the Project—or, rather, its velvet-gloved ruler. He was like a diplomat among natives. The natives, being helpless, seek to vent their resentment on the venerable personage, and sometimes, when their anger drives them, they may even tear something, or handle it roughly; but the diplomat easily tolerates such demonstrations, for that is the reason he is there, and he knows that even if he is insulted, the insult is not addressed to him personally but to the power he represents. Thus he can identify himself with that power—a convenient arrangement, since such impersonalization provides him with a sense of constant, safe superiority.

People who do not represent themselves but serve, instead, as a tangible, materialized symbol, a symbol fundamentally abstract though it may wear suspenders and a bow tie; who are a local, concrete instance of an organization that disposes individuals like objects—I detest such people, and am unable to transform the feeling into its comical or ironic equivalent. From the very beginning, sensing this, Nye gave me a wide berth, as one does with a vicious dog; otherwise the man would not have been able to fulfill his function. I showed him my contempt, and he definitely paid me back with interest, in his impersonal way, though he was always extremely polite. Which, of course, only irritated me the more. My human form was, in the eyes of people like him, a mere casing that contained an instrument needed for higher goals—goals known to them, inaccessible to me. What surprised me the most in him was that he apparently held actual views of some sort. But possibly they were only a good imitation.

Even more un-American and unsporting was Rappaport's attitude toward Nye—Dr. Saul Rappaport, that first discoverer of the message from the stars. He once read me an excerpt from a nineteenth-century volume describing the raising of pigs trained to find truffles. It was a nice passage, telling, in an elevated style typical of that age, how man's reason made use—in keeping with its mission—of the avid gluttony of the swine, to whom acorns were tossed each time they unearthed a truffle.

This kind of rational husbandry, in Rappaport's opinion, was what awaited the scientists; it was in fact already being put into practice in our own case. He made me this prediction in all seriousness. The wholesale dealer takes no interest in the inner life of the trained pig that runs about for the truffles; all that exists for him are the results of the pig's activity, and it is no different between us and our authorities.

The rational husbandry of scientists admittedly has been hindered by relics of tradition, those unthinking sentiments that came out of the French Revolution, but there is reason to hope that this is a passing phase. Besides the well-equipped sties—that is to say, the shining laboratories—other installations should be provided, to deliver us from any possible feeling of frustration. For example, a science worker might satisfy his instincts of aggression in a hall filled with mannequins of generals and other high officials specially designed for beating; or he could go to specific spots for release of sexual energy, etc. Availing himself appropriately of outlets here and there, the scientist-pig—explained Rappaport—can then, without further distraction, devote himself to the hunting of truffles, for the benefit of the rulers but to the undoing of humanity, as indeed the new stage in history will demand of him.

Rappaport made no attempt to hide these views. It was amusing to observe the reactions of our colleagues to his pronouncements (not made at the official meetings, of course). The younger ones simply laughed, which angered Rappaport, because the truth was that he thought and spoke entirely in earnest. But there was no help for it: one's personal experience in life is fundamentally unconveyable. Nontransmittable. Rappaport came from Europe, which is equated by the "military-senatorial mind" (as he liked to put it) with the Red Menace. Thus he never would have got into the Project had he not accidentally become its coauthor. Only the fear of possible "leaks" landed him in our team.

He had emigrated to the States in 1945. His name was known to a handful of experts before the war. There are few philosophers with a genuinely thorough schooling in mathematics and the natural sciences; he belonged in that rare category, and consequently turned out to be extremely useful in the work of the Project. Rappaport and I lived next door to each other in the hotel at the compound, and it was not long before we became more closely acquainted. He left his native country as a man of thirty, alone, the Holocaust having claimed his entire family. He never spoke about it, except one evening, after I had let him in on—and he was the only one—my and Prothero's secret. True, I am anticipating events in telling the story here, but I think this is indicated. Whether it was, oddly, to reciprocate my confidence with another, or for some unknown reason, Rappaport then told me how, before his eyes, a certain mass execution had taken place—the year was 1942, I think—in his hometown.

He was pulled off the street, a random pedestrian. They were shooting people in groups, in the yard of a prison recently shelled and with one wing still burning. Rappaport gave me the details of the operation very calmly. The executing itself could not be seen by those herded against the building, which heated their backs like a giant oven; the shooting was done behind a broken wall. Some of those waiting, like him, in his turn, fell into a kind of stupor; others tried to save themselves—in mad ways.

He remembered a young man who, rushing up to a German gendarme, howled that he was not a Jew—but howled it in Yiddish, probably because he knew no German. Rappaport felt the insane comedy of the situation, and suddenly the most precious thing to him was to preserve to the end the integrity of his mind, which would enable him to maintain an intellectual distance from the scene around him. However, he had to find—he explained this to me objectively and slowly, as to a man from "the other side" who could not be expected to understand anything of such experiences—some value external to himself, a prop of some sort for his mind. Since that was altogether impossible, he decided to believe in reincarnation. Maintaining the belief for fifteen or twenty minutes would be sufficient. Yet he could not accomplish that, not even in an abstract way, so he picked out from among a group of officers situated some distance from the place of execution one who, by his appearance, stood apart.

He described him to me, as though from a photograph. This was a young deity of war: tall, handsome, in battle dress, of which the silver borders seemed to have turned slightly ash-gray from the heat; he had on his full outfit, the iron cross under the collar, field glasses in a case on his chest, a deep helmet, a revolver with the holster conveniently moved toward the buckle of the belt, and in his gloved hand a handkerchief, clean and neatly folded, which he pressed to his nose now and then, because the executions had lasted so long—since that morning—that the flames had reached some of those cut down earlier in the corner of the yard, and from that place now belched the stench of burning flesh. But—and this, too, Rappaport did not forget—he grew aware of the presence of the sweetish corpse-smoke only when he observed the handkerchief in the hand of the officer he had singled out. He told himself that the moment he was shot, he would become that German.

He knew perfectly well that the idea was complete nonsense, even from the point of view of any metaphysical doctrine, reincarnation included, because the "place in the body" was already occupied. But somehow this did not bother him; in fact, the longer and more greedily he stared at the chosen man, the better he was able to cling to this thought that was to sustain him until the final moment. Already it was as if he were being given support— by the man. The man would help him.

This, too, Rappaport said calmly, but in his voice there was, I thought, a catch of admiration for the "young deity" who directed the entire operation so expertly, without moving from his place, without shouting or falling into the half-drunk trance of striking and kicking in which his subordinates worked, iron-chested. In that moment Rappaport understood even this: the subordinates had to behave that way; they were hiding from the victims in the hatred of them, but the hatred could not be produced in themselves except through acts of brutality. They had to batter the Jews with their rifle butts; blood had to flow from lacerated heads and crust upon faces, because it made the faces hideous, inhuman, and in this way—I am quoting Rappaport—there did not appear, in what was done, a gap through which horror might peer, or compassion.

But the young deity in the silver-braided uniform required neither these nor any other contrivances to act perfectly. He stood in a slightly elevated place, the white handkerchief applied to his nose with a movement that had something in it of the refined duelist. He was the master of the house and the commander, in one person. In the air floated flakes of ash, driven by the heat that pulsed from the fire; behind the thick walls, through the grated windows without panes, flames roared, but not a single ash fell on the officer or on his white handkerchief.

In the presence of such perfection, Rappaport managed to forget about himself, when suddenly the gate opened and in drove a film crew. Various orders were given in German, and the gunshots immediately ceased. Rappaport did not know then—or later, when he told me this—what had happened. Perhaps the Germans intended to film a pile of corpses, to use the footage in a newsreel depicting the enemy's actions (this took place near the Eastern Front). The slain Jews would be shown as the victims of the Bolsheviks. That may have been the case; Rappaport, however, offered no interpretation; he only related what he saw.

Immediately afterward came his failure. Those still alive were put in a row and filmed, whereupon the officer with the handkerchief asked for one volunteer. Rappaport understood at once that he should step forward. He did not know exactly why he should, but felt that if he did not, it would be terrible for him. The moment arrived in which the whole force of his will was exerted to make that one step—but he did not budge. The officer then gave them fifteen seconds to think and, turning his back on them, spoke quietly, casually, to some younger soldier.

Rappaport, as a doctor of philosophy, having earned his university degree with a brilliant dissertation on logic, hardly needed the entire apparatus of syllogisms to realize that if no one stepped forward, all would die: hence whoever now came forth from the line really would be risking nothing. It was simple, clear, and certain. He renewed his effort—this time, true, without conviction —and again did not budge. A few seconds before the time was up, someone presented himself, however, and disappeared with two soldiers behind a broken wall. Several revolver shots rang out. The young volunteer, smeared with blood, his own or not his own, then returned to the group.

It was dusk when the large gate was set ajar and, staggering in the cold evening air, the group of those left alive ran out into the empty street.

They dared not flee at first, but no one showed any interest in them. Why, Rappaport could not say. He did not attempt to analyze what the Germans did; they were like fate, which one did not have to explain.

The volunteer—need it be said?—had moved the bodies of the executed, and those still alive were finished off with the revolver. As if to see whether he was right that I really had not understood a thing about his story, Rappaport then asked me why the officer requested a volunteer and had been prepared, in the absence of one, to kill the lot of them, though that would have been "unnecessary"—on that particular day, at any rate—and why, moreover, he did not even consider announcing that nothing would happen to the volunteer. I did not, I confess, pass this test: I replied that perhaps the German had acted thus from contempt, scorning to enter into conversation with the victims. Rappaport shook his birdlike head.

"I understood it later," he said, "thanks to other things. Although he spoke to us, you see, we were not people. He knew that we comprehended human speech but that nevertheless we were not human; he knew this quite well. Therefore, even if he had wanted to explain things to us, he could not have. The man could do with us what he liked, but he could not enter into negotiations, because for negotiation you must have a party in at least some respect equal to the party who initiates it, and in that yard there were only he and his men. A logical contradiction, yes, but he acted exactly according to that contradiction, and scrupulously. The simpler ones among his men did not possess this higher knowledge; the appearance of humanity given by our bodies, our two legs, faces, hands, eyes, that appearance deterred them a little from their duty; thus they had to butcher those bodies, to make them unlike people's. But for him such primitive proceedings were no longer necessary. This sort of explanation is usually received metaphorically, as a kind of fable, but it is completely literal."

About this fragment of his past we never spoke again, nor did we touch on any others. But some time had to pass before I could stop remembering, whenever I saw Rappaport, the scene he had drawn so vividly for me, of the prison yard with bomb craters, the people with faces veined in red and black from blows to the head, and the officer whose body he wanted—fraudulently—to move into. I cannot say to what extent there remained in him a mindfulness of the annihilation he escaped. Rappaport was, in any case, a very sensible man—yet at the same time quite comical. I will incur his displeasure the most when I tell the way he left his room each day (though I did not mean to spy). In the hotel corridor, by the elevator, there was a large mirror. Rappaport, who had a bad stomach and stuffed his pockets with bottles of multicolored pills, when he left each morning always stuck out his tongue in front of the mirror, to see if it was coated. He did this so regularly that I would have thought it extraordinary had he omitted the practice.

At the meetings of the Science Council he was conspicuously bored, but proved particularly allergic to the utterances—seldom made, however, and generally tactful—of Dr. Eugene Albert Nye. If one did not want to listen to Nye, one could watch the mimicking accompaniment to the speech on Rappaport's face. Rappaport would scowl, as if suddenly aware of something vile on his tongue, would pull his nose, scratch behind his ear, squint at the speaker with an expression that seemed to say, "You can't be serious." But when Nye once, finally losing patience, asked him outright if he wished to take issue with some point, Rappaport, innocent and surprised, shook his head several times, held up his hands, and said that he had nothing, absolutely nothing to say.

I dwell on these descriptions to show the reader the central figures of the Project from a less official angle, and also to introduce him to the special atmosphere of a community sealed off from the world. Indeed, it was curious, that creatures as different from each other as Baloyne, Nye, Rappaport, and myself should have come together in a single place, with the mission of "establishing Contact," an ersatz diplomatic corps representing mankind vis-à-vis the Universe.

Although different, we joined to become an organism that studied the "letter from the stars"; we formed a group that had its own customs, tempo, and social patterns, with subtle variations on the official, semiofficial, and private levels. All this, taken together, created the "spirit" of the institution, but more than that, too—what a sociologist would take pleasure in calling a "local subculture." This aura within the Project—and the Project, after all, numbered nearly three thousand people in its most dynamic phase —was distinct and unique, and, in the long run, for me at least, wearisome.

One of the oldest members of the Project, Lee Reinhorn, who as a very young physicist had worked, once upon a time, on the Manhattan Project, told me that the atmospheres of the two undertakings were in no way comparable: the Manhattan Project had sent its people on an exploration typically natural-scientific, physical in character; while ours somehow remained implanted in human civilization and was unable to free itself from that dependency. Reinhorn called HMV a test of our culture's cosmic invariance—and thereby annoyed our humanist colleagues (in particular), because he was preening himself, with naïve good nature, for discoveries from *their* bailiwick. He studied, irrespective of the research of his own group (physics), material from all over the world, and from the preceding few decades—material primarily linguistic, devoted to the problem of cosmic communication, and especially to the aspect of it called the "cracking of languages of closed semantics."

Now, the uselessness of this pyramid of learned material—and the bibliography, with which I, too, acquainted myself, contained, if memory serves me right, about five and a half thousand titles— was obvious to every man in the Project. And the amusing thing was that such books and articles continued to appear in considerable numbers in the world, which, except for a small circle of chosen people, knew nothing of the existence of the "letter from the stars." Consequently the professional pride and sense of loyalty of the linguists who worked in the Project were put through the wringer when Reinhorn—receiving in the mail yet another bundle of relevant articles—filled us in, at the semiofficial research colloquia, on the latest from the field of "interstellar semantics." The worthlessness, the sterility of all those lines of reasoning, laced lovingly with mathematics, was really comical, though at the same time depressing.

Tempers flared; the linguists accused Reinhorn of maliciously mocking them. But friction between the humanists and the natural scientists of the Project was the order of the day. The former we called "elves," the latter "dwarfs." The internal jargon of the Project had a rich vocabulary; it could serve, along with the forms that the coexistence of both "parties" took, as a worthy subject for some future sociologist.

Fairly complicated factors inclined Baloyne to include within the frame of the HMV group a whole slew of humanistic fields: not least of which was the fact that he himself was, after all, by training and predilection, a humanist. But this rivalry could not very well take any productive form if our anthropologists, psychologists, and psychoanalysts, as well as the philosophers, refused to make use of the data as raw material for their research. Thus, whenever there was a seminar given in one of the "elf" sections, someone would write on the bulletin-board announcement, next to the title of the topic, the letters SF, for "science fiction." Unfortunately, this childish graffiti humor had justification in the barrenness of those sessions.

The general meetings almost always ended in open quarrels. The most petulant, I would say, were the psychoanalysts; they were especially aggressive in their demands—they wanted the appropriate experts to decipher the "literal layer" of the stellar message so that they could then set to work determining the entire system of symbols employed by the civilization of the Senders. Here, of course, came the inevitable rejoinder, in the form of a bold hypothesis, as, for example, that the civilization might reproduce asexually, which perforce would desexualize its "symbolic lexicon" and thereby in advance doom to failure any attempt at psychoanalytic penetration. The one who spoke thus would immediately be labeled an ignoramus, because modern-day psychoanalysis was no longer a primitive Freudian pansexualism. And if, at such a meeting, a phenomenologist also spoke up, there would be no end to the objections raised and countered.

For we had a veritable *embarras de richesses*, a quite unnecessary excess of "elfin" specialists—representing even such esoteric fields as psychoanalytic history and pleiography (for the life of me I cannot remember exactly what it is pleiographers do, though I am certain it was explained to me once).

It would appear that Baloyne was nevertheless wrong to have acceded, in this regard, to the Pentagon's wishes. Those advisers had mastered only one maxim, but that they mastered for all time: if one man dug a hole with a volume of one cubic meter in ten hours, then a hundred thousand diggers of holes could do the job in a fraction of a second. And likewise, just as such a multitude would crack one another's heads open with their shovels before they broke the first clod of earth, so our poor "elves" tussled and scuffled—mainly with themselves, but with us as well—instead of "producing."

But if the Pentagon believed results were directly proportional to the investment, that was that. The thought that our guardians were people who held that a problem that five experts were unable to solve could surely be taken care of by five thousand, was hair-raising. Our unfortunate "elves" suffered frustrations and complexes, because the truth of the matter was that they were condemned to complete idleness, albeit an idleness decked up in various appearances. When I arrived at the Project, Baloyne admitted to me, in private, that his dream—impossible—was to jettison all that academic ballast. But one could not even consider such a thing, for a very mundane reason: whoever entered the Project, once in, could not simply get up and leave; that would threaten us with the "breaking of the seal," i.e., the escape of the Secret into the wide, as yet unsuspecting world.

So Baloyne had to be a genius of diplomacy, tact. Now and then he even came up with things to do—or, rather, pretenses of things —for the "elves," and would be furious, not amused, at gibes directed at them, because that only opened up old wounds—as, for example, when in the suggestion box there appeared the proposal that the psychologists and psychoanalysts be transferred from their positions as researchers on the star letter to positions as doctors treating those who were unable to decipher the letter and consequently suffered "stress."

The advisers from Washington got in Baloyne's hair also. Every so often they would hit on a new idea—as when they kept insisting, for the longest time, on the organization of large, mixed sessions operating on the popular principle of "brainstorming," which replaces the mind of a solitary thinker, concentrating on a problem, by a large team that collectively, chorally, "thinks out loud," as it were, on a given topic. Baloyne, on his part, tried different tactics—passive, active, retaliatory—to resist this sort of good advice.

As one who gravitated naturally toward the "dwarfs," I will be regarded as partisan, but I must say that at the outset I was innocent of any bias. Immediately on my arrival at the Project I began studying linguistics, because that seemed imperative to me. I was soon amazed to learn that, when it came to the primary, most fundamental concepts in this field—a field supposedly precise, quantified, mathematized—there was absolutely no agreement. Why, the authorities could not come together on so basic and preliminary a question as what exactly morphemes and phonemes were.

But when I asked the appropriate people, in all sincerity, how in the world they could accomplish anything, given this state of affairs, my naïve question was taken as a sneering insinuation. I had got myself—not realizing it in those first days—in the middle of a cross fire; I had assumed that it was necessary to chop wood and let the chips fall where they might; and it was only the kindest, like Rappaport or Dill, who took me aside and filled me in on the complex psychosociology of the elf-dwarf coexistence, also called, at times, the "cold war."

Not everything that the elves did, I must say, was without value. The theoretical work of the interdisciplinary team of Wayne and Traxler, for instance, turned out to be very interesting; it was devoted to "finite automata deprived of an unconscious," that is, systems capable of "total self-description." A good many worthwhile studies came out of the elf milieu—except that the connection between those studies and the letter from the stars was either tenuous or altogether nonexistent. I say all this not to ride the elves—truly, that is not my intention—but only to show what an oversize and complicated piece of machinery was set in motion on Earth in the face of the First Contact, and how much trouble it had with itself, with its own workings, which certainly did nothing to further the attainment of its proper goal.

Inauspicious, also, as regards physical comfort, were the conditions of our day-to-day existence. At the compound we had no cars to speak of, because the roads that had once been built there were covered with dunes. In the housing area itself ran a miniature subway, constructed back when they needed it for the atomic testing ground. All the buildings stood on gigantic concrete legs—gray, heavy boxes with oblong sides—and beneath them, across the concrete of the empty parking lots, blew only the hot wind, powerful, as from a blast furnace, in such a closed-in space, driving that awful, reddish, unusually fine sand, which got into everything the minute you left your airtight quarters. Even the pool we had was underground; swimming would otherwise have been impossible.

But a lot of people preferred to go from building to building by the streets, in the unbearable heat, rather than use the underground means, because, as if it was not bad enough living like a mole, at almost every step one found grim reminders of the compound's past. Those giant orange double S's, for example—Rappaport, I recall, complained of them to me—which shone even in the day, indicated the way to shelter, standing for "shelter station," I think, but I am not sure now. And not only below ground, but also in our work areas glowed the signs EMERGENCY EXIT, ABSORPTION SHIELD. On the concrete disks at the entrances to the buildings was printed, here and there, BLAST CAPACITY, with numbers showing what force of impact from a wave front the given structure could withstand. At turns in the corridors and on stairway landings stood large, scarlet decontamination cylinders, and there were plenty of hand-held Geiger counters to choose from.

In the hotel, too, all the flimsier partitions, walls, or panes serving as dividers in the lobby were accordingly marked with large, flaming cautions that during the tests it was not safe to remain in that area, which had not been designed to withstand shock. And, finally, on the streets there were still a few enormous arrows that showed in which direction the propagation of a wave would be the strongest, and what would be the vector components, in the given spot, of its reflection. The general impression you received was that you were standing at the notorious "ground zero" and that any minute the sky would open up above your head in a thermonuclear explosion. Only a few of these signs were, with time, painted over. I asked why all of them were not removed. The people smiled and said that a great many signs had been removed, and sirens, and Geiger counters, and cylinders of oxygen, but the administration of the compound had asked that what was left not be touched.

As a new arrival I had heightened perceptions, and these souvenirs of the compound's atomic prehistory grated on me considerably at first. Later, when I became absorbed in the problem of the "letter," I ceased to notice them, like everyone else.

In the beginning these conditions seemed to me intolerable—and I am talking not only about climate and geography. Had Grotius told me, in New Hampshire, that I would fly to a place in which every bathroom was bugged and every telephone tapped, had I been able to observe Eugene Albert Nye from that distance, I would not only have understood theoretically, but also sensed, felt, how all our freedoms could vanish the moment we produced what was expected of us. And then, who knows, I might not have been so quick to agree. But even the College of Cardinals can be led to cannibalism, provided only that one proceeds patiently and by small degrees. The mechanism of psychological adaptation is inexorable.

If someone had told Madame Curie that, in fifty years, out of her radioactivity would come megaton payloads and "overkill," she might have been afraid to continue—she certainly would not have returned to her former tranquillity after hearing so dire a prophecy. Yet we have grown accustomed to this, and people who calculate corpses times ten to the eighth, to the ninth, to the tenth —no one considers them insane. Our ability to adapt and therefore to accept everything is one of our greatest dangers. Creatures that are completely flexible, changeable, can have no fixed morality.

5

THE WELL-KNOWN silence of the Universe—*silentium universi* —effectively drowned out by the din of local wars for half a century, was recognized by many astrophysicists as an inarguable fact, since persistent radio monitoring yielded nothing—from the Ozma Project to the many years of effort by the Australians.

And meanwhile, all that time, other specialists besides astrophysicists were at work: those who devised LOGLAN, LINCOS, and a whole series of other artificial languages as tools for the establishment of interstellar communication. Many discoveries were made, such as that of the economy of transmitting television images instead of words. The theory and methodology of Contact grew slowly into a library. It was known, now, exactly how a civilization would need to proceed if it wished to communicate with others. The preliminary step was to send call signals in a wide band, signals that were rhythmic, showing first of all their artificial nature, and then—by frequencies—where and in which kilo- or megacycle range to look for the true emission. And that would begin with a systematic presentation of grammar, syntax, vocabulary. It would be a guidebook composed for the entire Universe and valid even to the remotest nebula.

But it happened instead that the unknown Sender committed a dreadful faux pas, because his letter was without introductions, without a grammar, without a dictionary—an enormous letter, recorded on almost a kilometer of magnetic tape. When I learned of this, my first thought was that either the letter was not meant for us, that by pure chance we lay in the path of its transmission between two "conversing" civilizations; or else the letter was intended only for those civilizations that, having passed a certain "knowledge threshold," were able both to detect the cleverly concealed signal and to decode its meaning. According to the first possibility—that of accidental reception—the problem of "not following the rules" did not exist. According to the second, the letter took on a new, peculiarly enriched aspect: the information had been in some way (this was how I imagined it) made proof against the "unqualified."

To the best of our knowledge, without possessing the code units, or the syntax, or the vocabulary, the only way to decipher a message was by using the trial-and-error method, by sifting frequencies, whereby one might have to wait two hundred years for success, or two million, or a full eternity. When I found out that among the mathematicians in the Project were Baird and Sharon, and that the chief programmer was Radcliffe, I felt uncomfortable, and made no secret of it. It seemed strange—given their august presence—that I had been approached at all. But at the same time this gave me a little courage, because in mathematics there do exist insoluble problems, and they are insoluble for third-rate whizzes and first-order geniuses alike. And therefore there seemed to be a chance—because otherwise Baloyne would have stuck with Sharon and Baird. Apparently Sharon and Baird had concluded that if they could not carry the day in this extraordinary encounter, then someone else might.

The view of many notwithstanding, the conceptual convergence of all the languages of Earth's cultures, however varied they may be, is striking. The telegram GRANDMOTHER DEAD FUNERAL WEDNESDAY can be translated into any language you like—from Latin and Hindustani to the dialects of the Apaches, Eskimos, or the tribe of Dobu. We could even do this, no doubt, with the language of the Mousterian period, if we knew it. The reason is that everyone has a mother, who has a mother; that everyone must die; that the ritualization of the disposing of a corpse is a cultural constant; as is, also, the principle of reckoning time. But beings that are unisexual would not know the distinction between mother and father, and those that divide like amoebas would be unable to form the idea even of a unisexual parent. The meanings of "grandmother" thus could not be conveyed. Beings that do not die (amoebas, dividing, do not die) would be unacquainted with the notion of death and of funerals. They would therefore have to learn about human anatomy, physiology, evolution, history, and customs before they could begin the translation of this telegram that is so clear to us.

The example is primitive, because it assumes that the one who receives the message will know which signs in it carry information and which constitute their unessential background. With the letter from the stars our position was different. The recorded rhythm could have represented, for example, only marks of punctuation, while the actual "letters" or ideograms could have failed completely to affect the surface of the tape's magnetic coating, being impulses to which the machine was not sensitive.

A separate problem is the disparity between the levels of civilization. From the gold death mask of Amenhotep the art historian will read the epoch and its style. From the mask's ornamentation the student of religions will deduce the beliefs of that time. The chemist will be able to show what method was used then to work the gold. The anthropologist will tell whether the specimen of the species from six thousand years ago differs from modern man; and the physician will offer the diagnosis that Amenhotep suffered from a hormonal imbalance, acromegaly, that gave him his deformed jaw. In this way an object sixty centuries old provides us, in modern times, with far more information than its creators possessed—for what did they know of the chemistry of gold, of acromegaly, of cultural styles? If we turn the procedure around in time and send to an Egyptian of the era of Amenhotep a letter written today, he will not understand it, not only because he does not know our language, but also because he has neither the words nor the concepts to set alongside ours.

Thus were the general deliberations on the subject of the "letter from the stars." The information about it was compressed—in keeping with custom—into a sort of standard text and recorded on tape, and was played for the Very Important Persons who came to visit us. Rather than render it in my own words, I quote verbatim:

"The task of His Master's Voice is to study every aspect of and attempt to translate the so-called message from outer space, which is, in all likelihood, a series of signals sent intentionally and with the aid of an artificial-technological device, by a being or beings that belong to some undetermined extraterrestrial civilization. The medium carrying the specific communication is a stream of particles called neutrinos that have zero rest mass and a magnetic moment 1600 times less than the magnetic moment of an electron. Neutrinos are the most penetrating of the elementary particles known to us. Such particles reach Earth from every direction of the sky. Among them one can distinguish particles generated in stars (therefore in the sun as well) through natural processes such as beta decay and other nuclear reactions, and particles produced from collisions between neutrinos and the nuclei of atoms in Earth's atmosphere or in the crust of the globe. The energy of these particles varies from tens of thousands to many billions of electron volts. Shigubov's work has shown the theoretical possibility of building a so-called neutrino laser, or 'naser,' which could emit a monochromatic corpuscular beam. It is possible that the transmitter that sends the signals received on Earth operates on such a principle. Thanks to the work of Hughes, Lascaglia, and Jeffreys, there has been constructed, for the purpose of recording the separate energy levels in a neutrino emission, a device called an inverter or a neutrino transformer, based on the Einschoff Principle ('the pseudo-particle exchange'), which, making use of the Moessbauer-Tong Effect, is able to filter quanta of radiation to an accuracy of 30,000 eV.

"During the lengthy recordings of the low-energy quanta there was discovered, in the band of 57 million eV, a signal of artificial origin, made up of more than two billion units when converted into binary code. The signal is transmitted continuously, without breaks. It has a comparatively broad radiant, covering the entire region of α Canis Minoris and the star's vicinity in a radius of 1.5 degrees. The information it conveys is of unknown content and purpose. Since the redundancy in the communication channel is probably close to zero, the signal appears as noise. That this noise is a signal is confirmed by the fact that every 416 hours 11 minutes and 23 seconds the whole modulated sequence is repeated from the beginning, with a fidelity at least equal to that of the instruments used on Earth.

"For this artificial signal to be discovered and recorded, the following conditions have to be met: First, the corpuscular stream of neutrinos must be received by an instrument that has a resolution of at least 30,000 eV and is aimed at a radiant in the Canis Minor, with a possible deviation of 1.5 degrees in any direction from the α of that constellation. Second, one must filter out, from the entire neutrino emission of that sector of the sky, the band lying between 56.8 and 57.2 million eV. And third, the reception of the signal must be of a duration greater than 416 hours and 12 minutes, and then the beginning of the next emission must be compared with the beginning of the one preceding. If this is not done, the received signal will give no indication that it is anything other than a normal (natural) noise phenomenon. For a number of reasons, the constellation Canis Minor is a region interesting to neutrino astronomers. The first condition therefore may be met fairly commonly wherever there are such specialists who have at their disposal the right equipment. The selecting of the necessary band, however, has a lower probability, since the emission in that sector possesses 34 maxima in other energies (the number discovered at the present time). The maximum of the 57-million eV band in the spectrum of the entire emission does in fact display a sawtooth peak; that is, it is energetically sharper or better focused than the others, which are created by natural processes, but still it is not that noticeable; the singularity, in practice, will be found only *ex post facto*, i.e., when someone already knows that the signal at band 57 million eV is artificial and consequently directs his attention there.

"Let us assume that out of the world's forty observatories that have the Lascaglia-Jeffreys machine, at least ten are keeping the Canis Minor radiant under constant observation. The chance that one of these will filter for the signal works out to about 1:3 (10:34)—*ceteris paribus*. But a recording time on the order of 416 hours is considered rather long. One does not come across such recordings more often than once in every nine or ten research projects. Thus one can reasonably make the approximation that the discovery's chance of coming about was roughly 1:30-40, and that it could be repeated, with much the same probability, outside the United States."

I have quoted the whole text because its second part is also of interest. The probabilistic calculation is not offered very seriously; its inclusion was dictated by the policy, a bit cynical, of the directors of the Project. Their idea was to alarm the Very Important Persons, since a 1:30 chance is not what one could call astonomically small, and the Persons, alarmed, could use their influence to support an increase in the funding of the Project. (The greatest expense, apart from the large computers, were the machines for the automated chemical syntheses.)

To begin work on the "letter," one had to take a first step, and that was the worst thing. The tautology of the above sentence is superficial only. In history there have appeared, innumerable times, thinkers who believed that one could actually progress, in knowledge, from zero; they made of the mind a blank page and held that it could be filled with one and only one necessary order. This fiction has been the basis of awesome efforts. Yet such an operation cannot be carried out. It is impossible to commence anything without first making assumptions, and our awareness of this fact in no way diminishes its reality. Those assumptions inhere in the very biology of man, and in the amalgam of civilization which serves as the interface between the organisms and the environment; and this amalgam is permitted because the actions that must be taken in order to survive are not rendered unequivocal by the environment. The environment, rather, leaves the organisms a chink for freedom of choice, a chink spacious enough to include thousands of possible cultures.

At the beginning of the work on the stellar code, the initial assumptions had to be kept to a minimum, but one could not do without them altogether. If they proved false, the work would of necessity be in vain. One such assumption was that the code was binary. This agreed, by and large, with the recorded signal, but our own system of notation also contributed to this formalization. Not satisfied with the signal on the tapes, and physicists examined at length the neutrino emission itself, which was the "original" (the recording being only an image). They decided finally that the code could be considered binary "to a reasonable approximation." There was, in this pronouncement—inescapably—a Q.E.D. peremptoriness. The next problem was to determine to which category of signal the letter belonged.

To the best of our knowledge the letter could be "written" in some declarative-transactional language like our own, operating with units of meaning; or it could be a system of "modeling" signals, such as television; or it could represent a "recipe," that is, a set of instructions necessary for the production of a certain object. The letter, finally, could contain a description of an object —of a particular "thing"—in a code that was "acultural," one that referred only to certain constants in the world of nature, discoverable by physics and mathematical in form. The discreteness of these four categories of possible code is not total. A television image results from the projection of three-dimensional phenomena onto a plane, with a time distribution that conforms to the physiological mechanisms of the human eye and brain. What we see on the screen is not visible to organisms that are otherwise quite advanced on the evolutionary scale. A dog, for example, will not recognize on television (or in a photograph) another dog. In addition, the boundary between the "thing" and the "recipe for the thing" is not sharp. An egg cell is both a thing, as a material object, and the production recipe for the organism that will develop from it. Thus the relation that exists between the carrier of information and the information itself can be multivalent and tangled.

Knowing, then, the flimsiness of our classification schema, but having at our disposal none better, we proceeded to the task of eliminating, one by one, its variants. The easiest to test, relatively, was the "television hypothesis." For a while it enjoyed great success and was considered to be the most economical. In various combinations, then, the signal was fed into a picture tube. Not a hint of an image was obtained that represented anything; on the other hand, the result was not "complete chaos." On the white screen appeared black spots that increased, grew, flowed together, and vanished, and the whole gave the effect of "boiling." When the signal was run through a thousand times slower, the scene resembled colonies of bacteria in stages of expansion, mutual absorption, and collapse. The eye caught a certain rhythm and regularity in the process, though the rhythm and regularity said nothing.

Control experiments were also initiated, in which recordings of natural neutrino noise were fed into the television. What resulted was a formlessness without centers of condensation, a fluttering and flickering that dissolved into a uniform gray. It was possible to argue, of course, that the Senders had a different sort of television from ours—not optical, for example, but olfactory, or olfactory-tactile. Yet even if they were made differently from us, there could be no doubt that they were our superiors in knowledge, and therefore they would have had to realize that the chance of reception ought not to be made dependent on the addressee's physiological similarity to the sender.

The second variant-possibility was thus rejected. Testing the first was doomed to failure, because, as I pointed out, without a dictionary and a grammar it is impossible to crack a truly "foreign" language. So the two others remained. They were treated together, because (again, as I have said) the distinction between "thing" and "process" is relative. To make a very long story short —the Project began from precisely this position, achieved some results, "materializing" a small piece of the "letter" (i.e., successfully translating, as it were, a fragment of it); but then the work came to a standstill.

The task given me was to find out whether the assumption of the letter as a "thing-process" was correct. I could not refer to the results that had been obtained by beginning with the assumption, for that would have constituted a logical error (a vicious circle). It was not out of ill will, then, but precisely to keep me from approaching the problem with preconceptions that at the beginning no achievements were mentioned in my presence. They might have been, in a certain sense, the product of "misunderstandings."

I did not even know if the mathematicians of the Project had already made a stab at the task given me. I assumed that they had. If I knew their failure—I thought—then I could save myself some unnecessary trouble; but Dill, Rappaport, and Baloyne felt that the safest thing was to tell me nothing.

In a word, I was summoned to rescue the honor of the planet. I had to flex my mathematical muscles in earnest—a little nervous, but pleased. The explaining, the conversing, the sacramental entrusting of the recording from the stars took half a day. The "Big Four" escorted me then to the hotel, watching one another to make sure that no one, in my presence, would betray anything that for the time being I was not supposed to know.

FROM THE MOMENT I landed on the roof, through all the meetings and conversations, the feeling never left me that I was playing a scientist in a grade-B movie. The feeling was strengthened by the room—or, rather, suite—in which they put me. I cannot remember ever having at my disposal so many unnecessary things. In the study stood a desk of presidential proportions; opposite it, two television sets and a radio. The armchair had controls for being raised, turned around, and lowered, no doubt so that between bouts of mental struggling one could take a little nap on it. Near it there was a large shape beneath a white cover. At first I took this for some piece of gymnastic equipment or a rocking horse (even that would not have surprised me), but it was a brand-new, very handsome IBM cryotronic calculator, which indeed proved useful to me. Wanting to join man more closely to the machine, the engineers at IBM had him work it also with his feet. Every time I pressed the "clear" pedal I expected, by reflex, to drive into the wall—the pedal was so much like a car accelerator. In the wall cabinet behind the desk I found a dictaphone, a typewriter, and also a small, scrupulously furnished bar.

But the most peculiar thing was the reference library. Whoever had assembled it must have been absolutely convinced that the more a book cost, the more valuable it was. Thus there were encyclopedias, thick volumes on the history of mathematics and the history of science—even one on Mayan cosmogony. Perfect order reigned among the backs and bindings; and complete nonsense in the printed contents. During that whole year I did not use my library once.

The bedroom was also done up nicely. In it I found an electric heating pad, a medicine chest, and a small hearing aid. To this day I do not know whether this was a joke or a mistake. Taken together, everything expressed the careful execution of the order: "Top quarters for a top mathematician." Glancing at the night table, I saw a Bible and was reassured—yes, they truly had my welfare at heart.

The tome that contained the stellar code, delivered over to me with great ceremony, was not especially interesting—at least not at first reading. The beginning went: "000110101000111110011011111100101001010100." The rest was more of the same. The only additional information given me said that the code unit definitely was made up of nine elementary signs (zeros and ones).

Taking possession of this new abode, I put on my thinking cap. I reasoned more or less as follows: Civilization is a thing both necessary and accidental; like the lining of a nest, it is a shelter from the world, a tiny counterworld that the large world silently tolerates, with the toleration of indifference, because in it there is no answer to the questions of good and evil, beauty and ugliness, laws and customs. Language, the creation of civilization, is like the framework of the nest; it binds all the bits of lining and unites them into the shape that is deemed necessary by the occupants of the nest. Language is an appeal to the joint identity of the nesting beings, their common denominator, their constant of similarity, and therefore its influence must end immediately beyond the edge of that subtle structure.

The Senders had to know this. It was expected that the content of the signal from the stars would be mathematics. Great stock, as you know, was placed in the almighty Pythagorean triangles; we were going to greet, across space, other civilizations—with Euclid's geometry. The Senders chose another way, and I believed that they were right. With ethnic language they could not break free of their planet, because every language is pinned to a local foundation. Mathematics, on the other hand, is a severance too complete. It cuts bonds not only locally; it parts with the limitations that have become parameters for villainies and virtues; it is the result of a search for a freedom that dispenses with every tangible verification. It is the act of builders whose wish is that the world should never be able, not in any way, to disturb their work. Consequently, with mathematics one can say nothing about the world—it is called "pure" for the very reason that it has been purified of all material dross, and its absolute purity is its immortality. But precisely therein lies its arbitrariness, for it can beget any sort of world, as long as that world is consistent. Out of the infinite number of possible mathematics we have chosen one; our history decided this for us with its various unique and irreversible vicissitudes.

With mathematics one may signal only that one Is, that one Exists. If one wishes to act more effectively at a distance, the sending of a "production recipe" becomes inevitable. But such a recipe presupposes a technology, and technology is a transient, mutable condition, a passing from one set of materials and methods to another. And what of a description of an "object"? But an object, too, may be described in an infinite number of ways. It was an impasse.

There was one thing that bothered me. The stellar code had been transmitted in a continuous fashion, in uninterrupted repetitions, and this made no sense, because it hindered recognition of the signal as a signal. Poor Laserowitz had not been altogether mad: zones of periodic silence indeed seemed necessary—more, imperative—as an indication of the artificial nature of the signal. Periods of quiet would have drawn the attention of any observer. Why, then, was this not done? The question haunted me. I tried turning it around: the lack of interruptions seemed a lack of information, information indicating the intelligent source of the emission. But what if actually that was additional information? What could such a thing mean? That the "beginning" and the "end" of the message were nonessential. That one could read it starting at any point.

The idea fascinated me. I understood now why my friends had been so careful not to tell me anything about the ways in which the "letter" had been attacked. I was, as they wanted me to be, entirely without preconceptions. At the same time I had to wage the battle, so to speak, on two fronts at once: the main "opponent," of course, whose motives I tried to guess, was the unknown Sender, however, at the same time I could not help also thinking, at every step of my reasoning, about whether or not the mathematicians of the Project had taken the same path as I. All I knew about their work was that it had yielded no definitive result, not merely in the sense that they had failed to decipher the "letter," but in the sense, too, that they remained uncertain—in other words, they had not proved—that the "letter" belonged to the category of information that had been hypothesized: the "thing-process."

Quite like my predecessors, I felt that the code was overly laconic. It could have been supplied, after all, with an introductory part, showing, in simple statements, how one ought to read it. Or so it seemed. But the laconicism of the code was not an objective property of the code; it depended, rather, on the degree of knowledge of the receiver—or, more precisely, on the difference in knowledge possessed by sender and receiver. The same information could be found sufficient by one receiver and "too laconic" by another. Any object, the simplest object, contains, potentially, an infinite amount of information. Therefore, however much we detail a transmitted description, it will always be unnecessarily precise for some and fragmentary for others. The difficulty we were encountering only showed that the Sender was addressing parties more advanced than mankind at the given historical moment.

Information that is divorced from objects is not only incomplete; it invariably represents some kind of generalization. Its referent is never fully designated. On an everyday basis we are of another opinion, since this fuzziness in the designation of objects is, in ordinary life, barely perceptible. It is the same in science. Although we now know that speeds cannot be added arithmetically, we do not make a relativistic correction when we add the velocity of a ship to the car driving on its deck, because the correction, for speeds not near that of light, is so minuscule as to be meaningless. Now, there exists an informational equivalent to this relativistic effect: the notion of "life" is practically identical for two biologists, one of whom lives in Hawaii and the other in Norway. Yet the tremendous gulf between two alien civilizations has caused the seeming identity of many notions to fall apart. Certainly, had the Senders used, for designated objects, the set of heavenly bodies, there would not have been this problem. And if they designated atoms? Atoms as "things" to a considerable degree depend on one's knowledge of them. Eighty years ago an atom was "very similar" to a miniature solar system. Today it no longer is. Let us suppose that they send us a hexagon. In it one can see the plan for a chemical molecule, or for a bee's honeycomb, or for a building. An infinite number of objects correspond to that geometrical information. One can determine what the Senders have in mind only by specifying the building material. If, say, the material is to be brick, the class of solutions will indeed be narrowed down, and yet we will still have a set of infinite magnitude, because it is possible, after all, to construct an endless number of hexagonal buildings. The transmitted blueprint ought to be provided with precise measurements. But there exists a material of which the bricks themselves determine the exact measurements. Atoms. In their bonding it is impossible to bring them closer at will, or to move them farther apart. Therefore, having before me only a hexagon, I would think that the Senders meant a molecule of a chemical compound, one constructed of six atoms or of six groups of atoms. Such a statement very significantly limits the field of further searching.

Let us assume—I said to myself—that the "letter" is a description of a thing, a description, moreover, on the molecular level. The kernel of this preliminary thinking was the consideration of the letter's "content" as a thing having no beginning or end, and therefore circular. It could be either a "circular object" or a circular process. The distinction between the one and the other, as was pointed out, depends in part on the scale of observation. If we lived a billion times more slowly, and correspondingly longer, if a second—in this fancy—equaled an entire century, we would certainly conclude that the continents of the globe were processes, seeing with our own eyes how changeable they were, for they would be moving before us no less than waterfalls do, or ocean currents. And if, on the other hand, we lived a billion times faster, we would conclude that the waterfall was an object—because it would present itself to us as something highly immobile and immutable. The difference between "object" and "process," therefore, gave no need for concern. It was now only necessary to prove, and not merely to speculate, that the "letter" was a "ring," just as the molecular model of benzene is a ring. If I did not wish to send a two-dimensional image of that molecule, but chose, rather, to code it into some linear form, a series of successive signals, the place in the benzene ring from which I would begin my description would be unimportant. Every place would serve equally well.

It was from this position that I proceeded to the translation of the problem into the language of mathematics. What I did I cannot present plainly, since our everyday language lacks the required concepts and words. I can only say, in general, that I studied the purely formal properties of the "letter"—treating it as an object mathematically interpreted—for features that are of central interest in topological algebra and the algebra of groups. In doing this, I employed the transformation of transformational sets, which gives the so-called infragroups or Hogarth groups (named after me, since I was the one who discovered them). If I obtained, as a result, an "open" structure, that would still prove nothing, because it could be that I had simply introduced an error into my work, going on some false assumption (such an assumption might be, e.g., the assertion of the number of code signs in a single "unit" of the message). But it happened otherwise. The "letter" closed beautifully for me, like an object separated from the rest of the world, or like a circular process (to be more precise, like the DESCRIPTION, the MODEL of such a thing).

I spent three days setting up a program for the computer, and the computer carried out the task on the fourth. The result said that "something, in some way, closes." The "something" was the letter—in the totality of the interrelations of its signs; but as for the "how" of that closing, I could only make certain guesses, because my proof was indirect. The proof showed only that the "described object" was NOT "topologically open." But to reveal the "means of closure" with the aid of current mathematical methods was impossible for me; such a task was several orders of difficulty greater than the one I had managed to surmount. The proof, then, was very general—one could even say vague. On the other hand, not every text would have displayed this property. The score of a symphony, for example, or a linear coding of a television image, or an ordinary linguistic text (a story, a philosophical treatise) does not close in that fashion. But the description of a geometric solid closes, as does that of something as complex as a

86

genotype or a living organism. The genotype, true, closes differently from the solid. But by going into such distinctions and details I fear that I will be confusing the reader rather than explaining to him what I did with the "letter."

Let me just emphasize that from penetrating to the "sense"—or, to put it even more colloquially, to "what the letter was about"—I remained as distant as I had been before starting this work. Out of the innumerable features of the "letter," I recognized, and recognized only indirectly, one, one that had to do with a certain general property of the structure as a whole. Because I had succeeded so well, I later tried to attack that "second problem"—the resolution of the structure in its "closure"—but during my tenure at the Project I came up with nothing. Three years later, no longer with the Project, I renewed my efforts, because the problem had been pursuing me like a stubborn ghost. I achieved only this: I proved that using the apparatus of the topological and transformational algebras would NOT enable one to solve the problem. Which, of course, I had no way of knowing when I first sat down to the task. In any case, I provided a powerful argument in support of the contention that we had indeed received from the Cosmos the sort of thing to which could be attributed—considering the degree of concentration and cohesion that produced "closure"—the qualities of an "object" (that is, of the description of an object—I am abbreviating here).

I presented my work not without apprehension. It turned out, however, that I had done something that no one else had thought of—for the reason that during the preliminary discussions the idea had won out that the letter must be an algorithm (in the mathematical sense) and therefore a general-recursive function, and the search for the values of that function had swamped all the computers. This made sense to the extent that, if the problem were solved, the solution would carry with it information pointing, like a road sign, to further stages of translational work. But the order of complexity of the letter-as-algorithm was such that the problem was not solved. Meanwhile, the "circularity" of the letter had indeed been noticed, but it was considered of no great importance, not promising—in that initial period of great hopes—any quick or appreciable success. Then, later on, everyone became so mired in the algorithm approach that they could not free themselves from it.

One might think that I had achieved no little triumph at the very beginning. I proved that the letter was the description of a phenomenon, and inasmuch as all the empirical research was going in precisely that direction, I gave it, so to speak, the blessing of a mathematical proof, guaranteeing that this was the right track. I thereby brought together those who were divided, because between the information theorists and the information engineers a breach had grown. The antagonists, finally, were referred to me. The future was to show how little I had accomplished—emerging well from an encounter with only my terrestrial rivals.

7

IF YOU ASK a scientist what he associates with the concept of a circular process, most likely he will reply: life. The suggestion that we had been sent the description of something living, and which we would be able to reconstruct, was both unsettling and intriguing. For two months after the events described above, I passed my time in the Project as a student, learning what in the prior year all the "applied" groups had done. The applied groups were also called "shock troops." We had a great many of these—in biochemistry, biophysics, solid-state physics—which later were to some extent combined in the laboratory, for syntheses. (The Project's organizational structure, in the course of its existence, grew more and more complicated, until some said that it had become more complex even than the "letter" itself.)

The theoretical section, comprising the informationists, linguists, mathematicians, and theoretical physicists, operated independently of the applied. All the findings of all the research were assessed and collated on the highest level—in the Science Council, where the group coordinators sat, along with the "Big Four," which became five upon my arrival.

The Project, when I made my appearance, had two concrete achievements to show for itself; they were actually one and the same, repeated independently in the biochemistry and biophysics departments. In both places there was produced—first on paper, or, rather, in the memory banks—a substance that had been "read off" from the letter, though named, by that principle of autonomy, twice: "Frog Eggs" and "Lord of the Flies."

The duplication of effort might appear wasteful, but it had its good side. If two people not communicating with each other analogously translate an unknown text, one tends to think that they have truly got to its "invariants," that what they have obtained is objectively inherent in the text and does not merely reflect their personal preconceptions. Granted, this statement, too, can be debated. For two Mohammedans, the same small "fragments" of the Gospel are "true"—as opposed to all the rest of it. If people's preprogramming is identical, the results of their investigations may coincide, even though they have not consulted each other. Since limits are placed on what may be accomplished, in any given historical period, by the general level of knowledge. It is for this reason that the atomistic and independent conclusions arrived at by the physicists of East and West, for example, have been so similar, and that one side could not discover the principle of the laser and have that principle remain unknown to the other. Therefore we should not exaggerate the cognitive importance of such coincidence.

Frog Eggs—its name among the biochemists—was a semiliquid substance under some conditions, a gelatinous mass under others; at room temperature and normal pressure, and in not too great a quantity, it appeared as a shiny, sticky fluid, quite similar to the mucus-coated granules of the amphibian's spawn—hence the name. The biophysicists immediately manufactured about a hectoliter of the pseudo plasm, but it behaved—in an evacuated vessel —differently from Frog Eggs, and they christened it, alluding to a certain strange effect, with a more diabolical name.

Carbon played an important role in the composition of this artifact, but so did silicon, and heavy elements practically nonexistent in earthly organisms. The thing reacted to certain stimuli; it produced energy, which it dispersed in the form of heat, but had no metabolism—not in any biological sense. At first it appeared to be—a materialization of an impossibility—a *perpetuum mobile*, albeit in the form of a colloid and not a "machine." Standing in flagrant violation of the sacred laws of thermodynamics, it was subjected to very rigorous study. At last the nucleonics people found that the energy supporting it—supporting what was a kind of "circus trick," an acrobatic juggling of gigantic molecules that were unstable in isolation—was being drawn from nuclear reactions of the "cold" type. The colloid initiated them when it reached a certain critical mass. Important, in this, was not only the quantity of the substance, but also its configuration.

These reactions were difficult to detect, because the energy liberated through them—the radiant energy as well as the kinetic energy of the freed subatomic particles—was absorbed completely by the substance and used "for its own needs." To the experts this revelation was staggering. Basically, atomic nuclei are, within every terrestrial organism, "foreign bodies," or at least neutral. The life process never touches the energy potentials contained in them; it is unable to make use of that enormous, stored-up force. Atoms, in living tissue, are in effect only electron shells, because the shells alone participate in biological (chemical) reactions. Consequently, radioactive atoms that get into the system, carried there by water, food, or air, play the role of intruders "disguised" by their outer similarity (i.e., in their electron shells) to ordinary, normal—nonradioactive—elements, and the living tissue is not capable of telling the difference. Their every "explosion," any kind of nuclear decay of such an uninvited guest, constitutes for the cell a microscopic catastrophe—always damaging, though to a very small degree.

Meanwhile Frog Eggs could not do without such processes, which were its sustenance, the air it breathed, for it required no other source of energy, and indeed could make use of no other. Frog Eggs became the foundation for an edifice of hypotheses—a veritable Tower of Babel of hypotheses, unfortunately, because of the disparity between them.

According to the simplest, Frog Eggs was the protoplasm of which the Senders of the stellar code were composed. To manufacture it, as I indicated, only a small portion of the code was utilized —certainly no more than 3 or 4 percent—the portion that allowed itself to be "translated" into synthesis operations. The proponents of this first view believed that the entire code was the description of one Sender and that, if we succeeded in materializing him *in toto*, he would stand before us as a live and intelligent being from another civilization in the galaxy, telegraphed to Earth's receivers via a stream of neutrino emissions.

According to other, related, conjectures, what had been sent was not so much an "atomic blueprint" of an adult organism, as a kind of spore or egg capable of development, or even an embryo. The embryo would be suitably programmed genetically and, if materialized on Earth, could turn out to be as competent a partner for mankind as the adult specimen from the first possibility.

And there was no dearth of radically different approaches. According to another group, or family, of hypotheses (because the ideas of each circle were connected by their own consanguinity), the code described not an "individual" of any sort, but an "informational machine"—a type of tool rather than a representative of the race that transmitted it. Some conceived of such a machine as being a kind of library made of the stuff of Frog Eggs, i.e., a "plasmic container of memory," able to communicate the data stored in it or possibly even to carry on a "conversation" about the data. Others posited a "plasmic brain"—an analog, digital, or hybrid type—which would not be able to provide answers to questions concerning the Senders, but which would represent a sort of technological gift. The code, then, was the act of handing across space, to one civilization by another, the latter's finest instrument for the processing of information.

These hypotheses all had, in turn, their black or demonic variations, which arose—some said—from the reading of too much science fiction. Whatever had been sent, whether "individual," "embryo," or "machine," upon materialization would—according to these variations—attempt to take over the world. And, again, within this segment of beliefs was division—because some of the followers of the conquest-of-Earth theory held that this was a galactically planned "act of invasion," while others said no, an act of "cosmic friendship," this being the way in which advanced civilizations undertook to perform, with respect to others, an "obstetric intervention," facilitating the birth of a more nearly perfect social structure—for the local benefit, and not in the interest of the Senders.

All these hypotheses (and there were more) I considered not just wrong but ridiculous. In my opinion, the stellar code denoted neither a plasmic brain nor an informational machine nor an organism nor a spore, because the object it designated simply did not figure in the categories of our conceptualizations. It was the plan of a cathedral sent to australopithecines, a library opened to Neanderthals. In my opinion, the code was not intended for a civilization as low on the ladder of development as ours, and consequently we would not succeed in doing anything meaningful with it.

I was called a nihilist on account of this, and Eugene Albert Nye complained to his superiors that I was sabotaging the Project —of which I learned even without possessing my own network of hidden microphones.

I had been working almost a month on His Master's Voice when the matter took on a completely new light, thanks to the efforts of a team of biologists. We had at the Project what was called the Book of Canis Minor; in it anyone could enter his postulates, his criticisms of the theories of others, his own proposals or ideas, or the results of his research. The contribution of the biologists occupied a prominent if not central place there. It was Romney who came up with the notion of conducting experiments of a sort totally different from those that were absorbing his colleagues. Romney was (like Reinhorn) one of the few scientists in the Project of the older generation. Anyone who has not read his *Rise of Man* knows nothing of evolution. Romney searched for the causes of intelligence—and found them in combinations of accidents which, though neutral when they occurred, later took on a sardonic significance: cannibalism turned out to be a spur to mental development; the threat of glaciers, a prerequisite for civilization; the gnawing of bones, the inspiration for the origin of tools. And the junction of the organs of generation with those of elimination, taken from the fish and reptiles, became the topographic map not only for eroticism but for metaphysics, too, which oscillates between defilement and divinity. He drew from the zigzag course of evolution all its magnificence and wretchedness, and demonstrated how random series, in their deviations, turn into laws of nature. But the book is surprising most of all for the spirit of compassion that pervades it—though never given explicit expression.

I do not know how Romney hit upon his great idea. When asked, he would only mutter. His team directed its attention not to the letter recorded on the tapes but to the "original"—that is, the neutrino emission itself, streaming unceasingly from the sky. My guess is that Romney addressed the question of why it was *neutrino* waves that had been chosen by the Senders as the carrier of information. As I have said, there exists a natural neutrino emission in space, originating from the stars. The emission that, by means of the appropriate modulation, conveys the letter is a very narrow band in that totality. Romney must have wondered whether the band (corresponding to the notion of "wavelength" in radiotechnology) had been selected by the Senders randomly, or whether some special reason lay behind that decision. So he set up a series of experiments in which a great number of substances were exposed first to the ordinary neutrino radiation from the stars, and then to the stream of the letter. He could do this because the provident Baloyne, reaching deep into government coffers, had supplied the Project with a battery of high-resolution neutrino inverters. In addition, the radiation from the heavens was amplified several hundred million times—the physicists built the necessary equipment.

Neutrinos are the most penetrating of the elementary particles. They all, and particularly those at low energies, pass through galactic space and—with no greater difficulty—material objects, planets, stars; because matter is far more transparent to them than glass is to sunlight. The experiments really should not have produced any result worth mentioning. But they did.

In chambers placed at a depth of forty meters (quite shallow for an experiment with neutrinos) stood mammoth amplifiers connected to inverters. The increasingly concentrated neutrino beam, issuing from a metal cylinder the size of a pencil, hit various solids, liquids, and gases that were put in its path. The first series of tests, in which a great variety of substances was irradiated in this fashion by the natural emission from the sky, yielded nothing of interest—as was expected.

But the neutrino beam that carried the letter revealed an astounding property. Of two groups of macromolecular solutions, the more stable chemically turned out to be the one that had been subjected to the ray. The ordinary neutrino "noise," I should emphasize, did not possess such an effect. Only the stream that was modulated by information possessed it. It was as if its neutrinos, penetrating everything in an invisible rain, nevertheless entered into some interaction—for us imperceptible and unknown—with the molecules of the colloid and, in so doing, rendered the colloid less vulnerable to the factors that normally caused its decomposition, the unraveling and tearing of the seams of its chemical bonds. It was as if that neutrino emission "favored" large molecules of a certain type; as if it assisted the rise—in aqueous solutions saturated with particular substances—of those atomic configurations that constituted the chemical backbone of *life*.

The neutrino stream by which the letter reached us was too attenuated for the effect to have been discovered directly. Only its concentration by many hundreds of millions of times allowed the effect to be observed—in solutions, moreover, that had been irradiated for weeks on end. Even so, this suggested strongly that the emission, when not intensified, still had the same "life-favoring" property, except that the property would manifest itself in periods measured not in weeks but in hundreds of thousands—no, in millions—of years. Back in the prehistoric past, that all-penetrating precipitation increased the chances, in however fractional a way, of life forming in the oceans, because it wrapped certain types of organic molecules, as it were, in an invisible armor that made them resistant to the chaotic bombardment of Brownian motion. The stellar signal did not itself create life, but assisted in life's earliest, most elementary stage, hindering the dissolution of what had become combined.

Möller, a physicist and Romney's coworker, showing me the results of these experiments, used the image of comparing the Senders to a tenor who is able to sing a note in such a way that a glass held before his mouth will shatter from the created resonance. What the man sings *about* has no bearing, obviously, on this consequence of his song. Similarly, the cut, color, and weight of the paper on which a letter is written need have no particular connection with its content. But a connection can equally well exist between the information proper and its physical medium. When, for example, we receive a small, sky-blue, subtly perfumed note from a woman, we hardly expect to find in it a torrent of abuse or a diagram of the city's sewer system. The question of whether a connection exists, and whether its existence is of special significance, usually is decided by the culture, the context in which the communication takes place. The Romney-Möller Effect was one of our greatest achievements; yet at the same time, as was typical in the Project, it was a maddening puzzle that caused the scientists many a sleepless night. The number of theories that welled up on this score was no less than that of the theories that wound about, like a vine, the substance "derived" from the information itself, that is, from the content of the stellar message—the substance that was Frog Eggs. Whether between that "nuclear ooze" and the "biosympathy" of the neutrino code there was any connection—and if there was, what it meant—that was the question!

THOSE RESPONSIBLE FOR my being pulled into the Project were Baloyne, Baer, and Prothero. As I came to realize in the course of the first weeks, the task that was given me at the beginning, and crowned with a success that had been anticipated, was not the main reason they co-opted me onto the Science Council. The Project had plenty of specialists, and the finest, too; the rub was, it did not have the right specialists, for there were none in existence. I, who had already several times abandoned the purity of my mathematics, moving from one discipline to another across a vast area that stretched from cosmology to animal behavior, not only picked up in the process a great variety of information—that was not the important thing—but also had acquired the habit, in the course of these repeated relocations, of iconoclasm.

As a stranger from the outside, and therefore not bound emotionally to the sacred and time-honored rules of the territories I invaded, I found it easy to question what others, ensconced in their given science, never dreamed of challenging. Thus it happened that I did not build so often as I razed existing orders, the fruits of much labor and dedication. It was just such an individual that the directors of the Project wanted. The majority of the people in its ranks—the natural scientists, especially—were content to continue with their previous research, not overly concerned about whether or not that research would form a coherent whole relating to the informational Moloch that came from the stars, that begot a host of interesting, specific problems, and that actually led (as I have indicated) to important discoveries.

But at the same time the leadership—the Big Four—began to realize, if still somewhat dimly, that they were falling into the situation where the forest became harder and harder to see for the researching of the trees; that the established routine, now finely tuned and quite efficient in its performance of systematic operations, could engulf the Project itself, dissolving it in a sea of isolated facts and findings; and that in this way the chance would be lost of ever grasping what had taken place. Earth had received a signal from the stars, a message so packed with content that the few crumbs pecked from it were sufficient to nourish a multitude of research teams for years on end; and yet the message itself was wrapped in a haze whose impenetrability, veiled by a swarm of tiny achievements, grew less and less provoking. Perhaps at work here was simply a psychological defense mechanism; or perhaps it was the habit of people trained to uncover the laws behind a phenomenon and not pose questions as to what brought those and not other laws into the world.

To such questions philosophy and religion are traditionally supposed to supply answers, not the natural scientist, who severs himself from the temptation of trying to divine the motives behind Creation. But here it was just the opposite: the approach of the guesser of motives, so discredited in the historical development of the empirical sciences, became the last hope offered for victory. Granted, the attributing of anthropomorphic motives to the Causer of the properties of the atoms remained methodologically prohibited; but some similarity—even the most remote—between Those Who Sent the code and the code's recipients was more than a fantasy to comfort the mind; it was a hypothesis on whose cutting edge hung the future of the entire Project. And I was certain of this from the first, from the moment I set foot on the HMV compound—certain that a lack of any similarity would render futile all efforts to understand the stellar message.

Not for a minute did I put stock in any of the conjectures about the signal. The telegraphed individual, the blueprint of the "great brain," of the plasmic "informational machine," of the synthetic "ruler" who was to conquer Earth—all this was borrowed from the poverty-stricken repertoire of ideas which civilization, in its current technological form, had at its disposal. These imaginings were a reflection—much like the themes of science-fiction novels —of society, and of society primarily in its American version, whose export outside the States prospered around the middle of the century. They were either fashionable novelties or else conceptions built on the game principle "it's them or us"—and never did the insipidity of invention, its enchainment to Earth in the narrow channel of historical time, appear more obvious to me than when I heard these theories, seemingly bold but in reality pathetically naïve.

During the discussions held by the Project's chief information theorist, Dr. Mackenzie, when I had managed—by putting down such notions—to antagonize those present, one of Mackenzie's younger colleagues asked what, then, in my opinion, the signal was, for the vehemence of my refutations indicated that I must be in possession of the truth.

"Perhaps it is a Revelation," I replied. "Holy Scripture need not be printed on paper and bound in gold-embossed cloth. It can be also a plasmatic glob . . . such as Frog Eggs."

I was joking, but they, anxious to exchange their ignorance for something, for anything, as long as it bore the semblance of certainty, began to consider my words in all seriousness. And immediately, again, everything worked out nicely for them: the signal was the Word that becomes Flesh (meaning the effect that "favored biogenesis," the Romney-Möller Effect), and whatever the motives that inclined someone to support the development of life on the galactic scale, they could not be "pragmatic," selfish, technological . . . because, in order to take such action, one first had to regard biogenesis—throughout the Universe—as a phenomenon desirable and good. This was, so to speak, an act of "cosmic good will," which, when seen in that light, amounted to an announcement (but active, enacting) of "Good Tidings," remarkable in that it was capable of self-fulfillment—without the presence of cooperative ears.

I left them—they were in such a heat, they did not even notice —and went back to my apartment. The one thing I was certain of was the Romney-Möller Effect: that the stellar code increased the probability of the creation of life. Biogenesis was of course still possible without it, but a longer time would be required, and there would be, perhaps, a lower percentage of occurrences. This statement had in it something bracing—beings who operated like that, I could understand.

Was it possible to believe that the purely physical, life-giving aspect of the signal was completely independent of, totally divorced from, its content? That the signal should represent no information at all, no "sense" beyond its "protective" relation to life, was impossible—Frog Eggs, if nothing else, gave proof of that. Then could it be that the content was in some way parallel to what its medium effected? I knew that I was getting onto slippery ground. The notion of the code as a message which by its content as well was to "make happy," "do good," immediately suggested itself. And yet, as Voltaire put it, when the grain is shipped to the Sultan, does the Captain concern himself about the comfort of the mice on board?

Visitors from the outside were called by us not VIPs but "Feebs," for "feeble-minded." The pejorative was coined not so much to express the general opinion regarding the mental prowess of our illustrious guests, but simply because we had no end of trouble when problems typical of the Project needed to be explained to people who did not know the professional language of science. In order to give them some idea of the relation between the "life-causing form" of the stellar message and its "content"—from which at that time we had extracted only Lord of the Flies—I came up with the following analogy.

Let us suppose that a typesetter, on a linotype, composes a poem. The poem has a certain linguistic meaning. But in addition it may happen that if a sufficiently elastic stylus, one able to vibrate, is run across the metal letters, a sound will result, which by accident may have the value of a harmonic chord. It would be altogether improbable for sounds, arising thus, to combine to form —by sheerest chance—the first measures of Beethoven's Fifth Symphony. Were such a thing to occur, we would naturally think that the music was no product of chance but that someone had intentionally set the type in that way, selecting the right sizes of the letters as well as the spaces between them. What was, as an "incidental harmony," highly improbable for the cast printing type, was for the communication, the letter from the stars, an improbability equal to an impossibility.

In other words, the life-producing property of that communication could not be the work of chance. The Sender must have deliberately imparted to the neutrino beam such modulated vibrations as brought about the phenomenon of the supporting of biogenesis. Now, this coexistence of "form" and "content" seemed to demand, inexorably, some specific explanation, and the simplest assumption said that if the "form" favored life, then the content, too, ought somehow to be similarly "beneficial." If, on the other hand, one rejected the theory of a "universal good will" that to the letter's direct life-giving action added some corresponding message that benefited the addressee, then one was more or less condemned to accept the diametrically opposite formula, according to which the Sender of the benevolent, life-favoring message was enclosing (diabolically) a content that could lead the receivers to destruction.

If I say that one was condemned to the diabolical interpretation, it is not because such was my personal opinion; I simply note the actual train of thought within the Project. The stubbornness that manifested itself in the theorizing is evident throughout the published reports that tell the story of HMV. This stubbornness was always bipolar: either the letter was supposed to represent an act of "benevolent patronage," the giving of technological knowledge, which our civilization considers the highest good; or else it was an act of cunningly camouflaged aggression—whereby that which would arise from the materialization of the letter would strive to rule Earth, humanity, or even to annihilate it. I always stood in opposition to this paralysis of imagination. The Senders could have been, for example, rational beings who took advantage of an "energy opportunity": having earlier set in motion a "biophilic emission," and afterward desiring to enter into communication with the intelligent inhabitants of planets, they could have made use, out of simple economy, of the energy source already in operation instead of constructing special transmitters for the purpose; they could have superimposed on the neutrino stream a particular text that did not necessarily have anything to do with the stream's "life-causing" character. By the same token, the meaning of a telegram that we send does not stand in any one-to-one relation with the properties of the electromagnetic waves of the wireless telegraph.

Although such a thing was conceivable, ideas like this had no following among us. Some of the hypotheses were even highly ingenious—that, for example, the letter worked "on two levels." It effected life as a gardener casts seed upon the ground; but later it came around again, to see if the emergent crop was "right." And then the letter was to act, on its "second" level—that is, through its content—as the gardener's pruning shears: an agent that would remove "degenerated psychozoic enclaves." This meant that the Senders, summarily and without pity, sought to destroy those civilizations, evolutionarily arisen, which had not developed "properly," the sort, for example, that produced classes that were "self-devouring," "warlike," etc. Thus the Senders tended, as it were, the beginning and the conclusion of biogenesis, both the roots and the crown of the evolutionary tree. The content part of the letter was designed to provide a certain type of undersirable addressee with a razor, so that it could cut its own throat.

This fantasy, too, I rejected. The image of a civilization that was supposed to annihilate, in so unusual a way, the "degenerated" or "retarded," I dismissed as yet another projection—onto the unknown of the letter as an "association test"—of the fears characteristic of our age, and as nothing more. The Romney-Möller Effect appeared to indicate that the Sender held existence—in the form of life—to be a good thing. But I was not prepared to take the next step: either to attribute intentional kindness to the informational "layer" of the code as well, or to set a negative sign upon it. The "black" conceptions came to their creators automatically, because what had been given us by the letter they considered a Trojan horse, deserving only suspicion: an instrument, but one that would subjugate Earth; a being, but one who would rule us.

All these ideas beat between the diabolical and the angelic like flies between the panes of a double window. I tried putting myself in the place of the Sender. I would send nothing that could be used contrary to my intentions. To provide any kind of tool without knowing to whom would be like handing out grenades to children. What, then, had been sent? A plan for an ideal society, complete with "illustrations" presenting the energy sources for that society (in the form of Lord of the Flies)? But such a plan was a system dependent upon its own elements, that is, on the individual beings. There could exist no one plan optimal for all places and times. It would also have to take into account the particular biology—and I did not believe that mankind represented, in this respect, any sort of cosmic constant.

It seemed unlikely, at first glance, that the letter could be a communication that was a fragment of an interplanetary dialogue which we happened by pure accident to overhear, because that did not jibe with the constant repetition of the emission. A conversation, surely, did not consist in one of the partners' repeating, in circles, year after year, the same thing from the beginning. But, again, the time scale entered into play here. The communication had streamed to Earth, unchanging, for at least two years—that much was certain. Perhaps the "conversing" was being done by automatic devices, and the equipment of one side would keep sending its statement until it got the signal that the statement had been received. In which case, the repetitions could continue a thousand years, if the civilizations involved were sufficiently distant from each other. We did not know whether or not the "life-causing emission" could be the carrier of various contents—which was, *a priori*, quite possible.

Nevertheless, the "overheard conversation" version seemed very unlikely. When "questions" were separated from the "answers" they received by a time that was on the order of centuries, it was hard to call such an exchange a "dialogue." One ought to expect, instead, each of the parties to transmit to the other important facts about itself. Therefore, we should have been receiving not one emission but at the very least two. That, however, was not the case. The neutrino "ether," to the extent that the astrophysicists' instruments could tell, was completely empty—except for that one transmission band. This was perhaps the hardest nut of all to crack in the mystery. The simplest explanation was that there was no dialogue, no second civilization, but only the one, sending out an isotropic signal. After such a statement, you went back to racking your brains over the double nature of the signal . . . *da capo al fine*.

Yes, the letter could contain something relatively simple. It could, for example, be merely the diagram of a machine for us to use to establish communication with the Senders. It would be, then, the "blueprint of a transmitter," with the "components" the stuff of Frog Eggs. And we, like a small child puzzling over the plan of a radio kit, could manage to assemble nothing more than a couple of the most primitive screws. Or the letter could be an "incarnated" psychocosmological theory, showing how intelligent life in the Metagalaxy came to be, how it was distributed, and how it functioned. When one cast off one's "Manichean" prejudices, those *sotto voce* suggestions that the Sender had to wish us either good or evil (or good and evil at the same time, if, say, by his criteria his intentions toward us were "good," but by ours "evil"), the guessing spawned ideas more freely, ideas similar to the above, and became a morass no less immobilizing than the professional inertia that had caught the empiricists of the Project in the golden cages of their sensational discoveries. They believed—some of them, at any rate—that by studying Lord of the Flies one eventually could get to the bottom of the mystery of the Senders—like untangling a thread. I felt that this was a rationalization after the fact: since they had nothing except Lord of the Flies, they clung to it in their investigation. I would have allowed that they were right if the problem had belonged to the natural sciences—but it did not. From a chemical analysis of the ink with which a letter is written to us, we will never deduce the intellectual attributes of the writer.

Perhaps it was necessary to put a rein on ambitions and approach the intention of the Senders by gradual approximations. But here again came the burning question: Why had they combined, in one thing, a message meant for intelligent receivers *and* a biophilic effect?

It seemed strange—eerie, even. In the first place, general considerations indicated that the civilization of the Senders had to be incredibly old. The emission of the signal—by our best estimate—required a consumption of power on the order of at least a sun. An expenditure like that could not be a matter of indifference even to a society wielding a highly developed astroengineering technology. The Senders therefore must have acted in the conviction that such an "investment" paid—though not for them—paid in the sense of having real effectiveness in causing life. But at present there were relatively few planets in the entire Metagalaxy on which prevailed conditions that corresponded to Earth's of four billion years ago. Very few, actually. The Metagalaxy was a stellar-nebular organism well past its prime; in another billion years or so it would begin its decline toward old age. The youthful period of exuberant and violent planetary formation, from which had emerged, among others, our own Earth, was over. The Senders must have known this. It was not a matter of thousands of years, then, or even millions, that they had been sending the signal. I feared—how else to name the feeling that accompanied such a thought?—that they had been doing so for *billions* of years! But if such was the case, then—leaving aside the problem of our total inability to imagine what form a society would assume after the passage of such awesome geologic time—the reason for the "two-sidedness" of the signal turned out to be rather simple, if not trivial. They could have been sending, from the earliest times, the "life-causing factor"—and then, when they decided to take up interplanetary communication, instead of building special transmitters and technologies for that purpose, found it was sufficient to make use of the emission stream already pulsing through the Universe. All that was needed was the right modulation added to that carrier wave. Was it, then, for simple, engineering economy that they saddled us with this riddle? But surely the problems presented by the modulation program must have been technically and informationally monstrous—yes, for us they were, but for them? Here, once more, I lost the ground beneath my feet. Meanwhile the research went on: attempts were made, in endless ways, to separate the "informational component" of the signal from the "biophilic." None of them worked. We were baffled, but still unwilling to admit defeat.

BY THE END of August, I was mentally drained, more drained, I think, than I had ever been. The creative potential, the capacity to solve problems, changes in a man in ebbs and flows, and over this he has little control. I had learned to apply a kind of test. I would read my own articles, those I considered the best. If I noticed in them lapses, gaps, if I saw that the thing could have been done better, my experiment was successful. If, however, I found myself reading with admiration, that meant I was in trouble. Which is exactly what happened at the end of the summer. What I needed—and I knew this also from years of experience—was distraction, not a rest.

I began dropping in more often on Dr. Rappaport, my neighbor, and we talked sometimes for hours. About the stellar code itself we spoke rarely and said little. One day I found him amid large packages from which spilled attractive, glossy paperbacks with mythical covers. He had tried to use, as a "generator of ideas"— for we were running out of them—those works of fantastic literature, that popular genre (especially in the States), called, by a persistent misconception, "science fiction." He had not read such books before; he was annoyed—indignant, even—expecting variety, finding monotony. "They have everything *except* fantasy," he said. Indeed, a mistake. The authors of these pseudo-scientific fairy tales supply the public with what it wants: truisms, clichés, stereotypes, all sufficiently costumed and made "wonderful" so that the reader may sink into a safe state of surprise and at the same time not be jostled out of his philosophy of life. If there is progress in a culture, the progress is above all conceptual, but literature, the science-fiction variety in particular, has nothing to do with that.

My conversations with Dr. Rappaport were of value to me. Characteristic of him was a predatory and unceremonious manner of formulation, which I would have liked to make my own. The topics of our discussions were schoolboyish: we held forth on Man. Rappaport was a bit of a "thermodynamic psychoanalyst"; he declared, for instance, that really all the basic drives providing the motive force for human action could be derived directly from physics—but physics in the broadest sense of the word.

The urge to destruction is deducible from thermodynamics. Life is a fraud, an attempt at embezzlement, seeking to circumvent laws otherwise inevitable and implacable; insulated from the rest of the world, it immediately enters the path of decay, and that inclined plane leads to the normal state of matter, to the permanent equilibrium that is death. In order to continue living, life must feed on order, but because there is no order—none highly organized—other than life, it is condemned to consume itself. It must destroy to live, must take its nourishment from systems that are nourishment only to the extent that they can be ruined. Not ethics but physics determines this law.

Schrödinger was probably the first to observe this; but he, enamored of his Greeks, failed to consider what could be called, to quote Rappaport, the shame of life, the immanent stain rooted in the very structure of existence. I took issue, citing the photosynthesis of plants: they did not destroy, or at least did not need to destroy, other living organisms, thanks to their utilization of solar quanta. Rappaport replied that the entire Animal Kingdom parasitized the Plant Kingdom.

The second quality of man, and one he shared with nearly all organisms, sexuality, could also be derived—Rappaport went on —from statistical thermodynamics, in its informational aspect. Entropy, which lurked behind every ordered system, always caused information, whenever transmitted, to undergo loss. To counteract this fatal noise, to perpetuate this temporarily secured order, it was necessary to compare oneself constantly with a "hereditary text." Such collating, or "proofreading," whose purpose was to remove "errors," became the reason and justification for the rise of bisexuality. And therefore sex had its origins in the informational physics of transmission, in communication theory. The collation of the genetic material in each and every generation was imperative, a *sine qua non*, if life was to maintain itself; all the rest—the biological, algedonic, psychological, cultural—was the derivative, the forest of consequences that grew from that single hard kernel formed by the laws of physics.

I pointed out to him that by that argument he was universalizing bisexuality, making it a constant in the Cosmos. He only smiled; he never answered directly. In another age, another era, he would have been, I am certain, a stern mystic, a builder of systems; in our era made sober by an overabundance of discoveries, which tore apart like shrapnel every systemic coherence, an era which both accelerated progress as never before and was sick to death of progress, he was only a commentator and an analyst.

He told me once, I remember, that he had considered the possibility of creating something in the nature of a metatheory of philosophical systems, or for that matter a general program that would facilitate the automation of such a creation: an appropriately set machine would produce, first, the systems already in existence, and then, in the gaps left by oversight or insufficient rigor on the part of the great ontologists, it would create new ones—with the ease of a machine producing screws or slippers. And he even began work on this—put together a dictionary, a syntax, set up rules of transposition, categories, hierarchies, a sort of metatheory of types semantically extended—but then he saw that the task was an empty game not worth the effort, for nothing resulted from it but the possibility of generating those networks, checkerboards, edifices—those crystal palaces, if you like—built of words. He was a misanthrope, and I was not surprised to see by his bed—as by mine was the Bible—a book of Schopenhauer. The notion of substituting the concept of Will for the concept of matter seemed amusing to him.

"You might just as well call Will the mystery," he said, "and quantize, beam, diffract with crystals, and dilute and concentrate that. And if one should find that Will can be totally separated out from the interior of sentient beings, and in addition have attributed to it some kind of 'self-motion'—that predilection for eternal bustling about which is so exasperating in atoms, since it makes for nothing but problems, and I do not mean only mathematical—what, then, would keep us from agreeing with Schopenhauer?" He claimed that the time for a renaissance of the Schopenhauerian vision was coming. However, he was far from being an apologist for that small, rabid German.

"His aesthetic is inconsistent. But, then, perhaps he was unable to express this; the *genius temporis*, perhaps, did not allow it. In the 1950s I once had occasion to witness an atomic test. Did you know, Mr. Hogarth"—that was what he always called me—"that there is nothing more beautiful than the colors of a mushroom cloud? No description, no color photograph can do justice to that wonder, which lasts ten, twenty seconds. The dirt rises, pulled up by the suction when the fireball expands. Then the sphere of flame, like a runaway balloon, disappears in the clouds, and the whole world, for a moment, is a sculpture in pink—Eos Pterodaktylos . . . The nineteenth century firmly believed that what was murderous must be hideous. Today we know that it may be more beautiful than cherry orchards. Afterward, all flowers seem faded, dull—and this happens in a place where radiation kills in a fraction of a second!"

I listened, ensconced in an armchair, and now and then, I confess, I lost the thread of what he was saying. My brain, like an old horse pulling a milk truck, stubbornly returned to the same route, the code; I had to force myself not to go back to that ground, because it seemed to me that if I left it fallow, something might germinate there by itself. Such things happen sometimes.

I also had talks with Tihamer Dill—that is, with Dill Junior, the physicist. I knew his father, but that is a story in itself. Dill Senior taught mathematics at Berkeley. He was, in those days, a fairly well known mathematician of the older generation and had a reputation as an excellent teacher—even-tempered, patient, though demanding. Why I did not find favor in his eyes, I do not know. It is true that we differed in our style of thinking; I was fascinated by ergodic processes, a field that Dill made light of. Still, I always had the feeling that the problem had to do with more than mathematics. I went to him with my ideas—to whom else was I to go?—and he snuffed me out like a candle, brushing aside what I wished to present, distinguishing in the meantime my colleague Myers. He hovered over Myers as over a new rosebud.

Myers followed in his footsteps, and I have to admit that he was not bad at combinatorial analysis—a branch, however, that even then I considered to be dried up. The student developed the idea of the mentor, so the mentor placed his faith in the student—and yet it was not that simple. Could it have been that Dill felt an instinctive, animal antipathy toward me? Was I too forward, too sure of myself and of my future? Obtuse I most certainly was; I understood nothing. On the other hand, I bore absolutely no grudge against him. Myers, it is true, I detested. I can still remember the silent delight I experienced when, many years later, I happened to run into him. He was working as a statistician in some automobile company—General Motors, I think.

But the fact that Dill had failed so completely in his choice of protégé was not enough for me. It was not that I wanted him vanquished; I wanted him converted to a belief in me. I do not think I ever finished any larger paper in all my younger work without imagining Dill's eyes on the manuscript. What effort it cost me to prove that the Dill variable combinatorics was only a rough approximation of an ergodic theorem! Not before or since, I daresay, did I polish a thing so carefully; and it is even possible that the whole concept of groups later called Hogarth groups came out of that quiet, constant passion with which I plowed Dill's axioms under. And then, as if wanting to do something in addition, though now there was nothing really left to do, I played the metamathematician—in order to survey that entire anachronistic idea from above, as it were, in a kind of Olympian footnote. More than one of those who had already predicted a soaring flight for me were surprised at this marginal interest of mine.

Of course I did not reveal to anyone the real motive, the hidden reason behind that work. What did I actually expect? Not, certainly, that Dill would come to appreciate my worth, would apologize about Myers, would admit how greatly he had been mistaken. The thought of that hawklike, hale, seemingly ageless old man going to Canossa was too absurd for me to entertain it even for a moment. So I had nothing specific in mind as a dream to come true: the thing was too embarrassing and petty for that. Sometimes a person who is valued, respected, even loved by all, cares most, in the innermost recess of his soul, about the opinion of someone who stands uninterested outside the circle of admirers, and who may be, in the eyes of the world, of no particular importance, a mediocrity.

What was Dill Senior, in the final analysis? A rank-and-file professor of mathematics. There were dozens like him in the States. But such rational arguments would not have helped me, especially since at that time I had not acknowledged even to myself the meaning and aim of the idiosyncrasies in my ambition. And yet, when I received from the publisher the fresh, stiff copies of my articles, bright as if bathed in new glory, I would have lucid moments; before me would appear Dill, dry, thin as a beanpole, inflexible, his face like a portrait of Hegel—and I hated Hegel, I could not read him, because he was so sure of himself, as if the Absolute Itself spoke through his lips for the greater glory of the Prussian state. Hegel, I realize now, had nothing to do with it; I had put him in the place of another person.

A few times I saw Dill at conferences, from a distance; I steered clear, pretending not to recognize him. Once he himself began talking to me, politely, vaguely, but I excused myself, said that I was just leaving. There was really nothing I wanted from him now; it was as if he were necessary to me only in the world of the imagination. The publication of my major opus was followed by a shower of praise, by a first biography; I felt close to an unexpressed goal, and that was when our paths crossed. Rumors of his illness had reached me, yes, but I had not thought that it could alter the man so much. I saw him in a supermarket. He was pushing a cart filled with cans, directly in front of me. I followed. There was a crowd all around us. In a quick, furtive glance I noticed his pouchlike, swollen cheeks, and with the diagnosis came a feeling akin to despair. Here was a shrunken, pot-bellied old man with dull eyes and a slack jaw, dragging his feet in large galoshes. Snow melting on his collar. He pushed his cart, was pushed by the crowd, and I hurriedly stepped back and away, as though in fear; I wanted only to leave as quickly as possible—to flee. In an instant I had lost an enemy, who probably had no idea, ever, that he was an enemy. For some time afterward, I felt an emptiness, as if after the loss of someone very close. That kind of stimulating challenge, demanding the concentration of all one's mental power, was suddenly gone. Probably the Dill that followed me constantly and looked over my shoulder at the marked-up manuscripts never existed. When I read, years later, of his death, I felt nothing. But there long remained in me the wound of that vacated place.

I knew that he had a son, but I first met Dill Junior only in the Project. The mother, it seems, was Hungarian; hence that peculiar name, which brought to my mind Tamerlane. Though a junior, he was no longer young. He was one of those aging youths. There are people who are as if destined to be one age only. Baloyne, for example, is headed for a great patriarch; that appears to be his proper form, and he hastens to achieve it, knowing that not only will he not lose his vigor then, but in addition will wax Biblical and thus stand outside any suspicion of weakness. Then there are those who preserve the features of irresponsible adolescence. Dill Junior was that way. From his father he inherited an aspect of solemnity, a laboriousness of gesture: he certainly did not belong to the category of people who do not worry what their hands or face are doing at a given moment. He was what is called a "restless physicist," in somewhat the same way as I was a restless mathematician, because he repeatedly shifted from field to field. For a while he worked in Anderson's biophysics group. We struck up a friendship at Rappaport's place; this cost me a little effort, because I did not really like Dill, but I overcame my feelings for the sake of his father's memory. If this does not quite make sense to the reader, I can only say that it does not quite make sense to me, either, but that is the way it was.

Multispecialists, sometimes called by us "universalists," were greatly valued; Dill had been one of the creators of the Frog Eggs synthesis. But topics directly connected with the Project were, at Rappaport's evening colloquia, usually avoided. Before working with Anderson, Dill had been—under the auspices of UNESCO, I think—a member of a research team that was supposed to come up with proposals for counteracting the population explosion. He talked of this with satisfaction. There were a few biologists there, sociologists, and geneticists, besides the anthropologists. And, of course, celebrities in the form of Nobelists.

One of the last considered nuclear war to be the only salvation from a sea of bodies. His logic was flawless. Neither pills nor propaganda slowed the birthrate. Imperative was "management intervention" on the family level. The problem was not that every scheme sounded either gruesome or grotesque—as, for example, the proposition that a "child license" be granted only upon a citizen's accumulation of a certain number of points, points given for psycho-physical assets, for skills in rearing, and so on.

It was possible to devise various more or less rational programs, but it was not possible to put them into operation. In the end the thing always led to an infringement on those freedoms that no social order since the birth of civilization had dared to touch. Not one of the modern governments had sufficient power, or sufficient authority, for that. It would have meant doing battle with the mightiest of human drives, and with the majority of churches, and with the very foundation of the rights of man, hallowed by tradition. On the other hand, after an atomic cataclysm the strict state control of marriage and childbearing would be an immediate and vital necessity, for otherwise the genetic plasm damaged by the radiation would give rise to an endless number of monsters. This emergency control could then be replaced gradually by a legal system administering the propagation of the species, beneficially guiding its evolution and numerical force.

Nuclear war was, granted, a dreadful and heinous thing, but its long-term consequences could turn out to be salutary. It was in this spirit that one portion of the scientists spoke out; others objected, and no recommendation could be agreed upon between them.

This story upset Rappaport; and the more coolly Dill responded, with his faint smile, the more heated Rappaport became.

"Placing Reason on the throne as ruler," said Rappaport, "is equivalent to putting oneself in the hands of a logical madness. The joy of a father occasioned by the fact that his child resembles him has no rational basis, especially not if the father is an untalented, run-of-the-mill individual; ergo, we should establish sperm banks, whose donors will be the most useful to society, and will by artificial insemination breed children who are similar to such sires and therefore of value. The uncertainty connected with setting up a family can be seen, socially, as much wasted effort; ergo, we should pair up people according to selection criteria that provide for a positive correlation of the physical and psychological traits of the partners. Desires not satisfied give rise to frustrations, which disturb the smooth running of social processes; ergo, we should satisfy all desires, either naturally or by means of technological equivalents, or else, *enfin*, we should remove through chemistry or surgery the centers that produce those desires.

"Until twenty years ago, a trip from Europe to the States took seven hours; at a cost of eighteen billion dollars, that time was reduced to fifty minutes. It is known, now, that, given the expenditure of further billions, this flight time can be cut in half. A passenger, sterilized in body and mind (lest he bring into our great land either Asian flu or Asian ideas), pumped full of vitamins and videotapes, will be able to move from city to city, from continent to continent, and from planet to planet—with ever-increasing speed and security. And the vision of all this phenomenally efficient, solicitous machinery is supposed to take our breath away, so that we never get around to asking what exactly is gained by these lightning-fast peregrinations. Such speeds used to be too much for our old, animal body; travel from hemisphere to hemisphere, when too sudden, would disrupt its circadian rhythm. But, fortunately, a drug has been found to nullify that disruption. True, the drug sometimes causes depression, but there are other drugs to raise your spirits. They *do* cause heart disease. But, then, one can insert polyethylene tubes into the coronary arteries to prevent them from clogging.

"A scientist, in this sort of situation, behaves like a trained elephant made to face an obstacle. He uses the strength of his intellect the way the elephant uses its muscle—on command—which is most convenient, because the scientist can agree to anything if he is responsible for nothing. Science is turning into a monastery for the Order of Capitulant Friars. Logical calculus is supposed to supersede man as a moralist. We submit to the blackmail of the 'superior knowledge' that has the temerity to assert that nuclear war can be, by derivation, a good thing, because this follows from simple arithmetic. Today's evil turns out to be tomorrow's good; ergo, the evil is also, to some extent, good. Our reason no longer heeds the intuitive promptings of emotion; the ideal is the harmony of a perfectly constructed mechanism, an ideal that civilization as a whole, and its every member taken separately, must meet.

"Thus the means of civilization replace its ends, and human conveniences substitute for human values. The rule whereby corks in bottles give way to metal caps, and metal caps to little plastic lids that snap on and off, is innocent enough; it is a series of improvements to make it easier for us to open containers of liquid. But the same rule, when applied to the perfecting of the human brain, becomes sheer madness; every conflict, every difficult problem is compared to a stubborn cork that one should discard and replace with an appropriate labor-saving device. Baloyne named the Project 'His Master's Voice,' because the motto is ambiguous: to which master are we to listen, the one from the stars or the one in Washington? The truth is, this is Operation Squeeze—the squeeze being not on our poor brains but on the cosmic message, and God help the powerful and their servants if it succeeds."

With such evening conversations we amused ourselves during the second year of labor at HMV, in a growing atmosphere of foreboding, which was to be borne out shortly by a thing that gave Operation Squeeze a sense that was no longer ironic, but menacing.

10

ALTHOUGH FROG EGGS and Lord of the Flies were the
same substance, only preserved in different ways by the biophysicists and biologists, in each territory it was *de rigueur* to use the
local name exclusively. This, I thought, illustrated a certain small
but characteristic feature of the history of science, because neither
the fortuitous bends in the road of research nor the accidental
circumstances assisting at the birth of a discovery ever completely
detach themselves from its final form. Indeed, it is not easy to
recognize these relics, for the reason that, fossilized, they become
embedded in the heart of all later theories and formulations, like a
print of a coincidence which turns to stone, to an iron rule of
thought.

Before I could see Frog Eggs for the first time at Romney's lab,
I was given the now standard initiation required for all arrivals
from the outside world. First I listened to the brief, taped lecture
for VIPs, which I quoted earlier; then a two-minute ride on the subway took me to the chemical-synthesis building, where I was
shown a thing towering in a separate hall beneath a three-story
glass dome, resembling the skeleton of a dragonfly larva blown up
to the size of a brontosaurus; it was a three-dimensional model of
one molecule of Frog Eggs. The individual atomic groups were
represented by grapelike spheres of black, purple, violet, and
white, connected by clear polyethylene tubes. Marsh, a stereo-

116

chemist, pointed out to me the ammonia radicals, the alkyl groups, and, looking like strange flowers, the "molecular dishes" that absorbed the energy from nuclear reactions. These reactions were demonstrated by a machine that lit up, in turn, the fluorescent tubes and bulbs hidden inside the model, which gave the effect of a cross between a futuristic billboard and a Christmas tree. Because it was expected of me, I showed admiration, and then continued on.

The actual processes of the synthesis took place in the lower levels of the building, under the supervision of programming computers, in cylinders insulated with heavy shielding, because at certain stages fairly penetrating radiation was given off, though the radiation would subside when the synthesis reached its conclusion. The main synthesis hall occupied an area of four thousand square meters. From there the path led to the so-called silver vault, where —as in a treasury—lay the substance dictated by the stars. There was a round, windowless chamber there, with silver walls polished like mirrors; I once knew why this was necessary, but have forgotten. Bathed in the cold light of fluorescent tubes, atop a massive pedestal, stood a glass tank, like a large aquarium, empty—except that on the bottom of it rested a layer of a highly opalescent, motionless, bluish fluid.

A sheet of glass divided the room in half, with an opening opposite the tank. Mounted at the opening and heavily fortified was a robot manipulator. Marsh first lowered the beak of an instrument resembling surgical forceps to the surface of the liquid; when he lifted it, from the end hung a sparkling thread that did not at all resemble a sticky fluid. It looked as if the viscous substance had discharged from itself an elastic but sufficiently hard fiber that oscillated lazily like a string. When he lowered the manipulator again and shook it deftly so that the fiber fell off, the surface of the liquid, shining with reflected light, did not accept it. The fiber contracted, thickened, turned into a kind of gleaming larva, and began inching its way along like a caterpillar; when it touched the glass, it stopped and turned. This lasted about a minute. Then the curious creature blurred, its outlines dissolved, and it was sucked back into the parent.

This "caterpillar trick" was of little significance. When all the lights were turned off and the experiment was repeated in the dark, I observed, at a certain moment, a very weak but clear flash, as if between the bottom of the tank and the top there blazed, for a fraction of a second, a small star. Marsh told me later that this was not luminescence. When the thread was broken off, in that place a monomolecular layer resulted, which was no longer able to keep the nuclear processes under control, and one had then a sort of microscopic chain reaction—but the flash was a secondary effect, because the activated electrons, knocked into higher energy levels and leaving them instantaneously, gave off an equivalent amount of photons. I asked if they saw any chance of practical application of Frog Eggs. They had fewer expectations now than right after the synthesis, because Frog Eggs behaved like a living thing in the respect that, just as living matter utilized the energy of chemical reactions exclusively for itself, so did Frog Eggs not allow any expropriation of its nuclear energy.

On Grotius's team, which had manufactured Lord of the Flies, the protocol was quite different. There, one took extraordinary precautions to go down to the lower laboratory. I honestly do not know whether Lord of the Flies was placed two floors underground because of its name, or whether it had been so christened because it originated in subterranean quarters that brought to mind a kind of Hades.

First, one put on protective clothing: a large transparent suit complete with a hood and strap-on oxygen container. This involved a little trouble, which, for all its realism, had an element of ritual. As far as I know, no one has yet studied the behavior of scientists in the laboratory from the anthropological point of view, although there is no doubt in my mind that not everything they do is necessary. The same preparations and experimental activities can be carried out in many different ways, but once a certain procedure is established it becomes, in a given circle, in a given school, a custom with the force of a rule—of a dogma, practically.

I visited Lord of the Flies escorted by two people; the leader was little Grotius. We set out only after oxygen, with the turn of knobs, was let into our transparent outfits, so that each of us resembled a gleaming balloon with its own personal pit inside. Also before departure, the suits were checked for seal—very simply, by running the flame of a candle over particular spots where the pressure was a bit higher. The operation brought to mind some act of sorcery, with the burning of incense.

118

All this, taken together, formed a stern, solemn whole, a scene as if in ceremonial slow motion, caused no doubt by the fact that one could not move quickly in that shining balloon of polyethylene. Moreover, it was not particularly easy to converse, enfolded in such an envelope, and so communication by pantomime added to the growing impression that I was taking part in a religious service. One could of course argue that the suit offered protection against beta rays, that, while it may indeed have impeded movement, at the same time—being transparent—it allowed one to see well, etc., but I believe that I could have thought up, without much difficulty, another procedure, one less picturesque, perhaps, but at least free of subtle allusions to the symbolic sense of the name of Lord of the Flies.

In a special room with a concrete floor, a kind of stonework casing surrounded a vertical well. One by one we descended into it, down an iron ladder embedded in the stone, our suits rustling unpleasantly. Unpleasant also was the heat that built up inside those oversize fish bladders. At the bottom was a narrow tunnel, a little like a passageway in an old mine, illuminated at regular intervals by lamps with grates. But Grotius's people, I must admit, did not supply these trappings; the research team had simply made use of the underground part of the building, which at one time was to have served a more military purpose, connected with the thermonuclear explosions of the testing ground. After sixty or seventy yards the walls began to gleam; they were covered by a silver sheet metal, mirrorlike—the only detail the same as in the "silver vault" of the biophysicists. But this was not noticed, just as one does not notice the erotic aspect of nudity in a doctor's office: our perception is governed by the totality of the resultant effect and not the nature of its individual elements. The silver of the walls of the biophysicists evoked the sterility of a kind of sanctum of surgery, but in the underground corridor it took on a more mysterious character. As in some carnival funhouse, the reflections of our bladdered forms were multiplied and altered.

In vain I looked around; the corridor ended in a wide but blind recess. To one side, at the height of my head, I saw a tiny iron door, which Grotius opened, revealing a sort of embrasure or loophole in the thick wall; both my companions stepped aside, so that I might have an unobstructed view. The aperture was covered, on the other side, by a reddish slab, something in the shape of a slice of meat, pressed tight against the thick glass. Through the hood that went over my face, through the even blowing of the oxygen from the bottle, I felt, on the skin of my forehead and cheeks, a pressure that seemed to come not only from the heat. As I watched longer, I noticed a movement, extremely slow and not completely even, as if of the foot—skinned and glued to the glass —of a giant snail trying to crawl by futile contractions. The mass behind the glass seemed to push against it with unknown force— crawling slowly, but incessantly, in place.

Grotius politely but firmly moved me away from the opening, shut the small armored door, and took from the bag slung over his shoulder a flask, inside which were several common houseflies clinging to the sides. When he brought the flask near the closed hatch—and he did this in a measured, grave way—the flies at first froze, then opened their little wings, and in the next moment were whirling in the flask like black bullets gone mad. It seemed to me that I could hear their furious buzzing. Grotius moved the container a little closer to the hatch, and the flies beat with even greater violence. Then he returned the flask to his satchel, turned, and headed back to the kitchen.

Finally I learned the origin of the name. Lord of the Flies was Frog Eggs—but in a quantity exceeding two hundred liters. This transformation, however, took place by degrees. As for the truly remarkable effect with the flies, no one had the foggiest notion of its mechanism, particularly since, apart from the flies, very few hymenoptera displayed it, and spiders, beetles, and a multitude of other bugs carried patiently by the biologists down to this cavern showed no reaction whatever to the presence of the substance heated by the processes within it. There was talk of waves, of radiation—at least not, thank God, of telepathy. In flies whose abdominal ganglia were pharmacologically paralyzed the effect did not take place. But this finding was, after all, trivial. The poor flies were narcotized; every possible thing was removed from them in turn—now their legs were immobilized, now their wings—but all that was learned, in the end, was that a heavy layer of a dielectric effectively shielded the effect. This was, then, a physical, not a "supernatural" phenomenon. Well, of course. But what caused it remained unknown. I was assured that the thing would be explained—a special group of bionicists and physicists were working on it. If they discovered anything, I have yet to hear of it.

But Lord of the Flies presented no danger to the living organisms found in its vicinity. Even the flies, in the end, were not harmed.

11

WITH THE ARRIVAL of autumn—on the calendar only, because
the sun stood as high above the desert as it had in August
—I renewed my efforts, though I cannot say that it was with
renewed vigor, on the code. What was considered, in the Project,
the greatest success—and which definitely was that, from the technological point of view—the synthesis, that is, of Frog Eggs—I
not only neglected in my theorizing, but actually ignored, as if of the
opinion that that singular product was illegitimate. Those who had
created it accused me of having an irrational prejudice, a personal
aversion toward the substance, ridiculous as that sounded. They
also suggested—Dill, for one—that the somewhat theatrical pomp
and circumstance with which the people of both research teams
treated the "nuclear mucilage" had caused in me a coldness
toward Lord of the Flies itself; or that I resented the fact that
the empiricists had added to one mystery, that of the code itself,
a second, the mystery of a material whose purpose was unknown.

I did not agree. The Romney Effect, too, had increased our
ignorance, but in it I saw—at least then—a chance of getting
at the attitude of the Senders, and thereby at the very content of
the message. In the hope of enriching my imagination, I studied a
multitude of papers on the history of reading the genetic code of

122

man and the animals. At times it seemed to me, obscurely, that a parallel of the phenomenon confronting me was the "doubleness" of every organism, in the sense that an organism is both itself and the medium of information addressed, causally, to the future, since to its descendants.

But what could one do with such an analogy? The arsenal of conceptual ways and means that the era had to offer seemed to me appallingly bare. Our knowledge has grown to gigantic proportions only as far as man, not the world, is concerned. Between the cumulative, explosive, spearheading expansion of instrumental technologies and the biology of man there arises, before our eyes, an inexorably increasing gap; it divides humanity into a front line of foragers of information, with rear guards and reserves, and the abundant masses blessed with equilibrium because their heads are stuffed with informational pap, no less prefabricated than the variety made for the digestive tract. Now is beginning a great anthill proliferation, because the threshold has been crossed—exactly when, no one knows—beyond which the store of accumulated knowledge can no longer be encompassed by any single mind.

Not so much to amass still more knowledge as first to invalidate its vast deposits in those areas where less important and therefore superfluous information lies—that seems to me to be the first duty of contemporary science. The technologies of information have created, supposedly, a paradise in which anyone who desires to can know everything; but this is a complete fiction. Selection, tantamount to resignation, is as unavoidable as breathing.

If humanity were not being constantly goaded, provoked, and kindled by the local mutual gnawings of nationalisms, by collisions of interests (often more apparent than real), by surfeits concentrated at certain points on the globe alongside concentrations of want (yet surely by now we have the capability, in principle at least, among all our technological arts, of resolving such contradictions)—humanity, perhaps, might finally realize the extent to which these small, bloody fireworks, operated at a distance by the nuclear capital of the Superpowers, blind it to what meanwhile is taking place "by itself," what runs loose and is under no control. Politics views the globe exactly as it did in the preceding centuries (but now translunar space is included)—as a chessboard for contests. But all along, that board has been surreptitiously changing; it is no more a stationary ground, a foundation, but a raft, afloat and splintering under the blows of unseen currents that are carrying it in a direction *in which no one has been looking.*

Forgive me this flight of metaphor. But, yes, futurologists have been multiplying like flies since the day Hermann Kahn made Cassandra's profession "scientific," yet somehow not one of them has come out with the clear statement that we have wholly abandoned ourselves to the mercy of technological progress. The roles are now reversed: humanity becomes, for technology, a means, an instrument for achieving a goal unknown and unknowable. The search for the ultimate weapon has turned scientists into seekers of a philosophers' stone that differs from the alchemists' dream in one respect only, that it definitely exists. The reader of futurological papers has before him graphs and tables printed on glossy paper and informing him as to when hydrogen-helium reactors will appear and when the telepathic property of the mind will be harnessed for commercial use. Such future discoveries are foreseen with the aid of mass pollings of the appropriate specialists—a dangerous precedent, in that it creates the fiction of knowledge where formerly it was generally conceded that there was complete —but complete—ignorance.

One has only to look through the history of science to reach the most probable conclusion: that the shape of things to come is determined by things we do not know today, and by what is unforeseeable. The situation has been complicated in a new way by a "mirror *pas de deux,*" since one side of the world has been obliged to copy, as accurately and as rapidly as possible, everything that has been done by the other in the field of armaments. And often it is impossible to tell who takes a certain step first, and who merely imitates it faithfully. The imagination of humanity has become, in a sense, frozen in place, transfixed by the vision of atomic annihilation—which, however, has been sufficiently evident to both sides for them to abort its materialization. The fascination with scenarios of the thermonuclear apocalypse, written by strategists and scientific advisory councils, has paralyzed minds to such an extent that no attention is paid to other—and who knows if ultimately not more dangerous—possibilities hidden in progress.

Because the state of equilibrium is continually being undermined by new discoveries and inventions.

In the seventies, for a while, the ruling doctrine was the "indirect economic attrition" of all potential enemies; Secretary of Defense Kayser expressed this with the maxim "The thin starve before the fat lose weight." The competition-duel in nuclear payloads gave way to a missile race, and that in turn led to the building of more and more expensive "antimissile missiles." The next step in the escalation was the possibility of constructing "laser shields," a stockade of gamma lasers which would line the perimeter of the country with destroyer rays; the cost of installing such a system was set at four hundred to five hundred billion dollars. After this move in the game, one could next expect the putting into orbit of giant satellites equipped with gamma lasers, whose swarm, passing over the territory of the enemy, could consume it utterly with ultraviolet radiation in a fraction of a second. The cost of that belt of death would exceed, it was estimated, seven trillion dollars. This war of economic attrition—through the production of increasingly expensive weaponry that thereby placed a severe strain on the whole organism of government—although seriously planned, could not be carried out, because the building of super- and hyperlasers turned out to be insurmountably difficult for the current technology. This time merciful Nature, her own inherent mechanisms, saved us from ourselves; but this was, after all, only a fortunate accident.

Such was the global thinking of the politicians and the strategy of science dictated by it. Meanwhile, the entire historical tradition of civilization had begun to come apart on us, like the cargo of a ship rocked too violently. The great historico-philosophical concepts impaired at their foundations, the great syntheses based upon values inherited from the past, were turning into brontosaurs doomed to extinction; they would be shattered on the unknown shore of the next discoveries to come into view. There was now no longer any power, or any monstrousness, hidden in the bowels of the material world that would not be dragged out onto the scene as a weapon the moment it showed itself. So in reality we were playing not with Russia, but with Nature herself, because it was Nature and not the Russians that determined what discovery would next be bestowed upon us; and it would have been madness indeed to think that we were the apple of Nature's eye and that she would provide us only with those things which would promote the survival of the species. Any chance of the appearance, on the scientific horizon, of a discovery that would guarantee our total supremacy on the planetary scale would spur efforts and investments, because whoever reached that goal first would become the undisputed leader of the globe. People commonly spoke of this. But how could one believe that the weakened opponent would submit passively to the yoke imposed on him? No, this entire doctrine was self-contradictory, amounting to, at one and the same time, the destruction of the existing balance of forces—and its constant renewal.

We found ourselves, as a civilization, in a technological trap, where our fate was now to be decided entirely by the arrangement of certain relationships, not yet known to us, between levels of energy and matter. When I said such things, I was usually called a defeatist, especially among the scientists who were renting their consciences out to the State Department. Humanity, in a mutual clutching at hair and throats, as long as it went from camels and mules to chariots, carts, coaches, and to airplanes, steam engines, tanks, could still count on surviving—by breaking the fetters of this race. In the middle of the century a total fear paralyzed politics, but did not change it; the strategy remained the same. Days were put before months, years over centuries, but the reverse should have been done; the idea of seeing to the welfare of the species should have been written on the standards; the technological ascent should have been bridled, to keep it from becoming a fall.

In the meantime, the material gap widened between the Superpowers and the Third World—a gap called by the economists an "expanding harmony." Responsible personages, holding in their hands the fates of others, said that they realized that such a state could not go on indefinitely; but they did nothing, as if waiting for a miracle. It was necessary to coordinate progress but not to trust in it as in a machine, an accelerating automatic process. Surely it was madness, this faith that to do everything that was technologically possible was to act wisely and safely; surely we could not rely on a miraculous helping hand from Nature, more and more portions of which, turned into fuel for bodies and machines, we had incorporated in our civilization. And yet this incorporation may turn out to be a Trojan horse, a sugar-coated poison that poisons not because the world wishes us ill, but because we have proceeded blindly.

I could not ignore this background in my work. I had to keep it in mind as I pondered the two-sidedness of the message. The diplomats in their stiff tuxedos awaited, with a pleasant trembling in the knees, the Moment when at last we would be done with our unofficial, less important, preliminary labor, and when they, all in medals and stars, could fly off to the stars to proffer their letters of authorization and to exchange notes of protocol with a billion-year-old civilization. We were only to build the bridge for them. They would cut its ribbon.

But what really was the situation? In some corner of the Galaxy there appeared beings who, realizing the phenomenal rarity of life, decided to intervene in the Cosmogony—and correct it. The heirs of that ancient civilization possessed a Moloch of knowledge, beyond our conception, if they were able so precisely to combine a life-causing impulse with the utmost noninterference in every local path of evolution. The causal signal was not a Word turned to Flesh, because it gave absolutely no designation for what was to arise. The operation was, in its principle, very simple, but repeated over a time that was like an eternity; it represented two permanent riverbanks widely separated, between which the process of speciation was to proceed under its own power. The support was given with the greatest caution possible. No specifications, no concrete directives, no instructions of a physical or chemical nature—nothing other than the reinforcement of thermodynamically improbable states.

The probability intensifier was inexpressibly weak and worked only by virtue of the fact that, omnipresent, it penetrated every obstacle throughout an undetermined portion of the Galaxy. (Or perhaps the whole Galaxy? We did not know how many others of these invisible beams they were sending out.) This was not a single act but a presence whose permanence rivaled the stars themselves; yet, at the same time, it ceased the instant the desired process got under way. It ceased because the radiation's influence on formed organisms was virtually nil.

The duration of the emission frightened me. Yes, and it was possible, too, that the Senders were no longer among the living; that the process set in motion by their astroengineers within a star or group of stars would continue to run as long as the energy of the solar transmitters held out. The sneaking secrecy of our research seemed to me—by comparison—criminal. What mattered was not a discovery, not a mountain of discoveries, but the opening of our eyes to the world. So far we had been blind puppies. In the darkness of the Galaxy shined an intelligence, an intelligence that did not attempt to impose its presence on us; on the contrary, it concealed itself with great care.

The hypotheses popular before the existence of the Project seemed to me incredibly shallow; they ricocheted back and forth between the pole of pessimism, which called the *silentium universi* a natural state, and the pole of the mindless optimism that expected announcements clearly and slowly spelled out, as if civilizations scattered among the stars would communicate with one another like children in kindergarten. Yet another myth has bitten the dust, I thought, and yet another truth has ascended overhead—and, as is usually the case with truths, it is too much for us.

There remained the second, semantic, side of the signal. A child may understand separate sentences taken from a work of philosophy, but the whole he will not grasp. Our situation was similar. A child may be enchanted by the content of a sentence here, a sentence there—and we, too, marveled at small fragments that had been deciphered. Having pored long over the stellar text, communing with it through repeated efforts, renewed attempts, I grew at home with it in a curious way, and more than once I saw—although this was purely intuitive, with the feeling that the thing towered above me like a mountain—I saw, always obscurely, the magnificence of its structure. Thus I had exchanged, as it were, a mathematical perception for an aesthetic sense; but perhaps what took place was a merging of the two.

Every sentence in a book means something, even when pulled out of context; but within that context it mingles with the meanings of other sentences, of those that precede it and of those that follow. From such permeation, accretion, and focal fusion emerges finally the idea, frozen in time, that is the work. In the stellar code what mattered was not so much the meaning of the elements, of the "pseudo sentences," as their *purpose*, which I was unable to divine. But the code possessed an internal harmony, a purely mathematical harmony, the sort that is revealed in a great cathedral even to one who does not understand the cathedral's purpose, or know the laws of statics and the canons of architecture, and is ignorant even of the styles embodied, harnessed in the stone. I was that ignorant, open-mouthed spectator. The text was unusual in that it had no "purely local" properties. A keystone without an arch and a weight above is not a keystone; here is nonlocalness in architecture. The synthesis of Frog Eggs was preceded by the tearing, from the code, of its elements, which were then assigned atomic and stereochemical "meanings."

There was a sort of vandalism in this, as if on the basis of *Moby Dick* one were to begin slaughtering whales and rendering their blubber. It is possible to do this; the slaughtering is described in *Moby Dick*, although in a completely reversed, diametric way. But one can disregard that, and cut into pieces and rearrange as one pleases. And so, for all the wisdom behind it, was the code *that* defenseless? I was soon to learn that the situation could be worse; my fears would receive new fuel. Therefore, I do not disown in retrospect the sentimentality of these remarks.

Certain portions of the code, as frequency analysis indicated, appeared to repeat themselves like words in sentences, but each different neighborhood produced minute discrepancies in the shape of the impulses, discrepancies that were not taken into account by our *binary* informational version. The impatient empiricists, who could (after all) point to the treasures locked in their "silver vaults," insisted that these had to be distortions caused by the journey of the neutrino streams through many parsecs of space, a phenomenon—negligible, at that, considering—of the signal's desynchronization, its smearing. I decided to check this. I requested that a new recording be made of the signal—or at least of a large piece of it—and I compared the new text, received from the astrophysicists, with the corresponding segments from the five successive and independent results of the past reception.

It was strange that no one yet had done this precisely. If, in examining someone's signature for authenticity, increasingly powerful magnifying glasses are used, eventually the enlarged lines that are the ink marks on the paper begin to disintegrate—into elements spread out along the separate fibers, thick as rope, of cellulose; and it is impossible to determine just where, in the spectrum of magnification, the influence of the person writing ceases, the shape given to the letters by his "character," and where begins the realm of the action of statistical movements, the slight tremors of the hand, of the pen, the unevenness in the flow of ink, factors over which the person writing has no control. Still, one can make a determination, by comparing a series of signatures—a series, and not merely two, because then what is a constant, a regularity, will stand out and be distinguished from what represents the effect of completely variable fluctuations.

I was able to show that the "smearing," the "desynchronization," the "diffusion" of the signal lay wholly in the imagination of my adversaries. The accuracy of the repetitions reached the very limit of the resolution of the recording instrument used by the astrophysicists—and, because it was ridiculous to assume that the text had been transmitted with a setting for an instrument of precisely that calibration, this meant that the accuracy was greater than our ability to test it. So we could not know the maximum performance of the transmitter.

This caused something of a commotion. From then on I was called "the prophet of the Lord" or "the crier in the wilderness." Thus I worked, toward the end of September, in increasing solitude. There were moments, particularly at night, when between my wordless meditating and the text a bond of kinship was established, as if I had already grasped, almost, its totality, and in a sudden breathlessness, as before a bodiless leap, I sensed the other shore, but my utmost efforts were always insufficient.

These states, I think now, were a delusion. Today, of course, it is easier for me to see that not only was I incapable, impotent, but that the task was beyond the strength of any man. Then as now, I felt that the problem was not the type that would yield to a team assault; some one man would have to open that lock, casting off established habits of thought, some one man or no one. The apprehension of one's own powerlessness is certainly a sorry thing, and perhaps egoistic, too. It appears that I am seeking excuses. But if anywhere one ought to abandon his *amour propre* and forget the devil in his heart which worships success, I should think it would be in this matter. The feeling of isolation was at that time keen. The oddest thing is that that defeat, unequivocal as it was, left in my memory a taste of nobility, and that those hours, those weeks, are, when I think of them today, precious to me. I never imagined that this sort of thing could happen to me.

12

IN THE PUBLISHED records and the books there is very little or no mention at all of what was my most "constructive" contribution to the Project, because it was decided, in order to avoid all kinds of trouble, to hush up my role in the "antigovernment conspiracy"—a conspiracy that, or so I read somewhere, could have become the "greatest crime," and it was no thanks to me that it did not. I proceed now to the account of my offense.

Through the early part of October, the heat did not let up—during the day, that is, for at night the temperature in the desert fell below freezing. I would stay inside all day, and in the evening, before it grew too chilly, I would go out for short walks, always careful to keep in sight the towers of the compound, because among the high dunes of the desert, as I was warned, one could easily get lost. This actually happened once to some technician, but he returned around midnight; the glow of the lights had shown him the way. I was new to the desert. It was not at all like what I had imagined from films or books. It was, at one and the same time, totally monotonous and remarkably varied. What attracted me the most was the sight of the moving dunes, those great slow-motion waves that with their sharp, splendid geometry gave shape to the perfect solutions realized by Nature in those places where the clinging force of the biosphere, sometimes impertinent, sometimes furiously stubborn, did not impinge upon the realm of the inanimate world.

Returning one evening from such a walk, I encountered—not by accident, as it turned out—Donald Prothero. A second-generation descendant of an old Cornish family, he was the most English of the Americans I knew.

Seated, at the Council, between the enormous Baloyne and the beanpole Dill, in front of a fidgeting Rappaport and our fashion plate, Eugene Albert Nye, he was a figure curious in that there was nothing curious about him. The personification of averageness: an ordinary face, slightly sallow, long in the English way, with pronounced eye sockets and a strong jaw, and a pipe permanently fixed in his mouth; a passionless voice, an unaffected placidity, an absence of any emphatic gesturing—only in this way, by negatives, can I present him. And yet a mind of the first order.

I confess that he made me uneasy, because I do not believe in human perfection, and people who have no quirks, tics, obsessions, the touch of some minor mania, or points on which they turn rabid—I suspect such people of systematic imposture (we judge others by ourselves) or of totally lacking character. Certainly, much depends on the side from which we get to know a man. If, as usually happened to me, I first became acquainted with someone through his work—which in my profession is extremely abstract—and therefore, as it were, from the most spiritual side, the impact of meeting that entirely physical organism, which I had pictured instinctively as a kind of Platonic emanation, was always a shock.

To observe how pure thought or lofty detachment sweats, blinks, digs in its ear, how it manages, with varying success, its own machinery, which, supporting the soul, so often gets in the soul's way—this has always been for me an iconoclastic treat, malicious through and through. I remember how once I was being driven by a famous philosopher who admitted to solipsism, and he got a flat tire. Interrupting his discourse on the phantasmagoria of illusion which is all existence, he set about—in the most ordinary way, even with grunts—jacking up the car and hauling out the spare. I looked on with childish delight, as if seeing Jesus Christ with a stuffed nose. Using the illusion of a wrench, he removed,

133

one by one, the nonexistent nuts, then looked with despair at his hands covered with grease; the grease had no more substance than a dream, according to his doctrine—but somehow that did not enter his head.

As a child I honestly believed that there existed a category of perfect men; scientists, first and foremost, belonged in it, and among them the holiest had to be the university professors. Reality compelled me to part with such idealistic convictions.

Although I had known Donald for twenty years, there still seemed no getting around it: he really was the sort of scientist that only the most anachronistically enthusiastic individuals tended to believe in. Baloyne, also a great intellect, but a sinner as well, once pleaded with Donald—I recall—to come down to our level, at least on occasion (even once would do), by revealing some ugly secret about himself; and if that was impossible, to do something despicable that would make him more human in our eyes. But Donald only smiled from behind his pipe!

That evening, as we walked along a little valley between two rows of dunes, in the red light of the setting sun, and I was observing the projection of our shadows on the sand, whose grains—as in the paintings of the Impressionists—seemed to give off a lilac glow, like microscopic gas flames, Prothero began to tell me of his work on the "cold" nuclear reactions in Frog Eggs. I listened, out of politeness, and was surprised when he said that our situation reminded him of the Manhattan Project.

"Even if a chain reaction can be released in Frog Eggs on a large scale," I remarked, "the power of a hydrogen bomb, all the same, is technologically uncontrollable, so nothing, I think, threatens us from that quarter."

He then put away his pipe—an important sign. He reached in his pocket for a roll of film and handed it to me, open; the swollen red disk of the sun served as our light source. I knew enough of microphysics to recognize a series of pictures of ion tracks in a bubble chamber. Unhurriedly, standing next to me, he showed me several curious places. In the very center of the chamber was a tiny, pinhead-sized lump of Frog Eggs, and the star of a scattered nucleus, the trajectories of its fragments radiating outward, could be seen nearby—a millimeter or so away from the droplet of slime.

I saw nothing peculiar in this—but explanations followed, and more photographs. Something impossible had taken place: even when the droplet was enclosed on all sides by a lead shell, the tiny stars of splitting atoms appeared in the chamber—outside that armor!

"The reaction is remote," Prothero concluded. "Energy disappears in one place, along with the smashed atom, which reappears in another place. Have you ever seen a magician put an egg in his pocket and produce it from his mouth? This is the same thing."

"Yes, but that is a trick!" I still did not, and did not want to, understand. "The atoms, in the course of their disintegration, jump through the shield?" I asked.

"No. They simply disappear in one place and reappear in another."

"But that violates the principle of conservation!"

"Not necessarily, because they do this very quickly—something flies in here, something flies out there, you see. The balance remains unchanged. And do you know what transports them in this miraculous fashion? A neutrino field. And one modulated, moreover, by the original emission—a kind of 'divine wind.' "

I knew that such an effect was impossible, but I trusted Donald. If anyone in our hemisphere knew nuclear reactions, he did. I asked about the range of the effect. Yes, already, even before I was aware of it, came evil thoughts.

"I do not know what the range *might* be. It is, in any case, not less than the diameter of the chamber I used—six centimeters. I did this also at Wilson—twenty-five centimeters."

"You can control the reaction? Determine the endpoints of these 'changes of location'?"

"With the greatest precision. The terminus is a function of the phase—of where the field reaches a maximum."

I tried to understand what sort of process this was. The nuclei decayed within Frog Eggs, but the tracks of the decay simultaneously burst into view outside it. Donald said that the phenomenon lay beyond the frontiers of our physics; from the standpoint of physics, it violated all the laws. Quantum effects on such a macroscopic scale are not permitted—not within the pale of our theories. Gradually he spoke more freely. He had hit upon it by accident, while trying with his partner, McHill—blindly, really —to repeat Romney's experiment, but in a physical variation. He subjected Frog Eggs to the radiation of the emission, not knowing whether this would yield any result. It did. This happened right before he had to leave for Washington. In his one-week absence McHill constructed, according to their joint plan, a larger apparatus, one that would allow them to extend and focus the reaction to a radius of several meters.

Several meters. I thought that I had not heard him right. Donald, with the face of a man who has been told that he has cancer but is controlling himself phenomenally, said that nothing in principle stood in the way of their building an apparatus that would permit the effect to be increased millions of times—in strength and in range.

I asked who knew of this. He had told no one, not even the Science Council. He explained his motives. He had complete confidence in Baloyne, but did not want to place him in a difficult position, because Yvor was, among us, the one directly responsible to the Administration for all the research. And, that being the case, Donald could not then tell anyone else on the Council. He could vouch for McHill. To what extent, I asked. He looked at me, then shrugged. He was too intelligent not to see that a game was beginning, with the stakes so high that no man now could be vouched for. Although it had grown fairly cold, I was covered with sweat as the conversation continued. Donald told me why he had gone to Washington. He had written a memorandum-petition having to do with the Project and, without informing anyone of this, submitted it to Rush, and afterward took off to hear the answer; Rush had summoned him. There Donald explained to the Administration how harmful the secrecy of our research was. He argued that even if we acquired knowledge that increased our military potential, this would only augment the global threat. The present state was based on a fluid equilibrium, and regardless of in whose favor the scales tipped, if that tipping was too violent it could make the opposing side resort to desperate measures. The balance was preserved by the fact that every step taken by one side was parried by the other. So proceeded the arms race, and the global maneuvering. Although

I was a little put out that Donald had not consulted even with me, I kept this to myself and asked him only what sort of answer he had received. But I could easily guess.

"I spoke with a general. He told me that they were perfectly aware of the truth of what I had written, but that we had to continue to act as before, because we did not know whether or not the other side was conducting the exact same research as we . . . so that our eventual discoveries would not be disturbing the balance, but, on the contrary, restoring it. I got myself into a nice mess!" he concluded.

I assured him, though I knew better, that they would simply file his petition away. But this did not put him at ease.

"I wrote it," he said, "when I had nothing up my sleeve, absolutely nothing. In the meantime, while the petition already lay on Rush's desk, I hit on this effect. I even thought of withdrawing the miserable document, but that really would have looked suspicious to them! Well, you can imagine now how they will be keeping an eye on me!"

He meant our friend Nye. And I did not doubt that Nye had received appropriate instructions. I asked Donald what he thought about discontinuing the experiment, and disassembling the apparatus or simply destroying it. I knew, alas, what his reply would be.

"One cannot unmake discoveries. And, then, there is McHill. He will follow my lead while he is in this with me and we are working together, but I cannot say what he would do if I were to take the course you mention. And even if I could be sure of him, all that would be gained is a certain delay. The biophysicists have already set up their research plan for the coming year. I saw a rough draft of it. They want to do something similar to what I did. They have chambers, they have good nucleonics people—like Pickering—they have an inverter; they want to analyze the effects of microdetonations in the monomolecular layers of Frog Eggs, in the second quarter of the year. The equipment is all automatic. They will take a few thousand photographs a day, and the effect will stand out like a sore thumb."

"Next quarter," I said.

"Next quarter," he repeated.

What was there to add? We returned in silence across the dunes;

barely any light was given by the rim of the red sun sinking below the horizon. I remember that as I walked I saw the surrounding scene with such clarity, and it seemed to me so beautiful, it was as if I would be dying soon. Before we went our separate ways I wanted to ask Donald why he had chosen *me*. But I did not. There was really nothing that remained to be said.

13

THE PROBLEM, STRIPPED of its integument of professional terms, was simple. If Donald Prothero was not mistaken and further experiments bore out what the earlier experiments indicated, it would be possible to produce a nuclear explosion that, transmitted with the speed of light, would release its destructive energy not where it was detonated, but at any location one chose on the globe. At our next meeting Donald showed me a sketch of the apparatus, as well as his initial calculations, from which it followed that if the effect remained linear with an increase in power and distance, there would exist no limit to either. One might even blow the moon apart, by accumulating a sufficient amount of fissionable material on Earth and aiming the reaction, as at a target, moonward.

Those were awful days, and the nights were perhaps worse, because it was then that I turned the whole matter over and over in my head. Donald needed a bit more time to set up the apparatus. McHill went to work on that, while Donald and I tackled the theoretical analysis of the data, though of course this meant only their phenomenological formulation. We had not arranged to work together—the collaboration seemed to happen by itself. For the first time in my life I was obliged to apply to my calculations a certain "conspiratorial minimum"; that is, I destroyed all notes, always cleared the memory in the computer, and refrained from telephoning Donald even in neutral matters, since the sudden increase in our contacts could also attract unwanted attention. I was a little afraid of the perceptiveness of Baloyne and Rappaport, but we were seeing each other less often. Yvor had a multitude of things to do in connection with the approaching visit of the influential Senator McMahon, a man of great merit and a friend of Rush; and Rappaport at that time had got himself conscripted by the information theorists.

As a member of the Council—one of the Big Five, though "without portfolio"—I did not belong, not even formally, to any group, and so I was master of my time. The long nights I spent at the main computer, therefore, did not draw notice; besides, I had done much the same previously, though for other reasons. It turned out that McMahon would be coming before Donald could finish assembling the apparatus. Not wanting to place any specifying orders through the Project administration, Donald simply borrowed the devices he needed from other groups—which also was not an uncommon practice. But he had to think of something for the rest of his people to do, some task that would not seem unreasonable and raise questions.

Exactly why we felt we had to hurry with the experiment, it is hard for me to say. We hardly ever spoke about the consequences that would follow a positive (really, a negative) result of any large-scale test; but I confess that in the wanderings of my mind before sleep, seeking a way out, I considered even the possibility of declaring myself dictator of the planet, or seizing that power in a duumvirate with Donald—for the common good, of course, though we know that practically everyone in history has striven for the common good, and we know what such striving has become. A man standing at Donald's apparatus could in fact threaten all armies and countries with annihilation. However, I did not treat the idea seriously. It was not that I lacked the courage of desperation —in my opinion there was nothing now to lose—but I was quite sure that such an attempt would end, inevitably, in a cataclysm. Any such step could not bring peace to Earth—and I only mention this fantasy to show my state of mind then.

These events—and their sequel—have been described innumerable times, all in distorted versions. The scientists who understood our qualms or even personally sympathized with us—Baloyne, for one—presented the matter as if we had acted in accordance with the dictates of proper Project methodology, or at least as if we had no intention whatever of hiding our results. On the other hand, the tabloids (e.g., the well-known serial exposé by Jack Slezar, "The HMV Conspiracy"), using materials provided by our old friend Eugene Albert Nye, painted Donald and me as traitors, enemy agents. That this hue and cry did not bring us, the authors of the vile plot, before the avenging tribunal of some Congressional hearing, we owed to the favorable official versions, to the behind-the-scenes support of Rush, and, finally, to the fact that the business was, by the time it reached the public, rather stale.

True, I did not escape some unpleasant conversations with certain political figures. To them I repeated the same thing: all contemporary conflicts I considered to be *temporary* phenomena, as the reigns of Alexander the Great and Napoleon were temporary. Every world crisis could be viewed in strategic terms, as long as the consequence of that approach was not our potential destruction as a biological species. But when the fate of the species became one of the members of the equation, the choice had to be automatic, a foregone conclusion, and appeals to the American way, the patriotic spirit, to democracy, or anything else lost all meaning. Whoever was of a different opinion was, as far as I was concerned, a candidate for executioner of humanity. The crisis in the Project had passed, but there would be others. The march of technology would disturb the balance of our world, and nothing would save us if we failed to draw practical lessons from this crisis.

The promised Senator finally arrived with his entourage and was received with all due honors; he turned out to be a man of tact, because he did not enter into little chats with us, the usual "palavering" between white man and savage. With the new fiscal year and the budget much in mind, Baloyne wanted the Senator to be as well disposed as possible toward the work and achievements of the Project, so, trusting most in his own powers of diplomacy, he tried to monopolize McMahon. McMahon, however, cleverly slipped out of his grasp and invited me to have a talk. As I found out later, among the initiated in Washington I passed for the "leader of the opposition," and the Senator wished to hear my *votum separatum*. But I had no idea of this at dinner. Baloyne, cannier in this area of affairs and games, kept trying to give me the right cues, but since the Senator sat between us, Baloyne was confined to making faces that were supposed to be, at one and the same time, eloquent of meaning, discreet, and reprimanding. He had omitted previously to give me instructions, but now itched to amend that, and as we rose from the table he prepared to leap over to my side; but McMahon cordially put an arm around me and led me to his suite.

He offered me a very good Martell, which he had probably brought with him, because I did not recall seeing it in our hotel restaurant. He conveyed greetings from mutual acquaintances, jokingly expressed his regret that he could not personally benefit from the works that had brought me fame; then suddenly, but as if carelessly, he asked whether the code had or had not been solved. I had him now.

Our conversation took place in private; the Senator's entire contingent was being conducted through those laboratories we called "the tour."

"Yes and no," I replied. "Are you able to establish contact with a two-year-old child? Certainly, if you intentionally address it. But what will the child comprehend of your speech about the budget on the Senate floor?"

"Nothing," he said. "But, then, why do you say yes and no, if it is only no?"

"Because we do know something. You have seen our 'exhibits' . . ."

"I heard about your proof. You showed that the letter is a description of some kind of object, right? This Frog Eggs of yours therefore is a part of that object—am I correct?"

"Senator," I said, "please do not take offense if what I say is insufficiently clear. I can do no better. What seems, to the layman, the most incomprehensible thing in our work—or, rather, in our lack of success so far—boils down to this, that we supposedly 'cracked' a part of the 'code,' but then came up against a wall, while specialists in cryptanalysis insist that if a code is cracked in part, then the rest of the work has to be smooth sailing. True?"

He only nodded; I saw that he was listening carefully.

"There exist, speaking in the most general way, two kinds of language known to us. There are ordinary languages, which man makes use of—and the languages not made by man. In such a language organisms speak to organisms. I have in mind the so-called genetic code. This code is not a variety of natural language, because it not only contains information about the structure of the organism, but also is able, by itself, to transform that information into the very organism. The code, then, is acultural. In order to understand the natural language of people, one must ultimately become acquainted, at least a little, with their culture. Whereas, in order to know a genetic code, one need not have an acquaintance with any sort of cultural factor. For that purpose it suffices to have pertinent knowledge from the realm of physics, chemistry, and so on."

"Then the fact that you nevertheless succeeded, in part, shows that the letter is written in a language similar to the language of genetics."

"If that were all there was to it, we would be home free. The reality is worse, because it is, as usual, more complex. The difference between a 'cultural language' and an 'acultural language' is not an absolute thing, unfortunately. Our faith in the absoluteness of that difference belongs to a whole series of illusions that we find extremely difficult to give up. The fact that I was able to work out the mathematical proof that you referred to shows only that the letter was written in a language that does not belong to the category of the language we are now using. We do not know of languages beyond the genetic code and natural languages, but that does not mean there are none. I believe such 'other languages' exist and that the letter was composed in one of them."

"And what is this 'other language' like?"

"I can convey that to you only in a general way. Let me simplify. Organisms, in evolution, 'communicate' by 'uttering' certain sentences, which are genotypes, and the 'words' in them correspond to the chromosomes. But when a scientist presents to you the structural model of a genotype, you are no longer dealing with an 'acultural code,' because the scientist has translated the code of genetics into the language of symbols—chemical symbols, let us say. Now, to go straight to the heart of the matter, we begin to suspect that an 'acultural language' is something more or less like Kant's 'thing-in-itself.' One can fully grasp neither the code nor the thing. What comes from the culture and what comes from 'nature' —or from 'the world itself'—appear, when we examine any utterance whatsoever, as a two-component 'mixture.' In the language of the Merovingians, or in the political slogans of the Republican Party, the percentage of the 'culture' ingredient is very high, and what does not depend on culture—the ingredient 'straight from the world'—is present only in small quantities. In the language used by physics, we have, you could say, the opposite: there is much of 'what is natural,' of what comes from 'nature itself,' and little of what has been shaped by culture. But a state of complete 'acultural' purity in principle cannot be achieved. The idea that, in sending to another civilization an envelope containing models of atoms, it would be possible to eradicate from such a letter all traces of culture—that idea is based on an illusion. The trace can be greatly reduced, but no one, not in the entire Cosmos, is or ever will be able to reduce it to zero."

"The letter is written in an 'acultural' language, but still possesses an element of the culture of the Senders. Is that right? Is this where the difficulty lies?"

"Where one of the difficulties lies. The Senders differ from us both in culture and in knowledge, and let us call that knowledge scientific. For this reason the difficulty is at least two-level. We cannot divine their culture—not now, and not, I believe, in a thousand years. They must know this perfectly well. Therefore they have sent the sort of information for whose deciphering no knowledge of their culture is required. That is almost definite."

"And so the cultural factor should present no obstacle?"

"Senator, we do not even know *what* is presenting the obstacle to us. We have evaluated the entire letter with respect to its complexity. The complexity is such that it corresponds roughly to a class of systems known to us—social and biological. We have no theory of social systems, thus we were forced to use, as models 'placed against' the letter, genotypes—or, rather, not the genotypes themselves, but the mathematical apparatus employed in the study of them. We learned that an object even more similar to the code is a living cell—or a whole living organism. From which it does not follow that the letter is actually a kind of genotype, but only that out of all the things known to us which, for comparison, we 'set against' the code, the genotype is the most helpful. Do you see the tremendous risk this carries with it?"

"Not exactly. It would seem that the only risk is that if the code is not, after all, a genotype, then your deciphering will not succeed. There is more?"

"We are proceeding like a man who looks for a lost thing not everywhere, but only beneath a lighted street lamp, because there it is bright. Have you ever seen a tape for an automatic piano—a player piano?"

"Of course. It comes in a roll, with perforations."

"By chance, a program tape for a digital computer might also fit into a player piano, and although the program has nothing, absolutely nothing, to do with music—it might refer to some fifth-order equation—nevertheless, when it is put in the machine, it produces notes. And it might also happen that not all the notes thus produced will be in total chaos, but that here and there one will hear some musical phrase. Can you guess why I use this example?"

"I think I can. You believe that Frog Eggs is a 'musical phrase' caused by inserting in a player piano a tape that really belongs in a digital machine?"

"Yes. That is exactly what I believe. One who puts a digital tape in a player piano is making a mistake, and it is entirely possible that we have taken precisely such a mistake for success."

"Yes, but your two research teams, wholly independently of each other, produced Frog Eggs and Lord of the Flies—one and the same substance!"

"If you have a player piano in your house, and are unaware of the existence of digital computers, and the same is true of your neighbor, then, if you find some tape from a digital computer, it is very probable that both of you will do the same—you will conclude that the tape is meant for the player piano, because you possess no knowledge of other possibilities."

"I understand. This is, then, your hypothesis?"

"This is my hypothesis."

"You spoke of a tremendous risk. Where is it?"

"Substituting a computer tape for a player piano tape does not, obviously, involve risk; it is a harmless misunderstanding. But in our case it could be otherwise, and the consequences of a mistake could prove incalculable."

"How so?"

"I do not know. What I have in mind is the kind of error whereby someone reads, in a kitchen recipe, the word 'amanita' instead of 'amandine,' and concocts a dish that sends all his guests to their graves. Please keep in mind that we have done what lay within our power to do, and so imposed our knowledge—our perhaps simplified or erroneous notions—on the code."

McMahon asked how this was possible if it was so very like the breaking of a cipher. He had seen Lord of the Flies. Could one decipher a code incorrectly and *still* obtain such astounding results? Could the fragment of the translation that was Lord of the Flies be completely false?

"It is possible," I replied. "If we were to send, telegraphically, the genotype of a man, and the receiver were able to synthesize, on the basis of that, only white blood cells, he would end up with amoebalike things as well as an enormous amount of unused information. One cannot say that he who produces corpuscles, having before him the human genotype, has read the message correctly."

"The difference is on that order?"

"Yes. We made use of two to four percent of the entire code; but that is not all, because within that small percent there could be a full third that is guesswork: i.e., all that we ourselves put into the translation, from our knowledge of stereochemistry, physics, and so on. If the genotype of man were read to a similarly low degree, one could not even construct white blood cells. At the most, something in the nature of a lifeless protein suspension— nothing more. I think, incidentally, that conducting precisely such experiments with the human genotype—which already has been deciphered to about seventy percent—would be extremely instructive for us; but we cannot do this, because we have neither the time nor the resources."

When he asked me what I thought was the difference in development that separated us from the Senders, I said that although the statistics of von Hoerner and Brace indicated that the highest probability was for a first encounter to be with a civilization having an age of about twelve thousand years, I believed that there was a real possibility that the Senders were as much as a billion years old. Otherwise, the transmitting of a "life-causing" signal would not have any rational justification, since it could produce no effect in the course of a mere millennium.

"They must have governments with rather lengthy terms of office," observed McMahon. He also wanted to know my opinion as to the value of continuing the research, if matters stood as they did.

"Suppose a young thief robs you," I said, "of your checkbook and six hundred dollars in cash. Although he can do nothing with the checks and cannot touch the millions in your account, he will not consider that he has done badly, because for him six hundred dollars is a lot of money."

"And we are the young thief?"

"Yes. The crumbs from the table of the higher civilization can feed us for centuries . . . provided we behave sensibly."

I could have added something to this, but bit my tongue.

He wished to know my private view of the letter and the Senders.

"They are not practical—at least not in a way that we can understand," I said. "Do you have any idea, Senator, of what their 'personal expenses' must be? Let us say that they have at their disposal energy on the order of 10^{49} ergs. The power of a single star—and that is the power needed to send the signal—is for them what for us, in this country, would be the power of one large hydroelectric plant. Would our government agree to expend—for hundreds, for thousands of years—the power of a facility like Boulder Dam in order to make possible the emergence of life on the planets of other stars, assuming such a thing, given so microscopic a supply of energy, were possible?"

"We are too poor . . ."

"Yes, but the percentage of energy to be consumed in this deed of altruism would be the same in both cases."

"A dime out of a dollar is not the same, financially, as a million dollars out of ten million."

"And we have those millions, don't we. The physical space separating us from that civilization is less than the moral distance, because we on Earth have starving masses of people, while *their* concern is that life should arise on the planets of Centaurus, Cygnus, and Cassiopeia. I do not know what the letter contains, but—from this standpoint—it cannot contain anything that would bring harm to us. The one would be at too great a variance with the other. Yes, of course, it is possible to choke even on bread. This is the way I see it: if we, with our political systems and our history, represent a cosmic average, then nothing threatens us from the 'letter.' That is what you asked about, I believe? Because they must be well aware of this 'psychozoic constant' of the Universe. If we constitute a slight aberration, a minority, then that, too, they will take—must have taken, that is—into account. But if we are an extraordinary exception to the rule, a deviant form, a monstrous abnormality that occurs in one galaxy per thousand, once in ten billion years—such a possibility they would be right, in their calculations and in their intentions, not to take into account. In other words, one way or the other they will not be to blame."

"Spoken like Cassandra," McMahon said, and I saw that he was dead serious. But, then, so was I. We talked some more, but I told him nothing that might arouse the least suspicion, nothing that might indicate that the Project had entered a new phase. Still, I felt uncomfortable when we parted, having the impression that I had said too much—particularly toward the end. I must have been Cassandra-like in pantomime, in expression more than in words, because I had kept a tight rein on the words.

The Senator had not yet left when I returned to my calculations. I did not see Baloyne until after the Senator's departure. Yvor was morose.

"McMahon?" he said. "He came anxious, but left content. Do you know why? You don't? The Administration fears success—too much success. It fears a discovery that will have military application."

This astonished me.

"He told you this?" I asked. Baloyne threw up his hands at my naïveté.

"How could he tell me any such thing? But it is obvious. They are hoping and praying that we will fail completely, or at least that in the end it will turn out that all we have received is a postcard with greetings and best wishes. Yes, then they will announce this with great fanfare and furor and exaltation. McMahon went very far—you don't know him, he's an extremely cautious man. And yet he took Romney aside and grilled him on the long-range technological implications of Frog Eggs. Long-range, yet! And with Donald, too, the same thing."

"And what did they say?" I asked. About Donald I did not need to worry. He was like an armored safe.

"Nothing, really. I don't know what Donald told him, and

Romney only said to the Senator that he could confess his bad dreams but that was all, because, awake, he saw nothing."

"That's good."

I did not hide my satisfaction. Baloyne, however, showed every symptom of depression: he ran a hand through his hair, shook his head, and sighed.

"Lerner is supposed to come here," he said. "With some theory for us, some idea of his own. What exactly, I don't know, because McMahon mentioned it literally at the last moment, as he was getting in the chopper."

I knew Lerner—a cosmogonist, one of Hayakawa's former students. Former because, some said, he had outgrown his preceptor. What I did not understand was what connection his field could have with the Project—and how, anyway, had he learned of the Project?

"And where have you been? Don't you realize the Administration is duplicating our work? It's not enough that they keep looking over our shoulder—now this!"

I did not want to believe it. I asked him how he knew this. Was it possible that they had some Alter-Project, a kind of parallel verification of our activities? Baloyne, it seemed, knew nothing specific, and, because he hated to admit to ignorance, he worked himself up to the point that, in the presence of Dill and Donald, who came in, he exclaimed that really his duty, in the situation, was to tender his resignation!

Such threats fell from time to time, to the accompaniment of thunder—for Baloyne cannot live on a small scale, and a certain operatic panache is indispensable to his vital energy—but this time we joined in persuading him, until, acknowledging our arguments, he quieted down, and was about to leave when suddenly he remembered my meeting with McMahon and started questioning me about what I had said to the man. I repeated more or less everything, but left out the Cassandra part. And such was the epilogue to the Senator's visit.

Shortly thereafter, it became evident that the preparation would take Donald more time than he had thought. Things were not going that well for me, either—the theory became tangled; I set various little tricks in motion; the personal calculator console (that was what they called it) was insufficient; I had to keep going to the computer center, which was not the most pleasant thing, because the winds were hurricane-force then, and merely crossing a street —a hundred feet—was enough to get sand in your ears, mouth, nose, and down your collar.

The mechanism by which Frog Eggs absorbed the nuclear energy it produced was still unclear; equally unclear were its means of ridding itself of the residues of those microexplosions, and these were all isotopes emitting hard gamma rays—rare-earth isotopes, mainly. Donald and I put together a phenomenological theory that did not do too bad a job of predicting the results of the experiments—but only retrospectively, as it were, within the compass of what we knew already. As soon as the scale of the experiment was increased, the predictions parted company with the results. Donald's effect, named by him "TX" (tele + explosion), was remarkably easy to produce. He flattened a small blob of Frog Eggs between two panes of glass, and when the layer became monomolecular, the decay reaction moved across the entire surface; at greater "doses" the apparatus (the older, previous model) underwent destruction. But people, somehow, paid no attention: there was such a racket in the laboratory, there was so much shooting, it was like an arsenal testing out munitions. When I asked him, Donald explained—without cracking a smile—that his people were studying the ballistic wave propagation in Frog Eggs. That was the topic he had thought up for them, and with the cannonade effectively camouflaged his own endeavors!

Meanwhile the theory slipped through my fingers; I saw that actually it had been eluding me for quite some time, but I had not admitted this to myself. The work on it was extremely demanding —all the more difficult in that I had little stomach for it. As sometimes happens, the words I had spoken in my meeting with McMahon came back to haunt me. Often our fears are not altogether present, not dangerous, you could almost say, until we give them clear expression. This is exactly what happened to me. Frog Eggs without question now appeared to me to be a human artifact, the result of a false reading of the code. This was how I saw it: the Senders definitely had had no intention of sending us a Pandora's box; but we, like burglars, forced the lock, and stamped upon the plundered contents everything that in Earth's science was mercenary, predatory. And did not success in atomic physics (I thought) take place precisely in that area where the opportunity opened up for us to obtain the most destructive possible energy?

Nuclear reactors always limped behind the production of bombs; we had hydrogen warheads but still no hydrogen piles; the entire microworld revealed to man its interior—distorted by that one-sided approach—and therefore we knew far more about the strong interactions than about the weak. I discussed these topics with Donald; he did not agree with me, being of the opinion that if anyone should "shoulder the blame" for the "one-sidedness of physics" (though he did not believe in that one-sidedness, either), it was not we, but the world, by virtue of its structure. The simple fact was that it was easier, from any objective standpoint—easier if only by the law of least resistance—to destroy than it was to create. Destruction was a gradient consistent with the main direction of processes in the Universe, whereas creation always had to go against the current.

I reminded him of the Promethean myth. In his picture of things, the marches of science, worthy of respect and even reverence, should all converge, as at a source; but the myth praised not disinterestedly comprehending but seizing hold, not knowledge of but mastery over. This was the foundation of all empiricism. He said to me that with such suppositions I would delight a Freudian, seeing as I reduced the thirst for knowledge to aggression and sadism. I can see now that I had indeed lost a little of my common sense, my circumspection, and the coolness that comes from the directive of proceeding *sine ira et studio*—and that I had, with my speculations, shifted the "blame" from the unknown Senders onto humanity, incurable misanthrope that I was.

In the first week of November the apparatus began working, but the preliminary experiments, undertaken on a small scale, were unsuccessful: several times the detonation went so far out of control that it reached beyond the main shielding wall, and though it was minute, the leap in radiation hit 60 roentgens. It became necessary to put up around the shielding another, outer, barrier. Too massive a structure, now, to be concealed—and somehow Eugene Albert Nye, who never before had visited the physics labs, showed up several times at Donald's. The fact that he asked no questions, but merely looked on and poked around, did not bode well. Finally Donald asked him to leave, telling him he was in the way. When I rebuked Donald for this step, he replied, calmer than I was, that one way or another things would be decided soon, and until then he would not let Nye in the door.

When I look back now, I see how foolishly we both behaved—how mindlessly, even. I still do not know what ought to have been done, but that conspiratorial activity—there is no other way to say it—served only to preserve the illusion that our hands were clean. We got in deeper and deeper. We could neither hide our progress nor—in the face of the pointlessness of keeping the secret—suddenly one day announce it. The announcing had to be done either immediately after the discovery of TX—or never. Both of these ways out, logical though they were, were closed to us. The awareness that the biophysicists, in another quarter, would be moving onto that "hot" ground made us hurry. Our fear for the fate of the world—because nothing less, after all, was at stake—caused, truly by reflex, our concealment of the research. To come out of hiding now would be to invite such shocked questions as "Well, fine, but why do you come to us with this *now*?," "You have, of course, the final results?," and "But what was your reason for not telling us at the beginning?" I would not have known what to reply.

Donald harbored the vague hope that on the large scale the effect might manifest a kind of "recoil"—the initial theory had pointed to that. But, first of all, the initial theory turned out to be useless, and, second, it opened a door to the acceptance of certain assumptions, which further down the road led to undesirable probabilities.

Baloyne I avoided during this period as much as possible, because my conscience was not clean regarding him. But he had other problems. Besides Lerner, we now were expecting a second "outsider"; both were to enlighten us with their presentations at the end of the month. This clear admission by Washington that it possessed its own experts on His Master's Voice, and men, moreover, who had been working without any connection with us, put Baloyne in an extremely unpleasant and difficult position before all the research groups. Dill, Donald, and Rappaport (and I as well) felt, however, that he ought to carry his cross (that was the sort of language he used) to the end. Anyway, both of these visitors announced to us were minds of the first order.

152

There was no talk, now, of budget cuts for the Project. It appeared that if our uninvited consultants could not give the work a forward shove with their ideas (which seemed to me unlikely), the Project would go on by sheer inertia, because no one on high would dare to change the least thing in it—let alone talk of liquidating it.

Personal tensions developed in the Council: between Baloyne and Nye, first, since the latter must have known, we were convinced, of this spectral, second Project—His Master's Ghost—yet, for all the man's volubility, he had not once mentioned it. (But to Baloyne Nye was still the soul of politeness.) And there was tension between our "conspiracy of two" and, again, Baloyne, for he had got wind of something after all: sometimes I saw him following me with his eyes, as if waiting for an explanation or at least some hint. But I dodged the best I could—not too skillfully, I am sure, because playing such games had never been my strong point. Meanwhile, Rappaport held it against Rush that even he, the first discoverer, had not been informed of His Master's Ghost. Thus the sessions of the Council became more than unpleasant, in an atmosphere of short tempers, suspicions, and low spirits. I slaved away at the programs for the machine, a waste of my time and strength since any programmer could have done them, but consideration for the "conspiracy" won out.

At last, I finished the calculations that Donald needed, but still he was not ready with the apparatus. Finding myself idle, for the first time since my arrival at the Project I tried watching television, but everything on it seemed to me unutterably phony and devoid of sense, the news programs included. I went to the bar, but could not stay there, either. Nervous, unable to sit still, I finally went to the computer center, shut myself up carefully, and began doing calculations that no one, this time, had required of me.

I employed, once more, the defiled (so to speak) formula of Einstein for the equivalence of mass and energy. I worked out the power available to the inverters and transmitters of the explosions at a distance equal to Earth's diameter; some minor technical difficulties that cropped up with this occupied me—but not for long. An attack carried out with the TX effect made advance warning impossible. What would happen was simply that the ground under people's feet would turn to solar lava. One also

153

could produce an explosion not on Earth's surface but beneath it, and at any depth, whereby shields of steel plate as well as the whole massif of the Rocky Mountains, which was supposed to protect the chiefs of staff in their great underground bunkers, would become meaningless. There could no longer be even the hope that the generals—those most valuable members of our society, if personal worth was to be measured according to the means invested in the preservation of one's life and limb—would emerge, the only people left, on the radioactive, scorched surface of the planet, in order to begin the work (after removing their momentarily unnecessary uniforms) of rebuilding civilization from the bottom up. The most wretched denizen of the slums would be exposed equally now with the supreme commander of the nuclear forces.

I had brought about a truly democratic leveling of all who lived on Earth. The machine warmed my feet with a gentle flow of heated air that came from the slits in its metal register, and it tapped out rows of digits on the tapes, because it did not care whether they referred to megatons and body counts or to the number of grains of sand on the beaches of the Atlantic. The despair of the last weeks, which had gradually turned into a kind of stifling weight, suddenly lifted. I worked quickly and with satisfaction, no longer acting contrary to myself. No, now I was doing what was expected of me. I was a patriot. Now I put myself in the position of the attacker, and now of the defender, with perfect loyalty.

The problem, however, was without a winning strategy. If the focal point of the explosion could be moved to any place one chose on the globe—and from any equally arbitrary location—then it was possible to destroy life in an area of absolutely any size. The classical atomic blast was, from the standpoint of energy efficiency, a waste of resources, because at "ground zero" you had extreme "overkill." The molecules of buildings and bodies underwent a demolition that exceeded a thousandfold what was militarily necessary; while the force of the blow, attenuated over distance, permitted survival in fairly simple shelters a few or even several dozen miles away.

This uneconomical state of affairs became—under my fingers, as I programmed—a prehistoric mummy. TX was a totally efficient device. The fireballs of the classical explosions could be flattened, rolled out, as it were, into a death-dealing tinfoil, and one could spread that foil under human feet over all of Asia or the United States. The three-dimensionally fixed layer, chosen out of the continental shelf, in a fraction of a second could turn into a bog of flame. There would be released, for each man, just the energy required to kill him. But the command posts, perishing, would have ten seconds to send a signal to the submarines that carried the missiles. The dying side still could slay its enemy. And if it could, it would have to do so. And thus, finally, the technological trap snapped shut on us.

I kept looking for a way out, putting myself in the position of global strategist, but computation defeated each search in turn. I worked skillfully, but felt my hands shaking, and when I bent over the tapes that snaked slowly out of the machine, to read the results, my heart started pounding, and at the same time I felt a burning dryness in my mouth and bowels, as if someone had wrapped a cutting wire around my intestines. I observed these symptoms of visceral panic with a strangely cold irony, as if the terror affected only my muscles and gut, while a voiceless giggle quivered inside me, the same as half a century ago, unchanged and unaged. I felt no hunger or thirst, as if fed by the columns of numbers, for nearly five hours, programming the computer over and over again. The tapes I tore from their cassettes and stuffed into my pocket. But all this labor, ultimately, turned out to be unnecessary.

I was afraid that if I went to the hotel, the sight of the menu or of the waiter's face would cause me to burst into laughter. And I could not return to my own apartment. Yet I had to go somewhere. Donald, wrapped up in his work, was in a better position, at least for the time being. I went out into the street as if half asphyxiated. Night had fallen. The compound, bathed in the light of the mercury lamps, jutted its white outline against the darkness of the desert, and it was only high above the illuminated areas that one could make out, in the black sky, the stars. One more betrayal did not matter now, so I broke the promise made to Donald and proceeded to my hotel neighbor, Rappaport. He was in. I set the crumpled tapes before him and succinctly told him everything. He proved to be the right man. He asked three or four questions, no more, questions that showed that he had grasped immediately the gravity, the implications of the discovery. Our conspiracy did not surprise him in the least. He paid no attention to it.

I do not recall what he said to me when he put aside the tapes, but I understood from his words that he had expected something of the sort practically from the beginning. The anxiety had been with him constantly, and now that his premonition had come true, an intellectual satisfaction—or perhaps it was simply an awareness of the end—let him feel a certain sense of relief. I must have been more shaken than I thought, because he attended first not to Armageddon but to me. From his European wanderings he preserved a certain habit that I found amusing: he operated on the principle of *omnia mea mecum porto*, as if instinctively prepared for the necessity of another flight at short notice. That was how I explained the fact that in his suitcase he had a kind of "survival kit," complete with coffeepot, sugar, and crackers. There was also a small bottle of cognac—both the coffee and the cognac were much to the purpose. What began then had no name, but afterward we would refer to it as a funeral banquet or, more precisely, its Anglo-Saxon or Irish variant: a wake—a ritual watch held over a corpse. Granted, the deceased in question was still among the living, and had no knowledge, even, of his inevitable interment.

We sipped our coffee and cognac, surrounded by such silence, it was as if we were in a place of great desolation, as if the thing that was soon to happen had already come to pass. Quick to understand each other, exchanging fragments of sentences, we first plotted out the course of upcoming events. As scenario writers, we agreed. Everything would be thrown into the construction of TX devices. People like us would not see the light of day.

For their imminent demise the chiefs of staff would revenge themselves first on us—unconsciously, no doubt. They would not roll over and play dead; rational action becoming impossible, they would resort to irrational action. If neither the mountains nor a kilometer of steel sufficed to shield them from attack, they would declare the ultimate armor to be secrecy. There would follow a multiplication, a dispersion, and a burrowing into the earth of command posts, while headquarters would be moved—for certain —on board some giant atomic submarine or specially designed bathysphere, which would keep watch, snuggled on the ocean floor.

And the last shell of democratic forms would crumble, forms

whose substance had already been mostly gnawed away by the global strategy of the sixties. And this would show in the attitude toward scientists. There would be no desire, no time or place, to keep up appearances and treat them like clever but capricious children whom it was better not to frustrate.

When we had prophesied, roughly, our fate and the fate of others—in accordance with Pascal's maxim about the thinking reed that thirsts to know the mechanisms of its own annihilation—Rappaport told me of his efforts the previous spring. Before I came to the Project, he had presented to General Oster—the chief, at that time, of HMV—a plan for joining forces with the Russians. He proposed that we supply a group equal in number and expertise to a group that would be provided by the Russians, to work together on the translation of the letter. Oster explained to him good-naturedly how very naïve such a thing would be. The Russians would provide a group for show, but meanwhile work on the letter themselves.

We looked at each other and laughed, because the same thought occurred to both of us. Oster had simply told him a thing that we learned of only in the last few days. Even then, the Pentagon itself had adopted the principle of "doubling." We constituted the group that was "for show," and had been wholly unaware of it; the generals all the while had had another team at their disposal, one they apparently trusted more.

For a moment we paused to consider the mentality of the strategists. They never took people seriously, insisting that the important thing was the biological preservation of the species. The famous *ceterum censeo speciem preservandam esse* became a slogan like all other slogans: words to utter but not a value to be included in the strategic equations. By now we had imbibed enough cognac to amuse ourselves with the vision of generals who, as they were cooked alive, would issue their final orders into a silent microphone—because the ocean floor, like every other nook and cranny on the planet, would no longer offer shelter. The only safe place for the Pentagon and its people, we concluded, would be beneath the bottom of the Moscow River; but it was not too likely that even our daring eagles could manage to get there.

After midnight, we finally put such mundane subjects behind us, and the conversation grew interesting. We took up the Mystery of the Species. I dwell on this, because that dialogue-requiem in honor of Man the Wise, delivered by two representatives of the race who were woozy with caffeine and alcohol, and certain that the end was nigh, seems to me significant.

That the Senders were well informed about the state of things in the whole Galaxy, I opined, was beyond question. Our catastrophe was a consequence of their not having taken into account the specific situation on Earth, and they had not, because Earth was, in the whole Galaxy, an exception.

"These are old Manichean ideas, a dime a dozen," declared Rappaport.

But I was not at all claiming that the apocalypse was the result of any exceptional human "wickedness." It was simply that every planetary psychozoic enclave passed from a state of global division to one of integration. From bands, tribes, and clans arose nations, kingdoms, empires, world powers, and finally came the social unification of the species. This process almost never led to the emergence of two antagonists of equal strength, at least not immediately prior to the final joining; there would be, rather, a Majority in opposition to a weak Minority. Such a confrontation had much greater probability, even if only from a strictly thermodynamic point of view; one could demonstrate this by stochastic calculation. A perfect equilibrium of forces, an exact equals-sign between them, was a state so improbable as to be virtually impossible. One could arrive at such a balance only by coincidence. Social fusion was one series of processes, and the acquiring of instrumental knowledge was another series.

Integration on the scale of a planet could become "frozen" at a stage along the way if the discovery of nucleonics arose prematurely. Only in that case would the weaker side become equal to the stronger—inasmuch as each of them, wielding atomic weapons, could wipe out the entire species. Certainly social integration always occurred on a foundation of technology and science, but the discovery of atomic energy would ordinarily take place in the post-unification period—and then it would have no dire consequences. The self-imperilment of the species, or its tendency to commit involuntary suicide, was no doubt a function of the number of primitive societies that possessed the "ultimate weapon."

If on some globe there were a thousand hostile governments,

and each had a thousand nuclear warheads, the chance of a purely local conflict's snowballing into an apocalypse would be many times greater than if there existed only a few antagonists. Therefore, the relation between the two calendars—one calendar showing the sequence of scientific discoveries, and the other recording the progress of the amalgamation of the separate societies—determined the fate, in the Galaxy, of each individual Psychozoic. We on Earth definitely had bad luck: our passage from preatomic civilization to atomic took place atypically, too early, and it was this that had caused the "freezing" of the *status quo,* until the advent of the neutrino emission. For a planet united, the cracking of the letter would be something positive, a step toward entering the "club of cosmic civilizations." But for us, in our situation, it was a knell.

"Maybe," I said, "if Galileo and Newton had died of whooping cough in childhood, physics would have been delayed enough so that the splitting of the atom would not have come about until the twenty-first century. That whooping cough that never was might have saved us."

Rappaport accused me of falling into journalism: physics was ergodic in its development, and the death of one or two people could not have influenced its course.

"All right," I said, "then we might have been saved by the emergence, in the West, of some other dominant religion than Christianity—or, millions of years earlier, by a different formation of man's sexual nature."

Challenged, I took up the defense of this thesis. It was no accident that physics had arisen in the West as the "queen of empiricism." Western culture was, thanks to Christianity, a culture of sin. The Fall—and the first one had been sexual!—engaged the whole personality of man in melioristic pursuits, which provided various types of sublimation, with the acquiring of knowledge at the head.

In this sense Christianity favored empiricism, though, of course, unwittingly: it opened the possibility for it and gave it the chance to grow. Characteristic of the East and its cultures, on the other hand, was the category of shame—quite central—because a man's inappropriate action there was not "sinful" in any Christian sense, but at most disgraceful, and mainly in the external sense: having to do with the forms of behavior. Therefore, the category of shame

159

transferred man, as it were, "outside" the soul, into the realm of ceremonial practices. For empiricism, then, there was simply no place; the chance for it disappeared with the deprecation of substantive action, and instead of the sublimation of drives, their "ceremonialization" was provided for. Vice, no longer the "fall of man," became detached from the personality and was, so to speak, legally channeled into a separate repertoire of forms. Sin and grace were replaced by shame and the tactics of avoiding it. There was no penetration into the depths of the psyche: the sense of "what is proper," "what ought to be," took the place of the conscience, and the finest minds were directed toward the renunciation of the senses. A good Christian could be a good physicist, but one could not become a physicist if one was a good Buddhist, Confucianist, or follower of the Zen doctrine, because then one would be occupying oneself with the very thing those faiths deprecated *in toto*. With this as a point of departure, social selection gathered the entire "intellectual cream" of the population and allowed it to spend itself only in mystical exercises—yoga, for instance. Such a culture acted like a centrifuge; it cast the talented away from the places in society where they could initiate empiricism, and stoppered their minds with an etiquette that excluded instrumental pursuits as "lower" and "less worthy." But the potential of egalitarianism inherent in Christianity—though it came into conflict with class structures, though for periods it yielded to them—never altogether disappeared, and indirectly from it sprang physics, with all its consequences.

"Physics—a kind of asceticism?"

"Oh, it is not that simple. Christianity was a mutation of Judaism, which was a 'closed' religion in that it was intended only for the chosen. Thus Judaism was, as a discovery, something like Euclidean geometry; one had only to reflect on the initial axioms to arrive, by extrapolation, at a more general doctrine, one that under the heading 'chosen' would put all people."

"Christianity corresponds to a generalized geometry?"

"Yes, in a sense, on a purely formal level—through the changing of signs in a system that is the same with regard to values and meanings. The operation led, among other things, to the acceptance of the validity of a theology of Reason. This was an attempt not to renounce any of the qualities of man; since man *was* a creature of Reason, he had the right to exercise that faculty —and this finally produced, after a due amount of hybridization and transformation, physics. I am, of course, oversimplifying enormously.

"Christianity is a generalized mutation of Judaism, an adaption of a systematic structure to all possible human existences. This was a property of Judaism, purely structural to begin with. One could not carry out an analogous operation on Buddhism or Brahmanism, let alone the teachings of Confucius. So, then, the sentence was passed back when Judaism arose—several thousand years ago. And there is another possibility. The main problem of this world which every religion must confront is sex. It is possible to worship it—that is, to make it positive and central to the doctrine; it is possible to cut it off, to shut it out—neutrally; but it is also possible to see it as the Enemy. This last solution is the most uncompromising, and it is the one Christianity chose.

"Now, if sex had been a phenomenon of less importance biologically, if it had remained a periodic, cyclic thing only, as it is with some mammals, it could not have possessed central significance, being a transient, rhythmic occurrence. But all this was determined some one and a half million years ago. From then on, sex became the *punctum saliens* of really every culture, because it could not simply be denied. It had to be made 'civilized.' The man of the West always felt it an injury to his self-esteem that *inter faeces et urinam nascimur* . . . a reflection that, by the laws of Mystery, put Original Sin in Genesis. That is how it was. Another kind of sexual periodicity, or—again—another kind of religion, might have set us on a different road."

"To stagnation?"

"No—just to a delay in the development of physics."

Rappaport accused me of "unconscious Freudianism." Having been brought up in a puritanical family, he said, I was projecting onto the world my own prejudices. I had not freed myself, in fact, from the vision of everything in the colors of Damnation and Salvation. Since I considered Earthlings to be damned root and branch, I transferred Salvation to the Galaxy. My curse cast mankind into Hell—but did not touch the Senders, who remained completely good and without blemish. That was my mistake. In thinking of them, one first had to introduce the notion of a "fellowship threshold." All intelligence moved in the direction of more and more universal generalization, which was only proper, because the Universe itself approved that course. He who generalized correctly could control phenomena of increasing scope.

An evolutionary awareness—understanding that mind was the result of a homeostatic "mountain climbing" against the current of entropy—made one embrace, in fellowship, the evolutionary tree that gave rise to sentient beings. But one could not encompass with fellowship the entire tree of evolution, because ultimately a "higher" being was obliged to feed on "lower" ones. The line of fellowship had to be drawn somewhere. On Earth, no one had ever placed that line below the fork where the plants parted company with the animals. And in practice, in the technological world, one could not include, for example, the insects. If we learned that for some reason exchanging signals with the Cosmos required the annihilation of Earth's ants, we would certainly think that it was "worth" sacrificing the ants. Now, we, on our rung of development, may be—to Someone—ants. The level of fellowship may not necessarily extend, from the standpoint of those beings, to such planetary vermin as ourselves. Or perhaps they had rationalizations for this. Perhaps they knew that according to the galactic statistics, the Earth type of psychozoic was doomed to techno-evolutionary failure, so that it would not be so horrendous to add to the threat hanging over us, since in any case "we most likely would not amount to anything."

I present here the gist of that vigil on the eve of the experiment, not a chronological record of the conversation, which I do not recall that precisely. I do not know when Rappaport told me of his European experience—the one I described earlier. It was, I think, when we had finished with the generals but had not begun to seek the cause of the impending denouement. Now I said to him more or less the following:

"Dr. Rappaport, you are even worse than me. You have made of the Senders a 'higher race' that identifies only with the 'higher forms' of the Galaxy. Why, then, do they endeavor to spread biogenesis? Why should they sow life if they are able to carry out a policy of expansion and colonization? Neither of us can go, in our reasoning, beyond the concepts accessible to us. You may be right that I localize to Earth the reasons for our defeat because of the way I was raised as a child. Except that instead of 'human sin' I see a stochastic process that has driven us into a dead end. You, a refugee from a country of victims, have always felt too strongly your own innocence in the face of extermination, and therefore you situate the source of the catastrophe someplace else: in the domain of the Senders. We did not choose this ourselves—they did it for us. Thus concludes every attempt at transcendence. We need time, but we will not have time now.

"I have always said that if only there were a government wise enough to want to pull all humanity out of that hole and not just its own, we might eventually climb out. But funding from the federal budget has been readily available only to the seeker of 'new weapons.' When I told the politicians that we ought to launch a crash program in anthropology, build machines for the simulation of socio-evolutionary processes, using the kind of money they put into their missile and antimissile research, they smiled at me and shrugged. No one took it seriously, and at least now I have the bitter satisfaction of being right. We should have studied man first—that was our proper ordering of priorities. But we did not, and now what we know of man is not enough. Let us finally admit that this is the case. *Ignoramus et ignorabimus,* because now we do not have the time."

The good-hearted Rappaport did not try to argue with me. He led me—I was drunk—to my room.

Before we parted, he said, "Don't take it so much to heart, Mr. Hogarth. Without you things would have turned out just as badly."

14

DONALD WOULD PLAN the experiments as much as a week in advance, four runs a day. This was the maximum of which the improvised apparatus was capable. After each experiment it would suffer partial destruction, and repairs would be necessary. The repairs went slowly, because the work had to be done in protective suits—on material radioactively contaminated. We got under way after the "wake"—or, rather, he did; I was only a spectator. We knew now that the people from His Master's Ghost or the Alter-Project were coming in eight days. Donald originally intended to start first thing in the morning, because he wanted his people, still engaged in the bogus research that he had assigned them, to cover with their cannonade the unavoidable roar of the explosions, but, having everything ready late the evening before (in other words, while I was working out endless variations of global Armageddon at the computer center), he did not wait.

Actually, by now it did not matter *when* Nye—and, after him, our mighty protectors—found out. Fallen into a troubled sleep after Rappaport left me, I awoke several times and jumped up with the impression that I had heard the boom of a detonation, but it was a dream. The concrete of the buildings had been designed, way back when, for more than such explosions. At four in the morning, feeling like Lazarus, I dragged my aching bones out of bed and decided—since I was unable to stay in my room any longer—to dispense with the rest of our "conspiratorial" cautions and go to the laboratory. We had not planned it this way, but I simply could not believe that Donald Prothero, having everything ready, would quietly turn in for the night. And I was not mistaken: his nerves, too, had their limit.

I washed my face in cold water and went out. As I passed Nye's door at the end of the corridor, I noticed that his light was on, and involuntarily softened my footsteps. Conscious of the absurdity of this action, I smiled a crooked smile, which stretched the skin of my face—making it feel stiff and leathery, as if not my own—and ran down the stairs instead of summoning the elevator.

Never before had I left the hotel at that hour. The lobby was dark; I bumped into chairs set about; there was a full moon, but the concrete block at the entrance shut out its light. The street, on the other hand, looked uncanny, but perhaps it only seemed so to me. On the administration building shone the ruby lights that warned airplanes; other than that, there were only a few lamps at the intersections. The physics building was dark and appeared deserted, but, going the way I knew by heart through the half-open door, I made it to the main hall. Immediately I knew that the thing was over, because the signals that flashed red while the inverters were in operation were all dark. In the dimness of the hall the giant ring of the inverter made the place seem like the engine room of a factory or ship; the tiny indicator lights at the consoles were still blinking on and off, but I found no one by the chamber. I knew where Donald would be; the narrow passageway between the coils of the multi-ton electromagnets led to a small interior area in which there was a kind of cubicle, where Donald kept all his records, films, notebooks. And, in fact, I saw a light on. He jumped up when he saw me. McHill was with him. Without a word of explanation he handed me the scrawled sheets of paper.

I was not aware of the state that I was in until I found that I could not identify the symbols, though I was perfectly familiar with them—I stared stupidly at the columns of figures, trying to collect my thoughts. When finally the significance of the coordinates of the four runs of the experiment sank in, I felt a weakness in my knees.

By the wall was a stool. I sat on it and once again, carefully and slowly, went over the results. The paper suddenly went gray; some-

165

thing obscured my vision. This weakness lasted only a few seconds. When it passed, I was covered with a clammy sweat. Donald at last noticed that something strange was happening to me, but I said that I was better now.

He started to take back the notes, but I did not let him. I still needed them. The greater the energy was, the less accurate the localization of the explosion. Although four trials did not allow statistical analysis, the relation hit one in the face. Probably for charges over a microton (we cheerfully worked in units of nuclear ballistics) the error factor would equal half the distance between the point of detonation and the target. Three, at most four, more tests would be enough now to determine this exactly, and enough to make the uselessness of TX as a weapon a certainty. But I was already certain, because suddenly, with extraordinary clarity, I recalled all the preceding results as well as my wrestling to come up with a model for a phenomenological formula. The relation appeared before me, the true formula for the whole thing, incredibly simple; it was nothing but the transposition, to the TX effect, of the uncertainty principle: the greater the energy, the less the accuracy of the focus, and the less the energy, the more sharply one could focus the effect. At distances on the order of a kilometer, it would be possible to focus the effect to a target area the size of a square meter, exploding only a handful of atoms. No powerful blow, no destroying force, nothing.

When I lifted my eyes, I saw that Donald knew also. A few words sufficed. There was only one problem: further experimentation, at energies increased by an order of magnitude—necessary to put an end, once and for all, to the career of TX—would have to be dangerous, because the indeterminacy of the place where the energy would be released, its shifting—completely unpredictable— would imperil the experimenters. What we needed was some special proving ground, a desert . . . and an apparatus on far remote control. This, too, Donald had thought of. We said little; over us hung a naked, dusty light bulb. McHill, all this time, did not utter a word. It seemed to me that the man was not so much shocked as —almost—disappointed; but perhaps I am doing him an injustice.

We went through everything again, with extreme care; my thinking was so clear, I was able on the spot to trace out the dependence, extrapolating for even greater charges, those in the kiloton range, and then going in the opposite direction—for our previous results. The agreement was to three decimal places. At one point, Donald looked at his watch. It was already five. He threw the main switch to cut off the power from all the units, and together we left the laboratory. Outside there was daylight. The air was cold as crystal. McHill walked away, but we stood awhile in front of the hotel, in an unreal stillness and an isolation so complete, it was as if no one but us was left alive. The thought made me shudder—but now only in retrospect, a reflex of memory. I wanted to say something to Donald, something that would wrap it all up, that would express my relief, my joy, but suddenly I realized that I felt no joy. I was only empty, terribly exhausted, indifferent, as though nothing would or could happen now. I do not know whether he felt the same way. We shook hands, a thing we usually did not do, and went our separate ways. If someone lunges with a knife and the blade is deflected by hidden armor, he who struck the ineffective blow can take no credit.

15

WE DECIDED TO present the story of the TX effect at the Science Council, but after three days; a little time was needed to organize the results properly, put together more detailed observational records, and make enlargements of selected photographs. But the very next day, at noon, I went to Yvor. He took the news remarkably calmly; I had underestimated his self-control. Most of all he was offended that we had not let him in on the secret until the end. I said many things to him on this score, finding myself in a position opposite the one I had been in upon my arrival at the compound: that time, he had done his best to "explain" my prior exclusion. But this matter was of incomparably greater importance.

I used every conceivable argument to sweeten the pill—to the accompaniment of his grumbling. For a while he held a grudge, understandably, though in the end he came to appreciate our reasons, I think. In the meantime, Donald, in the same private way, informed Dill, so that the only one who found out about everything at the meeting was Eugene Albert Nye. As much as I detested the man, I had to admire him: he did not bat an eye during Donald's presentation, and I watched him the entire time. The man was a born politician, though not a diplomat—because a diplomat should not be vindictive, whereas Nye, almost a year after that meeting, when the Project had concluded its existence, with the help of a third party, a certain journalist, gave to the press a truckload of material in which the action Donald and I had taken, put in a certain light with typical commentary, occupied the place of honor. But for Nye, the matter never would have taken on the sensational aspect that obliged various high-placed people, among them Rush and McMahon, to come to our rescue.

As the reader can see, if Donald and I were guilty of anything, it was of illogic, because in one way or another our secret research eventually had to be grist for the Project's official mill. But the whole thing was depicted as an extremely harmful piece of bungling, as a heinous attempt to sabotage the Project: instead of going immediately to the qualified experts (which meant the Army's ballistic-missile people), we had puttered about like do-it-yourself handymen, on a small scale, thereby giving the "other side" an opportunity to overtake us—and get the jump on us, fatally.

I have skipped ahead like this to show that Nye was not so innocent as he appeared. The only thing that he allowed himself, during that notorious meeting, was to look several times over his glasses at Baloyne, whom without question he suspected of having a hand in our conspiracy. We tried to word our report in such a way that the secrecy of the work would seem dictated by the exigencies of methodology as well as by the uncertainty regarding success (by "success," of course, we meant the thing we most dreaded); but Nye was not taken in, not for a minute, by these justifications.

Then a discussion got under way. Dill observed, rather unexpectedly, that had TX worked out, it might have brought peace to the world and not annihilation, because it would have put an end to the doctrine of DEW ("distant early warning"), which was based on the interval of time between the firing of the offender's intercontinental rockets and their appearance on the defender's radar screens at the apogees of suborbital flight. A weapon that destroyed at a distance of the Earth's diameter and with the speed of light ruled out any early warning; it would place both sides in the situation of two men holding guns to each other's temples. And that could lead to global disarmament. But such shock treatment could just as well end altogether differently, Donald pointed out in reply.

Baloyne meanwhile felt himself the object of Nye's suspicion—and then began the conclusive collapse of the Council, which could not be healed or patched for the remainder of the Project's existence. Nye, from that point on, dropped the pose that he was some sort of neutral ambassador or observer from the Pentagon; this showed itself in various ways, none of them pleasant. For example, the invasion of Army specialists in the nuclear and ballistic fields, which commenced twenty-four hours after this meeting, was already in progress—like an occupation of enemy territory, with helicopters descending like locusts—when Nye telephoned Baloyne to inform him of the fact. At the same time, the visit of the notables from the Alter-Project was postponed. I was absolutely certain that the Army's nucleonics people, whom I did not consider scientists in any sense of the word, would only confirm our findings with tests on the proving-ground scale. But the way the data were grabbed out of our hands, along with the apparatus, film, and lab notebooks—whatever illusions I had left, that laid them to rest.

Donald, barely tolerated in his own laboratory, bore this philosophically, and even explained to me that it could hardly be otherwise, because if it *were* otherwise, the only appearances that would be kept up would be those that did not really matter . . . since such actions were the logical consequence of the world situation. And so on. In a sense he was right. But an individual came to me in the morning (I was still in bed) and asked for the sets of calculations. I inquired if he had a search warrant, and if he had come to arrest me. This restrained him somewhat, and I was able at least to brush my teeth, shave, and dress while he waited out in the hall. I had spoken, of course, from a sense of complete helplessness. But I repeated to myself that actually I ought to be glad, for what would have been the state of my soul if I had had to hand over calculations that promised *finis terrarum*?

We loitered about the compound like flies while the Army dumped from the sky its seemingly endless personnel and provisions. This operation most certainly had not been improvised at the last minute; they must have had it in readiness for a while, in some outlined form, not knowing, after all, what would pop out of the Project. Three weeks were enough for them to begin the appropriate series of microton blasts. I was not at all surprised that we learned of the results only thanks to leaks from the lower-echelon technicians who were in contact with our people. When the wind was right, the explosions could be heard all over the compound. Their negligible strength, on the payload range, meant there was practically no fallout. No special safety measures were taken. No one approached us, about anything; we were ignored, as if we did not exist. Rappaport said that this was because Donald and I had violated the rules of the game. Perhaps. Nye disappeared for days on end, commuting at supersonic speed between Washington, the compound, and the test site.

In the beginning of December, when the storms came, the installations in the desert were dismantled and packed away; the fourteen-ton helicopter-cranes, the passenger helicopters, and all the other hovercraft one day lifted off, and as suddenly and efficiently as it had arrived, the Army left us, taking with it—so I heard—a few dozen of the scientific-technical staff who were exposed to high levels of radiation in the last of the experiments, during which had been detonated—according to the rumors—a charge equivalent to a kiloton of TNT.

And then, as if an enchantment had been lifted from us—more or less as in "Sleeping Beauty"—we all grew active, and in a short time a great many things took place. Baloyne submitted his resignation; Donald Prothero and I demanded to be released from the Project; Rappaport, although very reluctantly, I believe, nevertheless followed suit, out of a feeling of loyalty. Only Dill did not resort to any demonstration; he advised us, in fact, to march around the compound waving appropriate signs and chanting. He did not take our action seriously, and I cannot deny that he had a point.

Our rebellious quadrumvirate was immediately whisked to Washington. We were spoken to individually and together; besides Rush and McMahon, and our general (whom I personally met for the first time), the President's science advisers also put in an appearance, and it turned out that our continued presence in the Project was absolutely vital. Baloyne—that diplomat, that politician—said at one of these meetings that, seeing as they had placed full confidence in Nye and less in him, they could let Nye now recruit better people and run the Project himself. They treated us, when such dicta fell thick and fast, like ill-tempered, spoiled, but beloved children. I do not know about the others, but I genuinely had my fill of the Project.

One evening Baloyne came to my hotel room; that day he had had a private *tête-à-tête* with Rush, and he told me the reason for the constant persuasion. The advisers had come to the conclusion that TX was only a misfire in a beginning series, that actually it pointed clearly to the fruitfulness of further research, and such research was now our be-all and end-all, a matter of life and death. Though I considered this reasoning to be nonsense, I realized, after a little reflection, that we could actually return, provided the Administration met our conditions, which then and there we began, Baloyne and I, to draw up. I knew that if the work went on without me, I would have no peace with myself and could not go back to my pure—that is, unsullied—mathematics, because my belief in a safety mechanism that the Senders had placed upon the stellar code was really only a belief and not certain knowledge. I put this more succinctly to Baloyne: Let us go by Pascal's aphorism about the frail reed. If we cannot oppose, we will at least know.

The four of us, putting our heads together, figured out why the Project had not been handed over to the Army. The Army had been raising its own special breed of scientist—under the table— the type that would carry out basic assignments and be capable of limited autonomy. When he knew where to start and where to finish, the Army scientist did excellent work. But cosmic civilizations, their motives, the life-causing effects of the signal, the relation between these effects and the signal's content—all this, for him, was black magic. "Yes, and for us as well," remarked the ever-caustic Rappaport. We agreed, finally, to continue with the work. We got our way: Eugene Albert Nye, L.L.D., vanished from the Project (that was one of our conditions). He was immediately replaced, however, by another civilian, a Mr. Hugh Fenton. In this way we exchanged an evil for an evil. The budget was increased, the people from the Alter-Project (the existence of which we also brandished in the faces of the slightly abashed men in command) were incorporated into our research teams, and the Alter-Project itself presumably ceased to exist—but that was not true, either, because according to the official version, it never had existed. So, then, having vented our spleen, having deliberated together, having set conditions that were to be followed to the letter, we returned "home"—back to the desert; and thus began, with the New Year already past, the next and final chapter of His Master's Voice.

16

AND SO EVERYTHING went back to the way it was before—
except that one new face appeared at the sessions of the Council,
that of Hugh Fenton. Fenton the Phantom, he was called, or the
Invisible Man, because he somehow existed microscopically—not
that he was small, but he kept himself in the shadows. Winter
meant frequent storms, but of sand, not rain. Rain hardly ever fell.
It was not difficult for us to jump back into our former routine of
work—of existence, rather. Again I went to Rappaport's to chat,
and again I sometimes met Dill there; it seemed to me that the
Project was my life, that the one would end with the other.

The only new thing were the weekly seminars, quite unofficial,
during which various topics would be discussed in turn—such topics as the prospects for the auto-evolution (that is, controlled
evolution) of intelligent beings.

What did that hold for us? Supposedly it would put us on the
track of the anatomy, physiology, and thereby the civilization of
the Senders. But in a society that had reached a level of development similar to ours, there appeared antithetical long-range trends
whose distant outcome could not be foreseen. On the one hand,
the technologies already formed exerted pressure on the existing
culture and, to some extent, inclined people to subordinate themselves adaptively to the needs of the instrumentalities set in motion. Thus you had indications of competition between intellectual

man and the machine, and also of various forms of symbiosis between the two—and both psychology and physio-anatomical engineering discovered "weak links," shoddy parameters in the human organism, and from there the path led to the planning of necessary "improvements." Out of this same trend came the idea of manufacturing "cyborgs," partly artificial people, designed specially for work in space and the exploration of planets whose conditions were drastically different from Earth's; and the idea of connecting a human brain directly to reservoirs of machine memory, of making devices in which an unprecedented marriage of man and instrument would take place, on the mechanical and/or intellectual level.

This whole stream of technological pressures threatened to cleave the biological homogeneity of the species, hitherto intact. It was not just a single civilization for all men that such changes could render a fossil from the dead past, but even the single, universal physical shape of man. Man might in effect transform his society into a psychozoic type of ant colony.

On the other hand, the sphere of instrumental technologies might be made subordinate to cultural influences, to social mores. This could result in the biotechnological extension of the factors that determined—for example—fashion. The technologies of fashion as yet did not go beyond the boundary of the human skin. Some claimed, true, that their influence went further, but this was only because at various periods different physical variations of man have been promoted as especially valuable, as models. One need only think of the difference between Rubens's ideal of feminine beauty and the woman of today. It might appear, to an outside observer of human affairs, that in women (who more obviously conformed to the dictates of fashion), in accordance with the requirements of the passing seasons, now the shoulders would widen, and now the hips, now the breasts would grow large, and now diminish, now the legs would fill out, and now they would again be thin and long, and so on. But such waxings and wanings of the flesh were an illusion only, produced by the selection, out of the variety of the entire set, of those physical types that gained the approval of the day. Such a state might be subjected to biotechnological correction. Genetic control would then shift the range of racial variety in the direction desired.

175

Of course, genetic selection for purely anatomical traits seemed a frivolous thing in comparison with a multitude of culture-creating transformations, yet at the same time a desirable thing for aesthetic reasons (the opportunity to make physical beauty universal). But we were speaking of the first steps along a path to which one could affix the sign: REASON IN THE SERVICE OF THE URGES. This, because the overwhelming majority of the material products of the mind were channeled into sybaritic pursuits. An ingeniously constructed television set dispersed intellectual garbage; sophisticated transportation technologies made it possible for a degenerate, instead of getting soused in his own backyard, to dress up as a tourist and do the same in the vicinity of Saint Peter's basilica. If this tendency were to lead to the invasion of the human body by technological contrivances, undoubtedly the idea would be to expand the gamut of pleasurable sensations to the maximum, and perhaps even to bring into being—besides sex, narcotics, culinary happiness—other, as yet unknown, kinds of sensual stimulation and gratification.

If we had, in the brain, a "pleasure center," then what prevented us from connecting to it synthetic sense organs that would allow the reaching of orgasms mystical and nonmystical, through actions specially designed and devised as triggers of multiphase ecstasy? The carrying out of such an auto-evolution would constitute a definitive closure in the culture and mores; it would entail a withdrawal from all things extraterrestrial. It would be an exceptionally pleasant form of intellectual suicide.

Science and technology without question would be able to come up with devices that would meet equally the requirements of both the first and the second paths of development. The fact that both seemed to us rather monstrous, each in a different way, as yet meant nothing.

Negative assessments of such transformations were quite groundless. The directive that one should not "overly indulge" oneself could be rationalized only as long as the satisfaction of one individual meant, at the same time, the detriment of another (or the detriment of one's own body or soul, which happened, say, in the case of drug addiction). This directive could be the expression of plain necessity, and then one had better submit to it without argument; but the whole thrust of technology was precisely to eliminate, one by one, all necessities that limited possible action. Those who said that civilization would always face certain necessities, in the form of limits to personal freedom, were in fact adherents of the naïve faith that the Cosmos was arranged not without thought to the "duties befitting" intelligent beings. This was a common extension of the Biblical injunction about working for one's daily bread in the sweat of one's brow. It was not, as such naïve people often thought, an ethical judgment, but one clearly ontological. Existence, as a habitat for us, was furnished in such a way that one could not, not by any discoveries, attain the situation of "dizziness with success."

But there was no way to base far-reaching forecasts on so primitive a faith. If not on "puritanical" and "ascetic" grounds, people sometimes voiced these sentiments out of a fear of change. That fear sat at the bottom of all scientific arguments that ruled out, to begin with, the possibility of building "intelligent machines." Humankind always felt most at home—though never comfortable—in situations that were slightly desperate: that spice did not bring solace to the body, but did appease the soul. But the call of "all forces and reserves to the front of science" was stirring as long as "intelligent machines" were not able to replace the scientists effectively.

Of the real nature of both directions—the expansive-"ascetic" and the "encysting"-hedonistic—we could say nothing sensible. A civilization could take either path: storming the Cosmos or cutting itself off from it. The neutrino signal seemed to prove, at least, that certain civilizations did not shut themselves away from the world.

A civilization as "spread out" techno-economically as ours, with the front lines swimming in wealth and the rear guard dying of hunger, had by that very spread already been given a direction of future development. First, the troops behind would attempt to catch up with the leaders in material wealth, which, only because it had not yet been attained, would appear to justify the effort of that pursuit; and, in turn, the prosperous vanguard, being an object of envy and competition, would thereby be confirmed in its own value. If others imitated it, then obviously what it did must be not only good, but positively wonderful! The process thus became circular, since a positive feedback loop of motivation resulted, increasing the motion forward, which was spurred on, in addition, by the jabs of political antagonisms.

And further: a circle would result because it was difficult to come up with new solutions when the given problem already possessed some solutions. The United States, regardless of the bad that could be said of it, undoubtedly existed—with its highways, heated swimming pools, supermarkets, and everything else that gleamed. Even if one could think up an entirely different kind of felicity and prosperity, this could still only be, surely, in the context of a civilization that was both heterogeneous and—overall—not poor. But a civilization that reached a state of such equality and thereby became homogeneous was something completely unknown to us. It would be a civilization that had managed to satisfy the basic biological needs of all its members; only then, in its national sectors, would it be possible to take up the search for further, more varied roads to the future, a future now liberated from economic constraints. And yet we knew, for a certainty, that when the first emissaries of Earth went walking among the planets, Earth's other sons would be dreaming not about such expeditions but about a piece of bread.

17

DESPITE THE DIFFERENCES of opinion that separated us in the affairs of the Project, we represented—and by "we" I do not mean only the Science Council—a sufficiently close-knit team so that the new arrivals, here and there already called "the Pentagon puppets," could be certain that their theses would be received by us with daggers drawn. Although I, too, was rather unfavorably disposed toward them, I had to admit that Lerner and the young biologist accompanying him (or astrobiologist, as he styled himself), pulled off an impressive thing; because it was difficult for us to believe that, after our year of tribulation, after the wringer to which we had collectively surrendered our brains, it was still possible to set forth, on the subject of His Master's Voice, hypotheses that were totally new, never even touched upon by us, and, moreover, different from each other and supported by a well-constructed mathematical apparatus (though not so strong regarding data). Yet this is precisely what happened. What is more, these new ideas, mutually exclusive to a degree, allowed for the establishing of a kind of golden mean, a novel compromise that brought them together not at all badly.

Baloyne, perhaps because he felt that it was not suitable, in a meeting with the people of the Alter-Project, to stick to our old "aristocratic" structure—the division between the all-knowing élite and the poorly informed pawns of the collective—or perhaps just because he believed that what we were to hear would be revelational—organized a lecture meeting for more than a thousand of our workers. If Lerner and Sylvester were aware of the hostility of those assembled, they gave no indication of it. In any case, their behavior was impeccable.

Their research—Lerner emphasized in his introduction—was purely theoretical in nature; they had not been given, except for the stellar code itself and general information about Frog Eggs, any details, and their purpose had not at all been to set up some "parallel experiment," or to compete with us, but only to approach His Master's Voice differently, having in mind exactly the sort of confrontation of views which was taking place now.

He did not stop for applause—just as well, since there would have been none—but went straight to the matter, and proceeded quite lucidly; he won me over with both his talk and his person—and won others, too, judging by the reaction in the auditorium.

Being a cosmogonist, he had worked on cosmogony—in its Hubblian variant and Hayakawan modification (Hayakawan, and mine, too, if I might say so, though I had merely done the mathematical wickerwork for the bottles into which Hayakawa poured new wine). I will try to give a sketch of his thesis and convey, if I am able, something of the tone of the lecture, which more than once was interrupted by remarks from the audience, because a dry summary would lack all the charm of the conception. The mathematics, of course, I omit—although it played its part.

"I see it this way," he said. "The Universe is a thing that pulses, that contracts and dilates in alternation, every thirty billion years. . . . When it contracts, it eventually reaches a state of collapse in which space itself disintegrates, becoming folded up and locked not only around stars, as in the case of the Schwarzschild sphere, but around all particles, the elementary included! Since the 'joint' space between the atoms ceases to exist, obviously the physics known to us also disappears, its laws undergo transformation. . . . This null-space cluster contracts further, and then—speaking figuratively—the whole turns inside out, into the realm of forbidden energy states, into 'negative space,' so that it is not nothingness, but less than nothingness—mathematically, at least!

"Our actual world does not have antiworlds—that is, it has them periodically, once in thirty billion years. 'Antiparticles' are, in our world, only the trace of those catastrophes, an ancient relic, and also, of course, an arrow pointing to the next catastrophe. But there remains—to continue the metaphor—a kind of 'umbilicus,' in which still pounds the remnant of the unextinguished matter, the embers of that dying Universe; it is a fissure between the vanishing 'positive' space, this space that is ours, and the other, the negative. . . . The fissure remains open; it neither grows nor closes, because it is continually forced apart by radiation—by *neutrino* radiation! Which is like the last sparks of the bonfire, and from which begins the next phase, because, when 'what was reversed' has come to the limit of its 'inside-out' expansion and created an 'antiworld,' and extended it, it begins to contract again and break back through the fissure, first in neutrino radiation, which is the hardest and most stable, because at that point there is no light yet, only, besides the neutrino radiation, ultrahigh gamma! What begins again to swell spherically and form the expanding Universe is a spreading, globe-shaped neutrino wave, and that wave is at the same time the matrix of creation for all the particles that will occupy the soon-to-be-born Universe; it carries them with it, but only potentially, in that it possesses sufficient energy for their materialization!

"But when this Universe is in full swing, with its nebulae flung wide, as ours is now, there are still stray echoes in it of the neutrino wave that brought it into being, AND *THIS* IS HIS MASTER'S VOICE! From the gust that forced its way through the 'fissure,' from that neutrino wave arose the atoms, the stars and planets, the nebulae and the metagalaxies; and this eliminates the 'problem of the letter.' . . . Nothing was sent to us by 'neutrino telegraph' from another civilization; at the other 'end' there is No One, and no transmitter, nothing but the cosmic pulse from that 'rupture.' It is only an emission produced by processes that are purely physical, natural, and totally uninhabited, therefore devoid of any linguistic character, of content, of meaning. . . . This emission provides a permanent link between the successive worlds, the expiring and the newly created; it connects them energetically and informationally; thanks to it, a continuity is preserved, there are nonaccidental, regular repetitions; therefore one can say that this neutrino stream is the 'seed' of the next Universe, that this is a kind of metagenesis or alternation of generations, separated by macrocosmic time, but in the analogy there is, of course, no biological content. Neutrinos are the seeds from disintegration only because, of all the particles, they are the most stable. Their indestructibility guarantees the cyclic return of genesis, its repetitions. . . ."

He put all this much more exactly, of course, supporting it, when possible, with calculations. During the lecture it grew very quiet in the hall; when he finished, the attacks began.

Questions were thrown at him: How did he explain the "life-causing" property of the signal? How did it originate? Was it, according to him, a "pure accident"? And, most of all—where did we get Frog Eggs from?

"Yes, I've thought about this," Lerner replied. "You ask me who planned it, composed it, and sent it. If not for that life-causing side of the emission, life in the Galaxy would have been an extraordinarily rare phenomenon! But now I ask in turn: What about the physical properties of water? Had water at a temperature of four degrees Celsius been lighter than water at zero, and had ice not floated, all bodies of water on Earth would have frozen bottom-to-top, and no aquatic creatures would have been able to survive outside the equatorial zone. And had water had a different dielectric constant, not as high, protein molecules would not have been able to form in it, and therefore there could not have been protein-based life. Yet does anyone ask, in science, whose helping hand intervened here, and who gave water its dielectric constant or provided for the relative lightness of its ice? No one asks, because we consider such questions to be meaningless. Had water had other properties, either a nonprotein form of life would have arisen or else no life at all. By the same token, one cannot ask who sent the biophilic emission. It increases the probability of survival for macromolecular bodies, and this is either the same sort of accident, if you like, or the same sort of inevitability that has made water a substance 'favoring life.' The whole problem should be turned around, set right side up, and then it will read as follows: Thanks to the fact that water possesses these properties, and thanks to the fact that in the Universe there exists a radiation that stabilizes biogenesis, life can arise and oppose the growth of entropy more effectively than it would otherwise. . . ."

"Frog Eggs!" came shouts. "Frog Eggs!"

I was afraid that at any minute a chant would start. The auditorium already had reached the heat of a boxing match.

"Frog Eggs? You know better than I that there was no success in reading the so-called letter as a whole, but only its 'fragments'—from which Frog Eggs came into being. This shows that as a meaningful whole the letter does not exist outside your imagination, and that Frog Eggs was simply the result of an extraction of information inherent in the neutrino stream, information that something could be done with. Through the 'fissure between the worlds,' between the one dying and the one being born, burst a ball of neutrino radiation, expanding like a soap bubble; this wave had sufficient energy to 'inflate' the next Universe, and the front of the wave is impregnated with information inherited, as it were, from the phase that has ended. Now, in this wave lies the information that created the atoms, as I already said, and the information that 'favors' biogenesis, and in addition it has segments that from our standpoint 'serve no purpose,' that are 'worthless.' Water possesses properties like those I mentioned, that 'favor' life, and properties that are indifferent to life, as for example transparency; water could have been nontransparent, and this would have had no significance for the emergence of life. Just as one cannot ask, 'And who made water transparent?' one cannot ask, 'Who wrote the program for Frog Eggs?' It is one of the properties of the given Universe, a property that we may study—like the transparency of water—but that has no 'extraphysical' meaning."

There was an uproar in the hall. Finally Baloyne asked how, then, Lerner explained the circular repetition of the signal, and the fact that all the rest of the emission spectrum for neutrino radiation in the sky was ordinary noise, while in that single, solitary band lay so much information.

"But that is simple," replied the cosmogonist, who seemed to be deriving pleasure from the general stir. "Initially the entire emission was concentrated precisely in that band, since it was precisely at that point on the spectrum that it was 'sharpened' by the 'fissure between the worlds,' and compressed, and modulated, like a stream of water in a narrow opening. At the beginning there was a needle-band, nothing more! Then, as a result of dispersion, scattering, desynchronization, diffraction, deflection, interference—a greater and greater amount became diffused, blurred, until finally, after billions of years of the existence of our Universe, from that primal information there resulted noise; and from the sharp focus there resulted a broad energy spectrum, because in the meantime the 'secondary' noise generators of neutrinos—the stars—had become activated. What we are receiving, as the letter, is the remainder of the 'umbilicus,' the remnant that has not yet undergone dissolution, that has not altogether merged with the countless reflections and currents that go from corner to corner of the Metagalaxy. The present (and omnipresent) norm is noise—not information. But at the moment of the creation of our Universe, at its violent birth, the neutrino bubble contained within it full information about all that physically was to arise from it; and precisely because it represents a relic of an epoch that has left no discernible trace of itself other than this, it seems to us astoundingly different from the phenomena of 'ordinary' matter and radiation."

It was clever, all right, the pretty, logically coherent construction that he put before us. Then followed the mathematical portion; he showed what features the "fissure between the worlds" would need to have in order to correspond exactly, as a "matrix," to the place in the neutrino spectrum where the emission, or what we called the "stellar code," was situated. It was a nice piece of work; he brought in resonance theory, and was even able to provide an explanation in his lecture for the constant repetition of the signal, and for the location—that radiant of Canis Minor—from which the alleged letter came.

I took the floor then and said that actually it was he who had stood the matter on its head, because he refashioned the whole Universe to fit the letter, simply making the "dimensions" of this fissure of his such that they would correspond to the *given* energetics of the signal, and he even altered the geometry of his made-to-order, ad hoc cosmos so that the direction from which the "signal" came would turn out to be a thing of chance.

Lerner, smiling, admitted that to a certain extent I was right. But, he added, if not for his "fissure" the successive worlds would come and go with no connection between them; each would be different—that is, might be different; or the Universe might remain permanently in the "antiworld," null-energy phase, and that would be the end of all creation, of all possible worlds—we would not exist, nor the stars above us, and there would be no one to rack his brains over what did *not* take place. . . . But it had, after all, taken place. The monstrous complexity of the letter was explained in this way: the unimaginable concentration of the "death throes" caused the dying world, just as a man gave up the ghost, to "give up" its information; this information did not suffer destruction; instead— owing to laws unknown to us, because physics must have ceased in that compression, that discontinuity-dissociation of space—it fused with what still existed: with the neutrino node within the very "fissure."

Baloyne, who chaired the meeting, asked us if we wished to begin a discussion then and there, or first hear Sylvester. We voted for the second, out of curiosity, of course. Lerner I knew a little, having met him once or twice at Hayakawa's, but Sylvester I had never even heard of. He was a small young man with a pasty face—which is of absolutely no importance.

He began in a vein surprisingly similar to Lerner's. The Universe was a pulsing entity, with alternating phases of blue contractions and red expansions. Each phase took around thirty billion years. In the red phase, that of the retreating nebulae, after a sufficient dispersal of matter and the cooling of planetary bodies, life formed on them and sometimes gave rise to intelligent species. When the dilation ended and the Universe began to converge centripetally, gradually, in that blue phase, there resulted enormous temperatures and increasingly hard radiation, which destroyed all the living matter that in the course of the preceding two billion years had succeeded in covering the planets. Obviously, in the red phase—as in this one in which *we* have come into being—there existed civilizations at varying levels of development. And there must have existed those that excelled technologically; those that, with their advanced sciences, including cosmogony, were cognizant of their own future—and the future of the Universe. Such civilizations—or, for convenience, let us say such a civilization—situated in some particular nebula, therefore knew that the process of organization would pass its peak and the process of universal destruction would commence, in growing heat. If the civilization possessed far more knowledge than we, it would also be able, to some extent, to foresee the continuation of events after the "blue end of the world," and if it enriched its knowledge even more, then it would be able to affect that future state. . . .

Again there was a buzz of voices. Sylvester was offering nothing more or less than a theory of the control of the cosmogonic process!

The astrobiologist assumed, along with Lerner, that a "two-cycle cosmic engine" was totally indeterminate—because, particularly in the compression phase, major indeterminacies would result from the changes, basically random, in the distribution of mass, and from the variable process of annihilation. Thus, what "type" of Universe would emerge from the next contraction could not be accurately predicted. We were acquainted with this difficulty on a miniature scale, because we could not predict, or calculate, the course of turbulence phenomena, the sort that gave rise to whirling (as, for example, in water breaking on a reef). Thus the particular "red Universes," that resulted, each in turn, from the blue, could differ so much among themselves that the type realized at present, in which life was possible, might constitute an ephemeral, never-to-be-repeated state, or one that would be followed by a long series of nothing but lifeless pulsations.

Such a horoscope might not suit that high civilization, and so it would undertake to change the vision of eternity as an everlasting graveyard, now heated, now cooling—to change it through appropriate astroengineering manipulations. Preparing itself for the extermination that awaited it, the civilization could "program" a star or a system of stars, modifying in a fundamental way the energetics of that system, turning it into a kind of neutrino laser ready to fire—or, rather, arranging that it would become such a laser only at the moment when the tensors of gravitation, the parameters of temperature, the pressure, and so forth exceeded certain maximum values—when physics itself, the physics of that given Universe, began to crumble! Then this dying constellation would be converted entirely, "triggered" by phenomena that would release its accumulated energy, into a single, black neutrino flash —programmed with the utmost precision and care! Being the hardest and most inertial of the radiations, this monotonic neutrino wave would serve not only as the death knell of the extinguished Universe but at the same time would become the seed of the next phase, because it would participate in the formation of the new elementary particles. Moreover, the directive "stamped in the star" would include biophilia—the increasing of the chance of the birth of life.

Thus, in this spirited picture, the stellar code was revealed to be a transmission sent into the sphere of our Universe—from the Universe that came before it. The Senders, therefore, had not existed for at least thirty billion years. They fashioned the "message" so well that it survived the annihilation of their Cosmos; and their message, joining the processes of the succeeding creation, set in motion the evolution of life on the planets. We, too, were Their children. . . .

An ingenious notion! The "signal" was no letter at all; its "life-giving" virtue did not represent one "aspect" as opposed to the "content." It was only that we, according to our custom, had sought to separate what could not be separated. The signal—or, rather, the causal pulse—began first with a "tuning" of the cosmic material, newly resurrected, in order that there would arise particles with the desired properties (desired from the point of view of that civilization, of course), and when astrogenesis had got under way, and with it planetogenesis, other structural features became "activated," features present at the beginning within the pulse but till now having no "addressee"; only then did they begin to manifest their ability to assist the birth of life. And since it was "easier" to increase the overall chance of survival for large molecules than to direct and govern the formation of the most elementary building blocks of matter, we discovered the first effect as separate and "nonsemantic," while giving to the second, the atom-creative part, the name of "letter."

We had failed to read it because for us, with our knowledge, with our physics and chemistry, to read it completely was impossible. Yet from pieces of the knowledge recorded in the pulse we made ourselves a recipe—for Frog Eggs! And therefore the signal *directed and did not inform*; it was addressed to the Universe and not to any beings. All we could do was try to deepen our knowledge by studying the signal itself—as we studied Frog Eggs.

When Sylvester finished, there was much consternation. Here was an *embarras de richesses*! The signal either was a natural phenomenon, a "last chord" of a dying Universe, hammered out by a "fissure" between world and antiworld onto a neutrino wave;

a deathbed kiss planted upon the front of the wave—or else it was the last will and testament of a civilization that no longer lived. An impressive choice!

And both views found adherents among us. It was pointed out that in ordinary—that is, natural—hard radiation there were fractions that increased the tempo of mutation and thereby could speed up the rate of evolution, while other fractions did not do this, from which it did not follow that the first fractions meant something and the second did not. For a while everyone attempted to talk at once. I had the feeling that I was standing at the cradle of a new mythology. A last will and testament . . . we as the posthumous heirs of Them . . .

Because it was expected of me, I took the floor. I began with the observation that through any number of points on a plane one could draw any number of curved lines. I had never considered it my objective to produce the greatest possible number of different theories, because one could come up with an endless amount of those. Rather than tailor our Universe and its antecedents to the signal, it sufficed to admit, for example, that our receiving apparatus was primitive in the sense that a radio of low selectivity was primitive. Such a radio would pick up several stations at a time, and the result would be a mishmash; but someone who did not know any of the languages in which the programs were being broadcast might simply record everything as it came out, and rack his brains over that. We might have fallen victim to just such a technological mistake.

Perhaps the so-called letter was a recording of several emissions at once. If one assumed that in the Galaxy automatic transmitters were operating on precisely that "frequency," in that band, which we were treating as a single channel of communication, then even the constant repetition of the signals could be explained. They could be signals used by societies in some "civilizational collective" to keep in systematic synchronization certain technological devices of theirs, possibly astroengineering devices.

This would account for the "circularity" of the signals. But it fit poorly with Frog Eggs; although, stretching things a little, one could put its synthesis also into this scheme. In any case, the scheme was more modest and therefore more sensible than the giant visions that had been unfolded before us. There existed a mystery *outside* the signal, namely, the fact that it was alone. There should have been a great many of them. But to refashion the whole Universe to "explain" this mystery was a luxury we could ill afford. Why, the "signal" could be declared to be a "music of the spheres," a kind of hymn, a neutrino fanfare with which the High Civilization would greet, say, the ascension of a supernova. The letter also could be apostolic: we had, here, a Word that became Flesh. And we had, in opposition to it, Frog Eggs, which as Lord of the Flies—the work, therefore, of darkness—indicated the Manichean nature of the signal, and of the world. To pursue any further this sort of exegesis should not be allowed. Basically, both ideas were conservative, and Lerner's in particular, because it boiled down to a defense, a desperate defense, even, of the empirical position. Lerner did not want to leave the traditional points of view of the exact sciences, which from their inception had dealt with the phenomena of Nature and not of Culture, for there does not exist a physics or chemistry of Culture, but only of the "stuff of the Universe." Not willing to give up treating the Universe as a purely physical object, devoid of "meanings," Lerner acted like a man prepared to study a handwritten letter as if it were a seismogram. In the final analysis, handwriting, like a seismogram, was a lot of complicated curved lines.

Sylvester's hypothesis I characterized as an attempt to answer the question "Do successive Universes inherit from one another?" He supplied an answer in which our "code," though remaining an artifact, ceased to be a letter. I concluded by showing the incredible number of assumptions that both had pulled out of the air: the negative umbilicus of matter compressed into information at the bottom of the contraction-well; the branding of the wave front with the "atom-generating" stigmata—it would never be possible to verify any of this, *ex definitione*, because presumably these things would occur where there would no longer be beings of any kind, or physics. This was a discussion about life after death, decked up in the terminology of science. Or it was a sort of "philosophy fiction"—by analogy to science fiction. The mathematical robe concealed a mythology. In this I could see the *signum temporis*, but nothing more.

Naturally, the discussion then took off like wildfire. Toward the end of it, Rappaport suddenly rose with "one more hypothesis." It was so original that I present it here. He defended the thesis that the difference between "artificial" and "natural" was not entirely objective, not an absolute given, but a relative thing and dependent on the cognitive frame of reference. Substances excreted by living organisms in the course of their metabolism we considered to be natural products. If I ate a great quantity of sugar, its excess would be eliminated by my kidneys. Whether the sugar in the urine was "artificial" or "natural" depended on my purpose. If I ate so much sugar intentionally, in order to eliminate it, knowing the mechanism involved and able to predict the effects of my action, the sugar would be "artificially" present; but if I ate it because I had a craving for it, and for no other reason, its presence would be "natural." One could demonstrate this. If someone examined my urine and if I had arranged this with him accordingly, the presence of sugar which he would discover could acquire the meaning of an informational signal. The sugar might signify, for instance, "yes," and the lack of sugar "no." This process of symbolic signaling would be as artificial as could be, but *only between the two of us.* Whoever did not know of our arrangement would learn nothing of it from an examination of the urine. So, then, in Culture as well as in Nature only the "natural" phenomena existed "really and truly"; the "artificial" were artificial only insofar as we related them, by agreement or action, in a definite way. Only miracles were "absolutely artificial," and they were impossible.

After this introduction Rappaport delivered the main blow. Let us suppose that biological evolution could take a double path: it could create separate organisms, and then, from them, intelligent beings; or it could create, on the other branch, biospheres that were "nonintelligent" but at the same time highly organized—and let us call these "forests of living flesh," or vegetation of still another type, one that in the course of a very long development would master even nuclear energy. The vegetation's evolution would master it, however, not in the way that we mastered bomb or reactor technology, but in the way that our bodies "mastered" metabolism. In this case the products of the metabolism would be phenomena of a radioactive type—and, at a later stage, even streams of neutrinos, which would be nothing but the "excretion" from such globes, of the organisms on them, excretion which we would receive precisely in the form of a "stellar code." In this case we would have a completely natural process, because beings would not be intending to send anything to anyone, or to communicate, and the streams in question would be only the inevitable result of their metabolic activity, an "excretory emission." But it could also be that other planetary organisms would learn of their presence by this "spoor" left in space. Then it would constitute a kind of signal between them.

Rappaport added that his hypothesis fit into the class of things native to science, because science did not divide phenomena into "artificial" and "natural," and therefore he had entered into the spirit of its rules. The hypothesis, in principle at least, could be tested (by detecting the presence, or merely proving the theoretical possibility, of "neutrino organisms"), because it did not refer us to "other Universes."

Not everyone grasped that this was more than just an exhibition of wit. It was possible, in principle, to predict and calculate any type of organic metabolism when one began with physics and chemistry, whereas it was not possible, beginning with the same physics and chemistry, to predict or calculate a culture in which certain beings would write and send "neutrino letters." This second phenomenon was of another, nonphysical, order. If civilizations spoke to one another in different languages, and their differences in development were considerable, at best those who were less knowledgeable would extract from the received communication only (or nearly only) what was physical in it (or natural, the same thing). They would understand nothing more. And in fact, with a sufficiently large gap between civilizations, the same concept-symbols, even if they functioned in both cultures, would have totally different referents.

There was discussed, among other things, the question of whether or not the probable "civilization of the Senders," either existing or (according to Sylvester) no longer among the living, was rational. And how could we say that a civilization that concerned itself about what would be "in the next Universe," thirty billion years away, was rational? Even for a fantastically wealthy civilization, what had to be the cost, the price paid in the fates of living beings, for it to become the helmsman of the Great Cosmogony? This also, analogously, held for the "life-causing effect." One might say that *for them* this was rational—or that there was no intercivilizationally constant sense of "rationality."

A dozen of us gathered at Baloyne's after the closing of the meeting, and talked long into the night. If Sylvester and Lerner failed to convince us, they definitely poured oil on the troubled waters of the past. There was discussion about what Rappaport had presented. He added to it and made clarifications, and from this emerged a strange picture indeed—of leviathan biospheres that "sent" into the Universe, unaware of what they were doing; of an advanced stage of homeostasis, unknown to us; of amalgamations of vital processes which, drawing upon the sources of nuclear energy, began to equal, in their metabolic conversions, the power of suns. The biophilia of their "neutrino excretion" represented an effect exactly like that of the plants, whose activity had filled the atmosphere of Earth with oxygen, thus making life possible for other organisms, organisms that did not know of photosynthesis. And surely it was unintentional on the part of the grass to give us the opportunity to exist! Frog Eggs and the whole "informational" side of the letter became the products of an incredibly complex metabolism. Frog Eggs was a kind of waste, a cinder whose structure derived from planetary metabolisms.

When Donald and I returned to the hotel, he said at one point that he felt basically cheated: the leash on which we ran in circles had been lengthened, but that changed nothing in our situation of confinement. We were spectators at a nice display of intellectual fireworks, but when the show was over, we were left empty-handed. Perhaps—he went on—something had even been taken away from us. Before, the *consensus omnium* had stood behind the concept of a "letter" in whose envelope was found a little sand (meaning Frog Eggs). As long as we believed that we had received a letter, however incomprehensible it was, however mysterious, the knowledge of the existence of a Sender had value in itself. But now, when it turned out that perhaps the thing was not a letter but a meaningless scrawl, nothing remained to us except the sand . . . and even if the sand was gold dust, we felt reduced to poverty— more, we felt robbed.

I thought this over when I was alone. I tried to figure out where the certainty in me came from which allowed me to dispose of other views, no matter how well buttressed by arguments they were. I was convinced that we had received a letter. It is very important to me to convey to the reader not just this belief of mine—the belief does not matter so much—but the reasoning behind it. If I fail here, I should not have written this book. For that was its goal. A man who, like myself, has grappled long and often, on many changing fronts of science, with the problems of solving "Nature's ciphers," truly knows more about them than you will find in his mathematically tidy publications.

On the authority of this unconveyable knowledge, I maintain that Frog Eggs, with its reservoir of nuclear energy, with its "tele-explosion" effect, should have been turned into a weapon under our hands, because we strove so very hard, and desperately, to do this. That we were unsuccessful can be no accident. We had succeeded—in other situations, which were "natural"—all too often. I have no difficulty imagining the beings who sent the signal. They said to themselves: We will make it undecipherable for all who are not yet ready; but we must go further in our caution—so that even a false reading will not be able to supply them with any of the things that they seek but that should be denied them.

Not atoms, not galaxies, and neither planets nor our own bodies has Anyone cordoned off with such a system of safeguards, and we bear all the dismal consequences of that Neglect. Science is the part of culture that rubs against the world. We scrabble out pieces from the world and consume them—not in the order that would be best for us, because No One was so kind as to arrange this, but in an order that is regulated only by the resistance that matter itself presents. The atoms and stars have no reasons; they cannot defy us when we fashion models in their image; they will not bar our way to knowledge that may possibly be lethal. Whatever exists outside man is like a corpse: it can possess no intention. But the moment the forces not of Nature but of Reason direct a message at us, the situation changes completely. The One who sent out the letter was motivated by a purpose that was definitely not indifferent to life.

From the first, what I feared the most was a misunderstanding. I was sure that we were not being sent an instrument of murder; but everything indicated that what we had received was the description of some instrument—and it is well known what use we put instruments to. Even man is a tool for man. Familiar with the history of science, I did not imagine that there was any perfect safeguard against abuse. All technologies were, after all, completely neutral, and we could assign to any one of them the goal of death. During that unimportant but desperate conspiracy—stupid, no doubt, yet by impulse inevitable—I believed that we could no longer count on Them, because They apparently had not been able to foresee what we might do with the information *mistakenly*. The safeguarding against what was planned and deliberate—that I could believe; but not against what constituted *our* error or our filling in the gaps with faulty substitutions. Even Nature herself, who for four billion years had instructed biological evolution in how to avoid "errors," how to operate under the protection of all possible safety measures, could not keep an eye on life's molecular slips and twists, its side streets, dead ends, and wrong turns, its "misunderstandings" —proof of which was the innumerable degenerations in the development of organisms, such as cancer. But if They succeeded, that meant that They had gone far beyond the perfection, unattainable for us, of biological systems. I did not know, however—how, indeed, was I to have known?—that Their systems, more effective than the biological, were so universally certain, so airtight: against trespass by the unqualified.

That night in the huge hall of the inverter, bending over the sheets of scrawled paper, I had felt a sudden weakness, a moment of dizziness, and it had grown dark before my eyes, not only because the dread hanging over my head for all those weeks unexpectedly melted away; but also because in that instant I experienced, palpably, Their greatness. I understood what a civilization could be based on, and what a civilization could be. We think of an ideal equilibrium, of ethical values, of rising above one's own weakness, when we hear the word "civilization," and we associate it with what is best in us. But it is, above all, knowledge, a knowledge that from the sphere of possible situations eliminates precisely those (common, for us) like this one: where the finest brains out of a billion beings address themselves to the task of sowing universal death, doing what they would rather not do and what they stand in opposition to, because there is no alternative for them. Suicide is no alternative. Would we have changed one bit the course of further research, the invasion of metal locusts from the sky, had the two of us killed ourselves? If They foresaw such situations, the only way that I can understand it is if at one time They were—or, who knows, perhaps still are—like us.

194

Did I not say at the beginning of this book that only a fundamentally evil creature knows what freedom it attains when it does good? There was a letter, it was sent, it fell to Earth, at our feet, and had been falling in a neutrino rain while the lizards of the Mesozoic plowed the mud of the Carboniferous forests with their bellies, while the paleopithecus, called Promethean, gnawed a bone and saw in it the first club. And Frog Eggs? In Frog Eggs I see fragments—distorted, caricatured by our ineptness and ignorance, but also by our knowledge, which is skewed toward destruction—fragments of what the letter provided for by its very delivery. I am convinced that it was not hurled into the darkness as a stone is into water. It was conceived as a voice whose echo would return—once it was heard and understood.

The by-product, so to speak, of a proper reception was to be a return signal, informing the Senders that contact had been established, and at the same time telling Them the place where this occurred. I can make only a vague guess as to the mechanism that was to do this. The energy autonomy of Frog Eggs, its ability to direct nuclear reactions upon itself, which served no purpose other than to continue the state that made this possible—is evidence, proof, of an error on our part, because in our further incursion we came upon an effect as mysterious as it was dramatic, able under completely different circumstances to liberate, focus, and hurl back into space an impulse of tremendous power. Yes, if the code had been read *correctly*, the TX effect, discovered by Donald Prothero, would have been revealed as a return signal, an answer directed at the Senders. What convinces me of this is its fundamental mechanism: an action traveling at the greatest cosmic speed, carrying energy of any magnitude across a distance of any magnitude. The energy, of course, is to serve the transmittal of information, and not destruction. The form in which TX made itself known to us was the result of a distortion that the knowledge recorded in the neutrino stream underwent during our synthesis. Error bred error —it could not be otherwise. This is only logical, yet I am still amazed by Their versatility, that could thwart even the potentially fatal consequence of mistakes—of more than mistakes, because ours was a premeditated effort to turn a ruined instrument into a deadly blade.

The Metagalaxy is a limitless throng of psychozoic enclaves.

Civilizations deviating from ours by a certain number of degrees, but, like ours, divided, mired in internal quarrels, burning their resources in fratricidal struggles, have for millennia been making —and still are making, again and again—readings of the code, readings as unsuccessful as our own. Just like us, they attempt to fashion the strange fragments that emerge from their efforts into a weapon—and, just like us, they fail. When did the conviction take root in me that this was the case? It is hard to say.

I told only those closest to me—Yvor, Donald—and before my final departure from the compound I shared this private property of mine with the acrimonious Dr. Rappaport. They all—a curious thing—at first nodded with the growing satisfaction of comprehension, but then, after some thought, said that for the world as it was given to us, my idea made too pretty and complete a picture. Perhaps. What do we know of civilizations "better" than ours? Nothing. So perhaps it is not suitable to paint such a panorama, in which we figure somewhere in the frame as a blot on the Galaxy, or as one of the embryos stuck fast in labor contractions that go on for centuries; or, finally, to use Rappaport's metaphor, as a fetus, quite handsome at birth, but strangling on its own umbilical cord, the cord being that arm of culture which draws the vital fluids of knowledge up from the placenta of the natural world.

I can present no incontrovertible proof in support of my conviction. I have none. No evidence in the stellar code, in its information, nothing to indicate that it was produced for beings somehow better than us. Can it simply be that, stung for so long by humiliations, forced to work under the command of the Osters and the Nyes, I spun for myself—in the image and likeness of my own hopes—the only equivalent available to me of holiness: the myth of the Annunciation and Revelation, which I then—also to blame —rejected as much out of ignorance as ill will?

If a man no longer worries about the movement of the atoms and planets, the world becomes defenseless with regard to him, since he can then interpret it as he pleases. He who wields the imagination shall perish in the imagination. And yet imagination is supposed to be an open window on the world. For two years we examined a thing—at its destination, from the final results that streamed to Earth. I propose that we consider it from the opposite end. Is it possible, without falling into madness, to believe that we were sent puzzles, intelligence tests of a sort, charades of galactic descent? Such a point of view, in my opinion, is ridiculous: the difficulty of the text was not a shell that had to be pierced. The message is not for everyone: that is how I see it, and I cannot see it otherwise. First of all, the message is not for a civilization low on the ladder of purely instrumental progress, because it is obvious, surely, that the Sumerians or Carolingians would not have been able even to notice the signal. But is the limitation of the circle of receivers determined solely by the criterion of technological ability?

Let us look beyond ourselves. Enclosed in the windowless room of the former atomic test site, I could not help thinking about the great desert outside the walls, and the black canopy hanging above it, and that the whole Earth was being penetrated constantly, hour after hour, century after century, and eon after eon, by an immense river of invisible particles, whose current carried a communication that hit equally the other planets of the solar system, and other such systems, and other galaxies, and that this current had been sent from an unknown time past and across an unknown gulf—and that this was actually true.

I did not accept this knowledge without a fight; it was too much at odds with all that I had grown accustomed to. I saw, at the same time, our undertaking: the throng of scientists overseen discreetly by the government of which I was a citizen. Wrapped in a network of bugs and taps, we were supposed to establish contact with an intelligence that inhabited the Cosmos. In reality this was a stake in an ongoing global game; it became part of the pot, entered the pleiad of countless cryptonym-acronyms that filled the concrete bowels of the Pentagon; it was placed in some vault, on some shelf, in some file, with the stamp of TOP SECRET on the folder; yet another Operation, with the letters HMV, doomed in the bud, as it were, to insanity—this attempt to hide and imprison a thing that had been filling the abyss of the Universe for millions of years, in order to extract, as from lemon pits, information packed with fatal power.

If this was not madness, there is not and never will be madness. And so: the Senders had in mind certain beings, certain civilizations, but not all, not even all those of the technological circle. What sort of civilizations are the proper addressees? I do not know. I will say only this: if, in the opinion of the Senders, that information is not fitting for us to learn, then we will not learn it. I place great confidence in Them—because They did not let me down.

And yet, could not the whole thing have been only a series of coincidences? Absolutely. Was not the neutrino code itself discovered by accident? And could not the code in turn have arisen by accident, and by accident impeded the decomposition of large organic molecules, and by accident repeated itself, and, finally, by sheer chance produced Lord of the Flies? That is all possible. Accident can also cause such a swirling of waves at high tide that when the water recedes there will appear, on the smooth sand, the deep print of a foot.

Skepticism is like a microscope whose magnification is constantly increased: the sharp image that one begins with finally dissolves, because it is not possible to see ultimate things: their existence is only to be inferred. In any case, the world, after the closing of the Project, continued on its merry way. The popularity of statements made by scientists, political figures, and celebrities of the hour on the subject of cosmic intelligence has passed. Frog Eggs has been put to good use, so the millions from the budget did not go to waste. Over the code, now published, anyone from the legion of loose screws can rack his brains—those who used to invent perpetual-motion machines and trisect angles—and, in general, anyone can believe what he wants to believe. Particularly if his belief, like mine, has no practical consequence. Because it did not, after all, reduce me to dust and ashes. I am as I was before entering the Project. Nothing has changed.

I would like to conclude with a few words about the people of the Project. I already mentioned that my friend Donald is not alive. He suffered a statistical deviation in the stream of cellular divisions: cancer. Yvor Baloyne is not simply a professor and a dean, but a man so overworked that he does not even know how happy he is. About Dr. Rappaport I know nothing. The letter that I sent several years ago to the Institute for Advanced Study was returned. Dill is in Canada—neither of us has time to correspond.

But what, really, do these remarks signify? What do I know of the secret fears, ideas, and hopes of those who were my colleagues for a time? I was never able to conquer the distance between persons. An animal is fixed to its here-and-now by the senses, but man manages to detach himself, to remember, to sympathize with others, to visualize their states of mind and feelings: this, fortunately, is not true. In such attempts at pseudo merging and transferral we are only able, imperfectly, darkly, to visualize ourselves. What would happen to us if we could truly sympathize with others, feel with them, suffer for them? The fact that human anguish, fear, and suffering melt away with the death of the individual, that nothing remains of the ascents, the declines, the orgasms, and the agonies, is a praiseworthy gift of evolution, which made us like the animals. If from every unfortunate, from every victim, there remained even a single atom of his feelings, if thus grew the inheritance of the generations, if even a spark could pass from man to man, the world would be full of raw, bowel-torn howling.

We are like snails, each stuck to his own leaf. I retreat behind the shield of my mathematics, and recite, when that does not suffice, these final lines from Swinburne's poem:

> From too much love of living,
>   From hope and fear set free,
> We thank with brief thanksgiving
>   Whatever gods may be
> That no life lives for ever;
> That dead men rise up never;
> That even the weariest river
>   Winds somewhere safe to sea.
>
> Then star nor sun shall waken,
>   Nor any change of light:
> Nor sound of waters shaken,
>   Nor any sound or sight:
> Nor wintry leaves nor vernal,
> Nor days nor things diurnal;
> Only the sleep eternal
>   In an eternal night.

Zakopane, June 1967
Kraków, December 1967